ONE
TRUE
MATE · 4
Shifter's Innocent

LISA LADEW

Book cover by The Final Wrap <3

Cover model: Matthew Hosea

Photographer: Shauna Kruse

Muse by The Blurb Diva. My online bff. Hearts and unicorns and peen dreams.

As always, I must mention *Kristine Piiparinen for general awesomeness in the steamy romance world and Amanda Quiles for shifter guru-ness. Thank you both for your help.

No book thoughts would ever be complete without mentioning OTM's readers. I love that you get what I'm trying to do here, and that you dig this world as much as I do. I appreciate you so much. <3 <3 <3

Of course, I must mention my husband, John, for many things, including being a massive PITA, but of course, you've always supported me, always loved our boys, always had crazy ideas, and never backed down from a challenge, even when I say stuff like, "Ok, the bad wolf has to say something mysterious that makes the good wolf realize x, y, and z. What should that something be?" ha ha. Thank you.

GLOSSARY

Bearen – bear shifters. Almost always work as firefighters.

Citlali – Spiritual leaders of all *Shiften*. They are able to communicate with the deities telepathically, and sometimes bring back prophecies from these communications.

Deae – goddess.

Dragen – dragon shifter. Rare.

Echo – an animal with the same markings of a *shiften*. Usually seen as a harbinger of bad things, but could also be a messenger from the Light.

Felen – big cat shifters. Almost always work as mercenaries. They are also the protectors of Rhen's physical body and a specially-trained group of them can track Khain when he comes into the *Ula*.

Foxen – the *Foxen* were created when Khain forcibly mated with female *wolfen*.

Haven, The – final resting place of all *shiften*. Where The Light resides.

Impot – a *shiften* that cannot shift because of a genetic defect caused by mating too close to their own bloodline. Trent and Troy are not thought to be *impots* because they were born during a *klukwana*.

Khain – also known as the Divided Demon, the Great Destroyer, and the Matchitehew. The hunter of humans and the main nemesis of all *shiften*.

Klukwana – a ceremony where a full–blooded *shiften* who mates another *shiften* does so with both in animal form, then the mother stays in animal form during the entire pregnancy. The young in the litter are always born as their animal. *Wolven* from a *klukwana* always come in at least 4 to 7 young. *Bearen* are always two cubs, and *felen* are unpredictable, sometimes only one. *Shiften* born from a *klukwana* are almost always more powerful, bigger, and stronger than regular *shiften*, but many parents don't try it because of the inherent risks to the mother during the (shorter) pregnancy and the risk that the *shiften* young may choose not to shift into human form. A lesser known possibility is that the *shiften* young will have a harder time learning to shift into human form, especially if no one shifts near them in the first few days after birth.

KSRT – Kilo Special Response Team, or Khain Special Response team. A group of *wolven* police whose primary goal is to hunt down and kill Khain, if that can be done.

Light, The – The creator of the *Ula*, humans, Rhen, Khain, and the angels.

Moonstruck – Insane. *Shiften* who spend too long indoors or too long in human form can become *moonstruck* slowly and not even realize it.

Pravus – Khain's home. A fiery, desolate dimension that sits alongside ours.

Pumaii – a small group of specialized *felen* tasked with tracking Khain when he crosses over into our dimension.

Renqua – a discoloration in a *shiften's* fur which is also seen as a birthmark in human form. Every *renqua* is different. The original *renquas* were pieces of Rhen she put inside the wolves, bears, and big cats to create the *shiften*. Every pure-blooded shifter born since has also had a *renqua*. Half-breeds may or may not have one. Some *foxen* acquired weak *renquas* when they mated with *shiften*. Also called the mark of life.

Rhen – the creator of all *shiften*. A female deity.

Ruhi – the art of speaking telepathically. No humans are known to possess the power to do this. Not all *shiften* are able to do it. It is the preferred form of speaking for the *dragen*.

Shiften – Shifter-kind.

Ula – earth, in the current dimension and time. The home of the *shiften*.

Vahiy – end of the world.

Wolfen – a wolf shifter. Almost always works as a police officer.

Wolven – wolf shifters, plural.

Zyanya – When a *wolfen* dies, the funeral is for the benefit of humans, but the important ceremony is the *zyanya*. The pack mates of the fallen *wolfen* run in wolf form through the forest, heading north to show the spirit the way to the Haven. When they reach a body of water, they all jump in and swim to the other side, then emerge in human form.

CHAPTER 1

**Six weeks ago. Just beyond the city
limits of Serenity, Illinois.**

*C*erise bent over Zeus's neck, the fingers of her right
hand digging into his mane as he sped through the
forest. From behind her, Kaci dug her heels into
Zeus's side, trying to urge him faster still, but he didn't respond. They both knew they were racing the yellow glow just
barely starting to show in the east, because they might not
have another chance to hit this house until it was too late.
Tonight, or maybe never.

Cerise leaned forward to speak into Zeus's ear. "Faster,
Zeus, if you have anything left." She barely needed to speak
the first word and he showed her he did have a bit left. His
hooves flew, causing the wind to whip faster in her hair,
streaming it behind her like a strawberry blonde flag.

Kaci giggled, threading her arms tighter around Cerise's waist. Cerise felt like laughing herself, imagining they were flying, weightless, carefree, far above the problems of earthbound creatures. She tightened her knees and laid her body forward to move with the big horse.

Zeus's hooves pounded against the forest floor, occasionally punching through crusted snow that had fallen through a break in the boughs and collected in tiny white drifts. Ahead of them, the edge of the forest drew close. Cerise could see the house they were heading to. An old farmhouse, well taken care of, and miles beyond it, the first stirrings of the subdivisions that crept up to the edge of Serenity.

She spoke to Zeus again, rubbing his neck. "You can slow down now, big guy. Thanks for the ride. It was fun."

They broke through the trees and Zeus obediently dropped to a trot, then a walk. He swung his head and Cerise and Kaci both sat up straighter, Cerise feeling like swinging her head also. A bareback gallop through the forest in the dark and cold was exhilarating She hadn't slept so far, and she didn't feel tired at all.

Zeus maneuvered to the end of the driveway and stopped directly in front of a blue and white mailbox shaped like a tiny barn, then looked around, nickering softly, his ears flicking ahead, then behind. Cerise watched the house, wondering if anyone were inside gazing back at her. She was almost positive the only person who lived here worked nights and did not come home until nine or ten in the morning, but she did not know the man's days off from work. She could not escape from home often enough to do that kind of surveillance without Myles getting suspicious. She and Kaci took great care to only sneak out when he was at his most drunk, guaranteed to sleep for hours.

Cerise looked up and down the street from her high vantage point on Zeus's back. This house was one of the few left that hadn't sold off its land to developers. If no one were inside, there were no other houses close enough to see them. Forest lay on one side, open pasture on the other. The encroachment of Serenity, the closest city in any direction, was still a mile or two away to the east, the same way the sun would soon be shining from.

Cerise felt Kaci let go of her death grip on Cerise's hips and lean back confidently. Cerise swung a leg over to turn around on Zeus's back and face her little sister. Not really her sister, but Cerise would forever think of her as such. Cerise had raised Kaci like her own daughter, but was only ten or eleven years older. Unfortunately, she didn't know exactly how old either one of them was.

Kaci's eyes were tired, but no matter. They'd had a good night. Cerise hadn't been able to count their haul yet, but she thought they had at least a hundred dollars. Which put them much closer to making their escape. It would have to be soon. Myles looked at Kaci with more interest every day, and Cerise would never let that happen. She would steal Kaci out of the trailer as soon as they had $550. Enough so they could make it to California without hitchhiking. She hoped. Away from her dad forever. Ugh. She hated to think of him as that, preferring to use his given name, Myles. Disowning him in her mind. Dis-fathering him.

Cerise rubbed her temple lightly, fear creeping in with a pounding in her temple. Back when she'd been sick, she'd had migraines daily, and knew they meant a dark room, quiet thoughts, Kaci on her own in their tiny home, trying to cook food for Myles, if he was eating, and taking the beating if she got it wrong or if Myles simply felt like lashing out. Cerise pressed her lips together and took a deep breath, determined to hold off the migraine. She hadn't had one in months, had been getting better every single day. She had to stay functional.

Kaci's freckled face tightened as she watched Cerise put the hand to her head. Kaci knew exactly what it meant. Cerise winced as her probing fingers touched a fading bruise on her cheek that still hurt. Now Kaci's eyes traced the bruise and Cerise snatched her hand away. She didn't need to give Kaci anything more to worry about.

Cerise took a deep breath and rolled her shoulder muscles. "I'm going in alone but I'll call you if it's clear. What do you do if I'm caught?"

Kaci rolled her eyes. "Saaah-reeece," she said, butchering the pronunciation of Cerise's name for emphasis.

Cerise rolled her eyes right back. "Just tell me, Lemon. What do you do if I'm caught?"

Kaci sulked but answered. "Ride Zeus to the school and tell them Daddy beats me."

Cerise winced. It wasn't a lie, although Cerise tried to take most of the blows. She eyed the jagged cut of Kaci's hair and the too-large faded sweatshirt and too-small shoes she wore, everything full of holes and fraying at the edges. She had hope school officials would put more stock in the story than the police had the two times they'd already tried to escape their parents. "That's not strong enough by itself. What else does he do?"

Kaci rolled her eyes again and spoke in a huff. "He touches me. He makes me touch him. He makes me do stuff to him sexually."

Cerise ground her teeth together. *Not if I can help it.* "Good. And they are going to ask you exactly what he's done. You have to make it convincing."

Kaci shuddered. "Yuck. Why can't I just tell them the truth?"

Cerise swung a leg between her and Kaci and slid to the ground, then turned to stare back up at her little sister who really was no blood relation to her at all. "Because they won't believe it." She grasped Kaci's knee. "Now, ears open, eyes open, remember the signal, and pay attention."

Kaci nodded. Cerise turned and began to walk down the driveway. She would like to tell Kaci to ride Zeus under the cover of the forest, but Zeus didn't listen to Kaci very well. If Cerise was around, he wouldn't listen to Kaci at all. She could only pray that if she really did get caught, Zeus would somehow sense it and let Kaci take the reins for once. Ha ha. Reins. Good one. Like they weren't riding bareback and trying to steer him with their knees and fervent wishes.

Cerise walked straight to the house like she belonged there, but at the last minute, instead of mounting the steps to the front door, she swerved to the left and made her way down that side of the house, old snow crunching under her feet. A small white garage sat there and she peeked in the window. Empty. Perfect. Heading to the rear of the house, she picked the most-recessed and dark basement window, then knelt and tried to push it open. It was locked, but she could see the lock through the glass. A finger-pull kind, and very easy to open by breaking just one tiny pane of glass. Within moments, she was sliding inside quickly and decisively. She hated breaking into houses, but she'd learned months ago that if she was going to do it, hesitation never made it easier, better, or more legal.

Great. Just what she wanted to be good at. Being a criminal. Cerise rolled her eyes as her shirt hiked up to her breasts with the slide, then she landed neatly on the floor, pulling her ratty shirt down where it belonged.

She looked around in the almost nonexistent light to see an unfinished basement with boxes stacked from floor to ceiling against every wall. Cerise prowled toward the staircase leading upstairs, then stopped in the very middle of the room. Standing as still as possible, barely breathing, she listened, listened hard, finally deciding that the house sounded and *felt* completely empty. To her right, a box called to her, but she ignored it. She would check it on the way out.

She strode up the steps quickly, not careful at all. The sense she had about enclosed spaces hadn't been wrong yet. If it told her no one was in the house, no one was in the house.

At the top of the steps, she pushed open the door and peeked around at the dark house, then strode to the front door and unlocked it, opening it and motioning for Kaci to come in. Kaci nodded, sliding to the ground and enticing Zeus to follow her to the back of the house with a piece of apple she fished from her pocket.

Cerise watched her for a moment, her heart hurting at the snow pouring into the holes in Kaci's shoes as she walked. No jacket. Socks for gloves. Kaci didn't deserve the absolute nothing that she had. But Cerise had no way to give her more. *For now.* Cerise looked down at her own ratty tennis shoes and knew they weren't any better. Someday they would have nice things. Someday they would have coats and gloves to stay warm in the winter. Someday they would have a warm house and days of work and love and laughter. *Someday soon.*

Cerise walked slowly around the house, waiting for the money to call her. She'd discovered most people kept at least some money hidden in their house, and also that she was very good at figuring out where it was. She let her eyes slide over everything in the living room and the open kitchen beyond without settling on anything. A bookshelf called to her, but in a different way than money did and she tried to ignore it. She only *wanted* the books, but she *needed* the money.

Kaci pushed in the front door and sighed in relief as the heat from the house hit her. Cerise spoke to Kaci over her shoulder. "Money, only money. We aren't looking for anything else."

"What about DVDs?"

"Money, Kaci! Only the necessities."

Kaci said nothing but Cerise could sense her disappointment. Kaci moved to the stairs and Cerise felt a pang of fear, then stomped it down. Trust yourself. Only yourself. You know you're right, and this house is empty.

Unable to stop herself, Cerise drifted closer to the bookshelf. No money was calling to her, but the books were screaming. She ran her fingers over their spines, not looking at any of the titles. She didn't care what the titles were or what the words inside were about. Books were magic, all books, and she'd not seen many in her life.

Her fingers closed around a book at random and she drew it out, then lifted it to her face. It was fat and she loved that. Pocket Encyclopedia of World History. She sounded out the second word as best as she could, trying to figure out what sound the two Cs made. En-sy-slo-pee-dee-ah? Or En-kye-klo-pee-dee-ah? She'd never seen the word before and it fascinated her. It had to mean something exotic and amazing. Desire to know more gripped her, curling her fingers around the book. She had to have it. Which meant Kaci would get her DVD, if any were found.

Cerise flipped through a few of the middle pages of the book, delighted to see they were all short explanations of things she knew nothing about. She stopped at a random entry and read, struggling through the first few words, then letting her eyes wander over the accompanying picture. She didn't get out much; Myles never let them leave the farm and the last time either of them had been into the city had been years ago, the last time she'd tried to get Kaci away from Myles and Sandra, but even she could tell the Byzantine Empire had happened a long time ago by the pictures accompanying its entry.

Cerise tucked the book into the waistband of her pants at her back and strode into the kitchen, letting her eyes unfocus and feeling viscerally for the money that had to be there. Nothing. She pulled a few vases down from on top of the fridge and peeked inside them anyway, but she'd been right. No money jar.

She walked through the rest of the rooms, then made her way up the stairs after Kaci. "Anything?" she called out, then gasped when she saw what Kaci was holding.

A gun. A compact one with a swirly-blue grip, like a piece of jewelry. "Put that down," Cerise hissed.

Kaci held it carefully and turned it over in her hands. "We could really use this," she said, almost to herself.

"Lemon, put it down," Cerise admonished, her voice tight. "You'll shoot yourself."

"Okay, okay," Kaci said, and placed the gun on top of the dresser she was standing in front of.

"Anything?" Cerise asked again.

Kaci shook her head and pulled open another drawer, rifling underneath the clothes there. "Nothing so far."

Cerise turned away. It was no use searching up here. She felt nothing.

Cerise clomped down the stairs and was just about to call Kaci to her when she remembered the pull, almost like a beckoning voice in her head, that she'd felt in the basement.

Maybe there had been money in that box. It didn't make sense that money would be in a plain cardboard box, but she would look.

In a few minutes, she was in front of the box, with Kaci sitting on the bottom step, looking bored already. She hadn't found any DVDs upstairs and that was all she cared about, trusting all the other details to Cerise.

Cerise touched the box curiously, then pulled it open. But the box had gone silent. Cerise looked inside and found only Christmas decorations. She put the box aside, frustrated, even more frustrated to discover she could see around the basement better than she had been able to when they'd first entered. The sun was rising fast.

Something on the wall, behind where the box had been, caught her eye. It was a small plastic square embedded in the wall, with a faint light flashing on it, like some sort of alarm system. She stepped forward and looked at it, drawing her eye close. A beep sounded, making her pull her head back, and a door to her left slid open. A door that had been cleverly disguised as only part of the wall. As she stared, the door slid shut as quickly as it had opened. A draft of air pushed against her face, bringing with it a lovely smell of evergreen trees, warm leather, and pure masculine male. Cerise frowned. The only male she'd smelled in the last few years was Myles, and he smelled like rotten fruit. Not a good smell.

Cerise stared at the door, brows drawn, as Kaci pushed out a breath behind her and said, "Mega-cool!"

Cerise frowned. They didn't have time for this. But the tunnel called to her, and curiosity demanded she take another look.

She ran her hands over the plastic square, looking for whatever had triggered it to open the first time. She felt no grooves or buttons, so she hesitantly moved her eyes in front of it and again the door slid open. Then shut again. Cerise stared at it, trying to puzzle out what the door could possibly be. She'd seen a dark tunnel beyond that seemed to lead for miles.

Inexplicable desire to follow the tunnel clawed its way through her and she felt helpless to resist it. She dropped her head and thought furiously, trying to convince herself to go back upstairs, head out the door, and go home. They had a plan and they needed to follow it.

But her thoughts flew like a hurricane inside her head, trying to convince her to follow the tunnel, to see where it led. *It's good. He's good. He'll fix everything for you.* Cerise frowned again. She trusted no one, especially no man. Self-reliance was all that she had. Too bad she was almost entirely ignorant about the world outside their captive life. Just looking at the houses they broke into told her that. The person who lived in this house lived nothing like Kaci and Cerise lived.

The voice spoke up again. *Follow the tunnel. Follow the scent. Everything will be okay.*

Cerise looked to the broken window and the rising sunlight streaming in through it, then raised her gaze to the ceiling above her head, then looked over her shoulder at Kaci, who was gazing at her expectantly, waiting for Cerise to make the call. As naïve as Cerise was, Kaci was doubly so, and she knew it.

Cerise pressed her lips together. *No.* She absolutely could not risk everything they'd been working toward for months on the complete unknown behind that door.

Then why did she find herself beckoning Kaci to her, and trying to figure out her best plan of action to get them both through the door before it closed?

CHAPTER 2

"Where are we going?" Kaci panted.

Cerise tucked her elbows into her side and ran faster, trying to discourage talking. "I don't know, I told you."

"Then why are we doing this?"

"Lemon, just trust me, please."

Cerise could no more explain why they were doing this than where they were going. How could she explain the voice? The feeling she didn't even understand? The desire that made absolutely no sense? The anticipation of something wonderful, that she couldn't justify, much less bring words to?

Kaci snorted, but said no more. Their cheap shoes pounded on the concrete floor of the tunnel. Cerise eyed the next soft light in the distance. The lights were placed only every 50 feet or so, so that much of their forward progress was in complete darkness, but Cerise could tell they were alone in this tunnel. No animals. No people. No nothing, but them.

The tunnel smelled musty, but not as musty as she would have imagined, as if someone took care of it, cleaned up, kept it dry. The sounds of their passage through it was dampened but echo-y at the same time, making her frown and wonder exactly how long the tunnel was.

Ahead of them, a few feet past the next light, she could see a doorway. Her eyes focused on it, drawing her body there. That was where she was going. She could feel it. They'd gone maybe a mile to the east, towards town.

Cerise slowed her pace to a walk, her eyes on the door. Kaci let out a huff next to her. "About time," Kaci said, irritation obvious in her voice.

Cerise ignored her, and examined the door as they neared it. Next to it, another plastic square was affixed to the wall. This time, Cerise did not bother touching it, she just leaned in close and let it see her eyes. The door opened, then shut again too quickly for Cerise to react, but a breeze of scent bathed her face. She took a deep breath and sighed. The scent was dark and strong and she wanted more of it.

"Cool," Kaci said. "It's just like the other one. Let me try." Kaci stood on tiptoes but couldn't get her eye up to the height of the plastic box. "Give me a boost."

Cerise maneuvered behind her and bent in a slight crouch, then lifted Kaci a few inches, letting her climb on Cerise's leg. The box beeped again, but the sound was a harsh, denying sound, not the pleasant blip that signaled the door would open.

Cerise lowered a pouting Kaci back to the floor. Beyond the door, she had seen only darkness. Anything could be there. "You ready?"

"Yeah," Kaci said, excitement in her voice. Cerise knew she was surprised to even be let inside. Cerise tried to make her wait outside as often as possible, but it wasn't safe in this tunnel. Cerise had no idea what the tunnel was for, who built it, and who might be patrolling it. Kaci had to stay with her.

Cerise leaned forward, wrapping an arm around Kaci's shoulders. The box beeped pleasantly, and both of them stepped inside. Kaci tried to whisper, but Cerise shushed her.

She felt/listened in the darkness. Another basement. Empty, but the house itself was not. One person. Motionless and horizontal. Sleeping, two floors above them.

She bit her lip. They should not be in this house, but the desire rose up inside her again. *She had to be in this house.* She had to find out what it was that was calling to her. It couldn't be money, the call was different. It wasn't a cold, emotionless ping of paper and metal from a stationary spot, but more like a friendly hand curling around the nape of her neck, encouraging her to do something she wanted to do anyway.

"You stay here," she whispered to Kaci.

Kaci grabbed her hand tight and wouldn't let her go. "No way am I staying here in the dark," she whispered back fiercely.

Cerise blinked. Kaci had a point. She looked around and tried to see anything. Dark shapes loomed to their left and she could barely make out a clear path in front of them. She curled her fingers around Kaci's. "Okay, come on, but we aren't staying long. Just for a second."

Cerise took small, mincing steps across the floor until she sensed, and almost saw, a stairway ahead of them. She moved to its left and felt along the wall for a light switch. There. She snapped it on then turned to look around the basement. This one was finished with a thin carpet and only a few plastic boxes along one side. A clear plastic container of DVD cases drew her eye. She nodded to Kaci. "Look."

Kaci sucked in a breath. "I thought you said no movies."

"If you stay down here while I go see… something, I'll let you bring one home."

Kaci was already drifting that way. "Deal."

Cerise stared at the wooden stairs leading up to the house beyond. Who was she kidding? If she were caught, if anything bad happened here, Kaci was in a world of trouble. She couldn't get back out into the tunnels, couldn't get back to the house that Zeus waited patiently behind, and couldn't explain why she was here. And still that desire clawed inside Cerise. She *had* to see what (who) was upstairs.

Cerise ascended the stairs quickly and pressed her ear to the door, listening/feeling beyond. All was quiet. She eased the door open and stepped through, then closed it softly behind her. She lifted her nose and took a deep breath. The scent she was drawn to was everywhere, calming her, pushing her to find its source.

Her eyes passed over the small, neat kitchen, then traveled to her left. A dining room with table and chairs. To her right was a living room with a couch along one wall. She walked that way, tiptoeing on numb feet. *What was she doing?* Risking everything! Cerise grimaced. Just waking up was a risk for her and Kaci. She was doing *something*, and that was better than not doing anything. She had to believe it.

Along one wall, there was a couch, but no TV. She and Kaci had broken into twelve houses in the last three months and all of them had more furniture than this one did, all of it pointed at a huge, slim TV mounted on the wall, so different than the one she and Kaci watched at home. The tiny, boxy, awkward one they were lucky to have.

Her body tuned to the male she knew was in the house, she let her eyes travel over what else was different about this house. On every spare inch of wall, gathered in elaborate patterns, were pictures in simple wooden frames of all shapes and sizes.

The total effect of the images was to make Cerise forget her purpose for a moment. The number of pictures on the walls must have been in the hundreds, some bigger than a notebook, one as big as a window. Most were smaller, the size of half a piece of paper.

One of the biggest ones was of a city with brightly covered buildings rising from the ground. The second biggest one was a forest seen from the treetops, another a river winding between two bluffs, a fourth a bird in flight glancing back at the camera. Cerise held her breath and turned in a circle, taking in an overview of all the pictures that covered every wall in the room.

It took her a few minutes of staring to realize what was off about them, different about them from other houses she and Kaci had broken into. Every picture was shot from above, or from high in the sky, like they'd been taken from an airplane.

Cerise stopped spinning and stared at one wall, opposite the couch, her gaze caught by what was obviously the key piece of the collection, the one picture that was as big as a window. The background was blue, a sky with concentrated clouds whipping around a ball placed in the very center. She'd seen the earth as it looked from space in the opening credits of Sliders and this ball looked like that, but instead of continents and oceans, the ball was covered with skyscrapers and houses, and a wide river that cut right through the center of the man-made structures.

She stared at it for a long time, her breath snaking in and out of her lungs like an afterthought. She didn't know what city this was, but in the image, it was beautiful. She wanted to go there. To live there. Not for the first time, she wished she lived a different life.

Cerise shook herself, remembering why she was there, in that house, taking such a risk. She lifted her face to the ceiling and took a deep breath. Upstairs. She walked slowly through the living room, the picture room as she was already thinking of it, and found a staircase at the back of a short hallway.

Slowly, she tiptoed up the stairs, wincing at every creak they made under her feet. But the man never stirred, never moved, she could practically trace his outline in her mind. It was big. It made her shudder.

At the top of the stairs, she turned right, following her feeling of him, but at this distance she could have followed his scent. It was strong, and getting stronger. She passed uninteresting doors, heading for a partially open one at the end of the hallway.

As she peeked inside the room, enough light fell in the room from the window facing east that she could easily see what she'd come to find. A man lay sleeping on the bed, his back to her. Cerise stared at him, knowing he had been the reason she had felt compelled to come here, but still fighting that knowledge. The feeling said, *trust him*. Every experience she'd ever had in her life said, *no way!*

Her neck muscles tightened and her head began to pound harder as she resisted her inexplicable desire to go to him, to wake him, to tell him who she was and see if it meant anything to him. Men couldn't be trusted. Most men. All men. Especially men as big and muscular as this one was.

He looked like he could throw Myles across the room, and Myles was solid and tough as nails.

Her eye traveled over him even as her mind continued to rebel, taking in his dark hair in a military cut, the sculpted planes of his body, as his chest rose and fell under a single white sheet. The back of his arms and shoulders was covered with twisting tattoos she didn't pay much attention to, except the one that looked like a depiction of a storm you might see on a map, a circle with lines radiating out from it.

The pillowcases and sheets below his big body were also white and pristine-looking. On the empty pillow next to him was a camouflage cap set perfectly facing forward and at right angles to the creased lines of the pillowcase, like the last thing he'd done the night before was take it off and place it there. Her eyes scanned the room, looking for the rest of his clothes, but the floor she could see was bare. No pictures in here, only a dresser and a closed door she imagined led to a closet. She wondered what kind of clothes she would find if she pushed the door to the closet open, rummaged around in there. The thought confused her and filled her with more desire. She wanted to *know* this man, wanted to examine his life, and him.

The man turned over and made a distressed noise in his sleep. Cerise sucked in a breath and prepared to run, but his eyes remained closed, his breathing even. Behind his lids, she could see his eyes moving quickly. *Dreaming.*

His chest began to rise and fall more swiftly. "No," he said, and Cerise jumped, barely biting back a cry. "No Cole, not without you," he spat out, and his handsome face twisted with some emotion, but his eyes were still closed. *Not dreaming, nightmare-ing.*

She held her ground, staring as the man's heavy brows

shot close together and his fingers twitched. "Why?" the man moaned and the agony in his voice destroyed her. What was he seeing in his sleep?

He whimpered, a foreign sound she never imagined would come from someone so big and strong and she took a step forward, unbidden, against all her better judgment. His handsome face with the wide-set eyes and strong jaw twisted again, sweat rising on his forehead, his back bowing. "Please, he's my brother," the man panted, his eyes squeezed shut. Cerise's heart twinged in her chest, and she crossed to him, walking around the bed to face his back. She approached his bedside and lay a hand on his massive shoulder, the heat from his skin seeping into her hand at once.

"Shh," she whispered, but she needn't have spoken. With her touch, his forehead smoothed, his tensed muscles relaxed. He sighed, and half-smiled, one corner of his lips curling up as the sigh escaped them and he relaxed onto his back.

Her fingers stayed with him, moving to the strong muscles of his upper arm. She could no more stop touching him than she could stop breathing, stop thinking, stop *being*. His half-grin floored her, turning his face from dark and tortured to handsome beyond anything she'd ever seen or imagined.

A flood of feelings washed over her. Right. Good. *Trustworthy*. Cerise's eyes floated closed and she let the feelings and sensations come. Tingles marched across her skin as her hair tried to stand up on her head and arms. It felt so good that she never wanted it to end. Felt good in the way someone grazing their fingers lightly up and down your back felt good. She reveled in it, allowing sensation to overtake her.

With a jolt of dismay, Cerise realized her whole body felt different, more aware, more *there*. She could feel her pulse at her neck and in her chest and… between her legs? She licked her lips and pulled her hand away from the bare skin of the man in the bed in front of her, curling the fingers that had been touching him close to her body, wrapping them with her other hand.

She stared down at the sleeping man, trying to figure out exactly what was going on, but had no reference to start from. She had a rudimentary knowledge of where babies came from, knew men and women were supposed to stare at each other with lust and desire and would end up kissing and disappearing behind closed doors for *sex*. But what did any of that have to do with what was going on here? Why did he make her body pound with something she'd never felt before in her life? Why did thoughts of *sex* fill her mind when she looked at him?

Her mind fell silent for a moment as she noticed a scar furrowed above his right ear, a long, grooving scar almost a half-inch wide and five inches long, curving to the back of his head. Her fingers curled, wanting to touch it while her mind hungered, wanting to know the story behind it.

The room brightened incrementally and her intellect told her it was time to leave. Time to leave this man and run home before Myles woke up. If Myles found them both gone and even suspected they hadn't been in the yard, they would pay. He hadn't broken one of her bones in years and she wanted to keep it that way.

Cerise took a step away, then another, but her body carried her back to the bed for one last touch. Perhaps she wanted to know if she would feel the same things if she touched him again, she wasn't sure, but she didn't try to resist it. She lightly grazed his forearm and the good feelings returned, but they were already ebbing, not quite as strong. Her eyes slid shut and she let the sensations wash over her as her body tried to convince her how much she needed this man.

The thought sent a spear of fear through her and her eyes flew open. No. Self-reliance only, she needed no man, ever. Men were dangerous. Too big. Violent. At least the ones she knew.

Her gaze fell upon the part of his body covered by the sheet and she couldn't help but suck in a breath at what was standing there that hadn't been standing before. She knew what was supposed to be there, but had never seen it hard and jutting like that before, never quite tried to imagine exactly how the *sex* happened, but this new sight sent myriad images through her mind of how it could. She bit her lip and pulled her fingers away from him, ready to turn and run, scared at how her body and mind reacted to what she had seen, but before she could, his hand closed around her wrist. His eyes opened, and they were the loveliest shade of blue she had ever seen, like the afternoon sky as it deepened to evening.

"You here to kill me, darlin'?" he drawled, a slight grin on his face, showing white, even teeth with canines almost like fangs. *Sexy.*

"Oh no, no," she babbled, automatically curling her other hand around his fingers that were holding her. "Go back to sleep," she said, pushing with her mind in a way that felt both foreign and intimate to her. "Forget about me, I was never here."

His eyes slid closed and his hand dropped to the mattress, but the slight grin stayed on his face.

Cerise ran, not looking back.

CHAPTER 3

*B*eckett Oswego finished his tea and bourbon, signaling to the bartender for his tab. He'd only had one drink, but he'd bought a few rounds for the pretty ladies in the booth to his right. They'd smiled and cooed at him, welcoming him openly, but he wasn't feeling it. *Fuck.* His dick was in but his head was out, and that really sucked, since he'd gotten the idea that all three of the ladies would welcome him. Could have been a fun night.

He stood. His dick screamed at him but he ignored it, tipped two fingers in a salute to the ladies, and headed out the door. Two kids ran past him on the sidewalk at top speed, all pounding feet, shouts, and giggles, boys, probably ten or eleven. They turned a corner out of his sight, then a third boy followed, stopping near Beckett to put his hands on his knees and catch his breath.

"Hey mister, you see my friends run by?"

Beckett started for his truck, ignoring the kid completely.

"Fuck you very much," the kid muttered from behind him. Briefly, Beckett considered going back and showing him the wisdom of keeping his mouth shut when his elders and betters had real shit to attend to, but he scrapped it. He was in a foul mood, and that wouldn't help any.

But when he got to his truck, there were grubby hand prints all over the back window of the camper shell, smeared in the mud left there from last weekend's off-roading and drone piloting.

"I'm gonna kill those little bastards," he muttered, cranking on the door pull. It was still locked. He checked the windows, then pulled out his keys and opened the back. Betsy, his biggest and most awesome quad-copter was fine, and so was Zita, his smallest but most-useful drone. He checked the gift-wrapped present, too. Fine. They hadn't actually been in the truck, they'd just looked. No killing would be required today.

He could have used the distraction. He was not looking forward to what he was heading to, but he pulled himself behind the wheel of Cooter, his '83 lifted Chevy C-10. His only friend who had time for him anymore…

***

Beckett's mouth dropped open as he surveyed the yard and field behind Trevor's house, his housewarming present to Crew and Dahlia forgotten in his arms.

It looked like a massive battle had been fought there, maybe between dinosaurs, or *dragen*. Trees were ripped out of the ground, creating several massive holes in the forest, each scorched by fire, the trunks of the remaining trees blackened and charred and the ground twisted, dirt up-heaved. One monster blue spruce lay in the middle of a pasture as if thrown there by a giant.

In contrast to the carnage, tulips, daisies, mums, and other flowers he had no idea the names of, pushed through the snow two months too early, their blooms not closing, even though the sun was almost below the horizon.

Beckett turned in a circle, his mind pulsing. He'd heard the one true mates who had been found, who lived on this property with their males, had been practicing with their powers, but he couldn't imagine how they had done this. The tree in the middle of the pasture had to weigh thousands of pounds by itself.

One of them did that with her mind? He ran over their powers. Ella, the first to be found, and Trevor's mate, had some ability to fight and repel Khain. Trevor was the head of the KSRT, the all-*wolven*, or all wolf-shifter, police team he belonged to, fighting tirelessly to protect the humans from Khain, a demon with a penchant for fire and explosions and killing humans, who lived in a hell-like dimension alongside the real world. Beckett eyed the blue spruce, wondering if it had been Ella who had uprooted and thrown it.

Heather had been the second mate to be found, fated to Graeme, the *dragen*, or dragon shifter, who'd come to them from Scotland, seeking to find a way to end his impossibly long life, but finding instead a reason to live. As far as Beckett knew, her power was to start fires with her mind, and she could not be burnt.

Then Dahlia had been found, just over a month ago. Dahlia was the mate to Beckett's best friend, Crew. Dahlia's powers were harder to explain, but apparently she could create things with her mind. He bent to pluck a flower from the ground and hold it to his nose. It smelled right. Felt like a real flower. What if she'd told spears to jut from the ground instead, or monster-sized scorpions? Would they have come as easily as the blooms seemed to have?

A spate of laughter from the just-finished cabin he was heading to caught his attention. He tucked his gift under his arm and continued that way, his mind on the implications of the powers the one true mates had been born with. Had the angel that had fathered all of them intended for them only to be able to protect themselves? Or to fight? Female *wolven* had fought, been police officers alongside the males, but now that there were none left, he had to imagine any males blessed enough to find their one true mates would be hard-pressed to want them fighting Khain, unless they proved to have some sort of regenerative powers.

The snow crunched under his feet as he stepped over flowers until he reached the cleared path that led to the co-zy-looking log cabin. He approached the door, then knocked soundly, smiling a little at Crew's laughter he heard from inside.

It was good to hear Crew laugh, but it hurt, too. Until Crew had found Dahlia, Beckett had been Crew's best friend, maybe his only friend. Beckett had been the only person who used to be able to make serious Crew laugh, or even crack a smile.

But Beckett hadn't seen Crew for more than five min-utes in the last six weeks, since he'd returned from that other world with his mate, and finally stopped disappearing when he slept. It had suddenly become all Dahlia, all the time. Beckett *got* it, he really did, but that didn't mean he wasn't hurt, wasn't missing his friend.

He pounded on the door again, the smell of dinner

drifting to him from inside. Roast beef, mashed potatoes, gravy, and some sort of sweet dessert. Pie? Maybe. No, cake. Angel-food cake. Interesting. Someone's idea of a joke? He had no idea who was cooking, didn't even know if his best friend, Crew, cooked or not. They'd only eaten TV dinners and fast food and drunk beer when they'd hung out.

Still no answer. From inside, male and female voices laughed and talked and called out to each other. Beckett was about to knock again, when he thought better of it and simply opened the door. He stepped inside and put his gift down, scenting to get the lay of the house and occupants. He couldn't see anyone yet because the entryway was blocked from the kitchen and dining area by a partial wall of hand-hewn logs, but he could hear them, laughing and joking and sounding like a family.

Family. The word made him wince and he wondered why he had agreed to come here tonight. He could be out at the bar right now, drinking his weight in whiskey and beer and picking up a willing female or three to take home to his bed.

But the bar was different to him these days. Without the pursuit of the female, the rest of it just didn't make as much sense. And his desire to bed female after female had started waning when Trevor had found Ella, then taken another hit when Graeme had been paired with Heather. Once Crew had fallen in love with Dahlia, Beckett had found himself unable to look at a woman without stacking her up against his own mate. Whoever she might be.

He heard Dahlia's voice and Crew's answering banter, then laughter and he winced again. He might not belong at the bar, but he didn't belong here, either.

He looked around the small entryway for a piece of paper and a pen. He would leave Crew a note and take off, but before he could, Heather rounded the corner and leaned against the wall opposite him, fanning herself and taking off her shirt in one swift motion.

Beckett froze, then sighed in relief when he saw she had another shirt underneath it. A tank top, like it was summer. Heather leaned against the far wall and smiled at him. "Beckett, I didn't know you were here. Everyone's in the dining room."

Beckett grinned at her in reflex, because that's what he did. "Smells good."

Heather smiled back, still fanning her face. "Is it hot in here?" she said, her head drooping. "I'm so hot."

Beckett shook his head. The temperature was comfortable.

Graeme came around the corner, looking for Heather. "Leannan, what ails you?"

She smiled and held out a hand to him. "I'm good, just hot."

Graeme eyed her for a moment, then turned to Beckett. "Beckett! Good man. Good wolf. Everyone's around the corner."

Beckett nodded and pointed to Heather. "I'm peachy. Take care of your female."

Graeme gave him a distracted smile then hurried to Heather's side, peering into her face, looking for anything wrong there.

"I'm just so hot," Heather said, wiping her face with the shirt she held in her hand. "Do I feel like I have a fever?"

Graeme's expression twisted, closing down slightly as he placed both his hands on Heather's cheeks, gently looking her up and down. "It cannae be," he whispered.

"What?"

Graeme held her at arm's length and glanced at her stomach, then held a trembling hand to it.

"What?" Heather said again, then understanding, and maybe a bit of fear, filled her face.

"Crew," Graeme called, his voice urgent, his brogue suddenly thick. "I need ye!"

Beckett grimaced. That was his friend, not Graeme's. His cheeks heated at the thought. Crew wasn't his ball and Beckett wasn't a toddler, unable to share. If only Beckett wasn't so *alone*, now, he could be a more understanding friend. But Beckett had been *alone* since he'd been twelve years old, Crew the only real light in a lonely life.

Crew entered the room, his face smiling wider than Beckett had ever seen, new laugh lines wrinkling his eyes.

He held up a hand when he saw Beckett. "Beck! You came!"

Graeme commandeered Crew's attention immediately, not giving Beckett a chance to respond. "Crew, I know ye could tell when Ella was pregnant, could ye-could ye check on Heather?" His voice trailed off and Beckett could hear the fear and hope there in equal measures.

Crew's expression showed surprise for only a moment and then he nodded quickly. He stepped closer to Heather, holding out a hand. Heather raised her own hand in return, wonder on her face.

Crew stepped back before their hands met, and joked, "Maybe I should sit down first." Another wonder. Crew had never had much humor about his powers, or anything, before.

They moved to a bench along one wall, boots lined below it, Graeme practically carrying Heather, then Crew took her wrist in his fingers. Beckett watched Crew, something like dread eating at him. Crew's expression stilled, then his eyes went wide. "The baby—she's on fire in there," he breathed, his expression tight and scared.

Heather's eyes also grew wide, but Graeme threw back his head and laughed, a rich, full sound that brought relief to both Crew and Heather's expressions.

Graeme stood up, pulling Heather into his arms, then threw his head back and roared up at the ceiling. A roar of celebration. Of triumph.

All conversation in the dining area ceased, then Trevor, Ella, Dahlia, Trent, and Troy piled into the small entryway. Seven people and two full-sized wolves, as big as Great Danes. The room barely held them.

"What is going on?" Ella cried, her eyes alight, as if she suspected.

Graeme grasped Crew's hand and pumped it up and down. "I'm sorry to upstage your housewarming." He dropped Crew's hand and threw his arms wide, facing the newcomers. "Heather's pregnant. She's pregnant and the bairn lives. And it's a GIRL."

Graeme laughed again as congratulations began to flood them both. Troy sat back on his haunches and howled while Trent watched them all with flat eyes.

When the melee quieted slightly, Heather spoke up, tugging at Graeme's sleeve to get his attention. "Graeme, he didn't really mean on fire?"

"It wouldn't surprise me at all, leannan. I've told ye they come out on fire, but how was I to ken how long they are like that inside yer body?"

Heather grabbed him by the shoulders. "Girl," she said softly. The couple stared into each other's eyes, then Graeme dropped his mouth to Heather's for a sweet kiss. Beckett felt like throwing himself outside into the snow to avoid seeing what should have been a private moment between them.

He turned away, concealing his emotions behind his

typical grin. Why were they all excited that shortly they would have a huge liability thrust into their lap? Why was everybody in such a hurry to bring completely helpless pups into the world? Or whatever baby *dragen* were called.

Someone knocked on the door and Beckett turned to open it, anything to ignore the uneasy feeling in his chest.

But when he opened it, Mac stood there, hand empty. Leave it to Mac to show up at a housewarming party with no gift. Behind him were Bruin, Wade, Harlan, and Jaggar. Beckett lifted his eyebrows, surprised to see Jaggar. The male normally shunned events like this, anything that wasn't work. Like so many of them.

Beckett stepped back, allowing them entrance into the room. The place suddenly felt twice as small. Mac lifted his chin at Beckett. "Say hey, hardhead."

Beckett ignored him. Hardhead was better than redneck. Maybe that was Mac's gift. He would keep his mouth on a leash all night.

Wade held up a bottle of wine. "Do I sense something worth celebrating?"

Everyone began to talk it once and when Wade figured out what was going on, he held up what was in his other hand. A wooden box. He gave it over to Graeme. "These were for Crew, but I don't think he'll mind if I give them to you instead." He looked at Crew. "I'll bring you another box tomorrow."

Crew clapped him on the back. "It's no problem. It's not every day a male finds out he's going to have a pup."

"Wyrmling," Graeme said, his smile broad. Heather just looked dazed. And hot. Temperature-wise, not attraction-wise. She was cute and all, but she was Graeme's and did not appeal to Beckett.

Beckett wondered how long he would have to stay, and how long they were going to all cram into this tiny room. Crew came close to him, the uncharacteristic smile pasted on his face. "Dahlia's next," he said and Beckett knew he was right, but the thought filled him with dread, not joy. Crew clasped hands with him, then gave him a one-armed hug. "Your one true mate show up yet?"

Beckett shook his head.

Crew looked at him closer, obvious confusion on his face. "Are you positive?"

Beckett stared at him, irritated all of a sudden. Done with being there. Crew might have that whole foresight thing going on, but Beckett would know if he had met his one true mate. "I'm positive. I haven't met any women at all since you told me about her."

Crew raised eyebrows, but didn't say a word. Beckett scowled and looked away, then back as a thought hit him. "Hey, are you sure you weren't seeing the future?"

Crew shook his head, speaking louder to be heard over the din of everybody else talking at once in the room. Everyone except Jaggar, who looked as miserable as Beckett felt, hiding in one corner. "The only time I ever saw the future was when Khain showed it to me. That's not what this was. You've met her. You've *touched* her. I would bet my life on it."

Frustration ripped at Beckett. He could use his one true mate right about now, and he knew exactly what she would be like, too. She would be a party girl, someone he could take dancing all night, someone who did not want babies. Not right now, maybe not ever. Something in his chest tightened at the thought but he ignored it. What the hell good were pups, anyway?

Beckett addressed Crew. "You said I saw her six weeks ago, right?"

Crew nodded.

"And you said I asked her if she was going to kill me?"

Crew nodded again, his expression tight.

Beckett shook his head slightly. "Why would I do that?"

Crew looked up, but the answer wasn't written on the ceiling. "I don't know. It didn't make any sense to me either."

"What does she look like?"

Crew stared away from him for a long time before answering.

"It's not quite like that. I saw her through your eyes, but only your emotional perception of her at the time. All I can really say is…" His voice trailed off for a moment, then he spoke one word.

"Innocent."

CHAPTER 4

*C*erise stepped over the burnt patch in the carpet in their tiny trailer, remembering how Sandra had flung the kerosene lantern at Myles as he smashed her TV to get back at her for dumping his last fifth of whiskey down the sink. Cerise couldn't remember why Sandra had waged war on his liquor in the first place, the original slight forgotten over time. The whole place would have burnt down if the lantern hadn't been almost empty, and maybe it still would have if Cerise hadn't put the flames out with her bare feet. She winced as she always did when she remembered how bad the burns had hurt, but somehow her feet had healed without scars.

She thought that had been three years ago, but she had no way of knowing for certain. TV had taught her time was counted in months, weeks, days, hours, minutes, and seconds, but she'd never seen a clock in real life, or a calendar. There were none in the small trailer home she lived in. Sandra and Myles had never worked, Cerise had never been to school, or even a doctor.

She and Kaci marked the passage of days with marks on the peeling, rotting flooring that lay underneath the carpet in the room they shared. They had 912 marks there, which meant almost three years, but 240 marks were from before she got sick, and the rest from after. How long she'd been sick for was anybody's guess. Cerise thought maybe as long as six months. Kaci had been too stricken to remember to record the days while Cerise had lain on the floor of the bathroom, for entire weeks sometimes.

Cerise pushed the door of their room open whispering, "It's just me."

Kaci peeked at her from the closet and motioned her over, a DVD box held tightly in her hands. "Can I put it in?" she whispered, her eyes shining, her expression eager.

Cerise nodded. "I counted ten empties around him and he just broke into the 'shine. Keep it on low for about an hour but I think we'll be good tonight."

Kaci grinned and pulled the blanket off their tiny TV, pushed way in the back of the closet, then plugged it in to their only electrical cord that snaked in through the slightly-open window with rags stuffed all around. They'd found the TV on the side of the road with a FREE sign on it one night, years ago, long before Zeus had wandered into their yard. It was tiny and old-fashioned, compared to what they'd seen in the houses they'd been raiding, but it had a DVD attached, which made it worth its weight in gold and their only way to know what went on in the world outside their trailer.

Myles had been somehow stealing electricity from the power company for years, and they lived in fear of the day that he wandered outside while they thought he was good and passed out, and discovered they were piggy-backing off his wires.

Their DVD collection was small and they had watched every video in it at least a few hundred times, having nothing else to do, especially in the winter, but it still gave them a way to escape and a glimpse at something they had no other way of experiencing. *Until tomorrow.*

Cerise turned away from her delighted sister and the movie after she saw which one it was. *Heathers.* Kaci's all-time favorite.

Cerise knelt on the floor in the corner put her hand on the carpet there, running her fingers over it. She felt/listened for Myles and found him still sitting in his chair at the other end of the house. Good. She turned up one corner of the carpet and lifted the board out from below to reveal their hidey-hole and inventory the contents, something she did nightly.

First came out her book, the encyclopedia. She had read it from cover to cover in the last six weeks, even though she didn't know what many of the words meant or how to pronounce them. The puzzle that was reading fell into place for her more every day. If only they had more books in the trailer, but Myles didn't believe in them. He didn't believe in anything that didn't come out of a bottle, apparently. She wondered briefly if Myles even knew how to read, then put it out of her mind. Who cared? After tomorrow, they would be done with him forever.

Would she miss him? Her eyes fell on the fading bruises on her upper arms and she shook her head. No, she wouldn't miss him, just like she didn't miss Sandra since she'd disappeared.

Something's wrong with you, she tried to tell herself, but that quiet voice spoke up again, negating what she'd just thought. It didn't matter that they were her parents, neither had said a kind word to her or treated her nicely in all the time she could remember. Her entire life. They'd been nicer to Kaci, but only when she was a baby. When Kaci had turned two and three and wanted to run and explore, the abuse had begun. Not to mention what they'd done to Kaci as a baby. That first insult that Cerise could never forget. Stealing her out of her home, away from her parents to live this life of hell.

She put aside the encyclopedia and pulled out all their cash, counting through it as best she could. She did not know if she was completely correct in her assumptions about the money, but she'd seen enough in their movies to know she had the right idea.

She laid out her stacks of twenties, tens, fives, and ones, and counted through them quickly. $633, just like it had been last night. They also had a bag of coins but she was less confident in knowing what they were worth, because of the difference in nomenclature. Nomenclature was a word the encyclopedia had taught her and she repeated it often inside her head, loving the weight and length of it. Nomenclature. From what she could tell, it meant how the money was named. But the problem with the coins was she didn't know exactly what portion of a dollar they represented. She'd found a book in a trash pile behind their closest neighbor's house called, *My Big Book of Dollars and Cents*, but the back half had been torn off and most of the pages removed. She'd studied what had remained intently, but still knew her knowledge was inadequate.

If only she knew how much a train ticket to California would cost! Or a bus ticket. She needed two of them and if the

$633 wasn't enough money, she didn't know what they were going to do. Not hitchhike, that had already ended in disaster.

Cerise carefully wrapped the money back in its bag and pulled out her second most prized possession. A faded and smeared folding map of the United States, that had also been dug out of the trash pile. She put it on top of the money. Next came a piece of lined paper with Cerise's painstaking handwriting on it. She let her eyes travel over the first two entries.

- Grey house. pink mailbox. First to east on Granger Street. $42.
- Two story white house to the south in middle of Pike's field. $14

Cerise hated stealing anything at all, but she had spent months and years worrying over their situation and could see no other way out of it. She kept the list because she planned on returning to the area someday and paying everybody back every bit of money they had taken.

At the very bottom of the hole were two more books, both stories that she had stared at over and over again, teaching herself to read them after she'd memorized the relationship of the captions on the TV to the words coming out of the actors' mouths.

Placing everything but her encyclopedia back in the hole, and the map at the very top, she glanced at Kaci. The TV was still muted, but Kaci was whispering every line.

"Great, it's Heather." Kaci's face changed as she took on the persona of the next person who was speaking. Cerise loved to watch her do it. She had a talent for becoming another person.

Kaci's eyebrows pulled low over her eyes and her chin

jutted out. "Oh, shit." Then Kaci pulled her shoulders back and looked down her nose, her air haughty. "Hi, Courtney. Love your cardigan." Again her demeanor changed, relaxing, becoming easier. "Thanks, I just got it last night at The Limited. I totally blew my allowance." Back to Heather. Cerise could hear the twang in her whisper. "Check this out. You win $5 million…"

Cerise watched for a few more minutes, her fingers rifling through the pages of the book she held. She looked at it slowly, and her mind went to the man in the bed. The man with the scar on his head, who she would never see again. The thought pained her but she wrestled with it. Getting Kaci home was more important than anything else, especially more important than some random guy she didn't know.

"You ready?" she whispered to Kaci. "We go in the morning, just before the sun comes up." Myles would sleep until noon if he drank as much as he normally did, and he wouldn't come looking for them until he wanted food, which wouldn't be until later in the evening. They could have a twelve-hour head start on him, easily.

Kaci turned to her slowly and Cerise saw both fear and excitement in her eyes. "Fuck me gently with a chainsaw. Do I look like Mother Teresa?"

Cerise smiled. Kaci was twelve, or close to it, and Cerise knew she was too young to be swearing like that, but she would never tell her not to do it. Swearing was Kaci's favorite thing and one of the only pleasures she had in her life. Kaci deserved much better than what she got and if repeating swear words she heard on the tiny TV gave her some small measure of happiness, then Cerise would never breathe a word against it.

Besides, if Cerise was even remotely harsh with Kaci, the

girl refused to talk to her, sometimes for weeks. Her feelings could be hurt so easily, and Cerise was her entire world.

Cerise didn't have to worry about her swearing around Myles, because Myles had never heard Kaci talk. No one had, except Cerise.

"Oh!" Cerise cried. The phrase *Mother Teresa* jogged something in her mind. She thumbed through the book she held in her lap and went straight to a paragraph she'd read earlier. Kaci crawled over to her excitedly. "What?"

Cerise found what she was looking for and held the page open. "Look, it's Mother Teresa! She was a real person!"

Cerise read haltingly, sounding out words she didn't quite understand. "Mother Teresa, known in the Catholic Church as St. Teresa of Calcutta, was an Albanian Indian Roman Catholic nun and missionary and consecrated virgin."

Cerise read it all again silently, then continued to the next paragraph. Kaci was already crawling away, back to the TV in the closet. "Cool," Kaci said under her breath, then stopped crawling and looked back to Cerise. "Wait, people talk about whether or not someone is a virgin?"

Cerise shook her head and read that line over again. *Weird.* "I guess."

Kaci looked stricken and scared again.

Damage control. Cerise launched into the argument she always used when she could tell Kaci was terrified to leave even this poor excuse for a life. "Look, Kaci, we're going to find your real parents. Living with them is going to be way better than living here. No one's going to hit you or yell at you."

Cerise licked her lips, praying that was true. She didn't know for sure, but kids on the TV were hugged and kissed and smiled at, and given presents on their birthday. She had no idea when her or Kaci's birthday was. They'd taken to celebrating them at random every few months, especially on days when Kaci slumped in the closet and stared at the ceiling, refusing to talk for hours. Cerise would run outside and gather pine cones, or flowers or anything to try to make her smile. One such *birthday* had resulted in Cerise weaving together sticks to make a basket that Kaci had carried around full of flowers or bugs until it had fallen apart.

"I'll take you shopping," Cerise said quickly.

Kaci smiled at that. "I shop, therefore I am."

Cerise leaned forward, hands on knees. Another Heather's quote. "Yes, you can get all those nice clothes that the Heathers wear. And Veronica, too. The plaid blouses with the shoulder pads."

Kaci made a face. "I hate those shoulder pads. They look so ugly. Besides, they aren't *in* anymore," she said with authority.

Cerise turned away to hide her smile. Kaci had to be right, they hadn't seen anybody wearing shoulder pads in any of the pictures of the houses they'd been in. All the girls wore them in Heathers, and sometimes the women wore them in the few Knight Rider DVDs they had, but none of the other shows.

Kaci spoke, her voice soft and whispery, but still, Cerise could tell how scared she was. "You're going to stay with me, right?"

Cerise nodded and forced a smile. "Of course," she said brightly. *Maybe.* She'd have to come back and pay back the people she'd taken the money from, but she'd have to make the money first. She could get a job in California. "I'm sure your parents would let me stay close by and visit you every day."

Kaci pouted. "If they won't, then I won't live with them."

Cerise was about to explain why that wouldn't work, when Kaci spoke again. "What if we get caught, like last time?"

Cerise shook her head. "I'm over 18 this time. The cops will leave us alone, I know it." *I hope.*

"We won't hitchhike?"

Cerise shook her head, forcing herself to look Kaci in the eye. She wasn't telling a lie, her plan was not to hitchhike unless it was their only option. "We won't hitchhike. We have enough money to get us to California, I know we do."

Tears formed in the corner of Kaci's eyes. "I don't want to go to foster care again." Cerise crawled over to her, squeezing inside the closet, and pulled her into a hug. "I know. Jail wasn't any fun, either."

"What about the big cop? The crazy one? What if he finds us again?" Kaci asked and Cerise pulled her in tighter. "I promise you he won't show up this time. He doesn't even know where we are." That was the only good thing about the last time they'd tried to escape and been caught. Sandra and Myles had moved them away from that man with the intense eyes, all the way across the country, and they'd never seen him again. He'd scared Cerise as much as he had Kaci.

Cerise rolled her eyes heavenward. Please God, let her be right. If that cop found them again, who knew what he would do.

CHAPTER 5

*B*eckett sat at Crew's new dining room table, on a bench, next to Troy and Trent, thankful that Trent was next to him and not Troy. Trent ate fastidiously, even though he had no hands to bring the food to his mouth, slowly lowering his head and delicately picking his way around his plate.

Troy ate like the dog he looked like, wolfing his food without regard to what mixed with what or how he looked or how much flew off his plate onto the tablecloth.

Beckett didn't mind it too much, but Heather, who was directly opposite them, looked positively green and hadn't touched a bite of her salad or roast. Her pregnancy surprise, or Troy's table manners? Beckett bet on the table manners. Heather still seemed to feel nervous around the two wolves.

Everyone at the table spoke over each other except for Trent and Troy, Heather, Beckett, and Jaggar.

Beckett finished his last bite of beef and dropped his fork, wondering how quickly he could escape. Did he have to wait until after dessert?

His gaze fell on the picture he had brought as a gift, already hanging on the wall directly above the table. A place of honor. It was the overhead view of Chicago he had taken from his drone in a circling panoramic before drones were cool. Crew had always loved that picture, so Beckett had taken it off the wall of his own house, gifting it to his friend.

Besides his truck, Beckett had nothing to spend his money on but his drones, and he'd been fascinated with drone photography from his very first flight. That picture had been one of the first *good* shots he'd ever taken. Professional quality.

Beckett would never have given that picture to anyone else, except maybe his own brother. But his brother was dead and Crew was the only substitute for him that Beckett had. Beckett clamped down on the feelings that came with that thought and tried to pay attention to something, anything else. Desperate, he focused on Troy, watching him lick his plate clean, then start on the tablecloth.

Wade cleared his throat, his face serious. "Can I say something?" He addressed his question to Crew and Dahlia.

Crew nodded, his expression questioning, and Dahlia smiled her agreement.

Wade thought for a moment before he began. "I want to get this out of the way, so we can enjoy the rest of our evening. We have much to talk about as a group, and this is the first time we've all been together in many weeks. We're missing Canyon, Timber, and Sebastian, but they already know most of this, and what they don't know, I'll make sure to tell them."

He pulled a piece of paper out of his pocket and stared at it. "On the subject of the one true mates, there is nothing new to report." He looked pointedly at Beckett but Beckett shook his head, still not knowing if Crew's vision was wrong, or if he had somehow lost a day of his life. "Maybe I was drunk," he mumbled, even as he knew he hadn't been that drunk in years, not since he'd first been old enough to scrounge up liquor and see if forgetfulness was stored at the bottom of a bottle.

Wade gave him a look, then dismissed him. "Khain crossed into the *Ula* today." Wade held up his hands to quell the noise that had erupted at that statement. Trevor, Graeme, Crew, and Troy all had begun speaking at once, or, in Troy's case, barking.

When they quieted, he went on. "We didn't call you because you couldn't help. He was only over for a moment, and you all have your jobs here to do. I've said many times that we are gearing up for something, and what he did today only proves it, although it does change our focus slightly."

Trevor spoke up. "What exactly did he do?"

Mac swore and shook his head, snarling his words. "Fucker materialized inside a prison and made a *foxen* prisoner disappear. Poof." *Foxen* were *shiften* who could shift into foxes, and who *wolven*, *bearen*, and *felen* did not quite trust, mostly because their origins were suspect. They were not part of the original creation story, and some *shiften* thought they could be fathered by Khain.

The mood around the table changed, and Beckett watched Crew's face closely. He had been on a honeymoon of sorts for the last six weeks, but that was over now.

Wade held up his hands again. "I hate to say it, but that's not the worst of what I have to tell you this evening. Jaggar has finally been able to decode about half of the messages found in Ella's aunt's basement."

Beckett sat up straighter. He hadn't heard this yet. He'd spent his day sitting in a prison cell, babysitting a different *foxen* inmate and praying Khain chose him to abduct next. Rhen knew Beckett could use a good battle with Khain. Anything to break up the monotony of work without Crew around.

Wade cleared his throat and glanced at Jaggar before continuing. "I'll let Jaggar tell you exactly what he's been able to discover so far, but now we know why he had such a hard time decoding the messages. They are based on languages, but different languages. Jaggar has cracked two of them so far, and once he figures out what languages the other ones are based on, he'll be able to crack them, too."

Wade stopped talking and looked to Jaggar to tell the rest of the story. Jaggar swallowed and glanced down at his plate. After a moment, Trevor broke in, speaking softly. "How did you figure that out, Jaggar?" His tone implied what a feat it had been.

Jaggar shook his head and pulled at his collar, but finally spoke. "That's not important. What's important is what they said. He wrote each page in a different code language, so I was only able to translate every fourth or fifth page, but what I did translate is scary." He looked up and met Trevor's eyes. "And sick."

"Wait." Beckett held up a hand. "Who's this *he* that we are talking about?"

Jaggar raised his eyebrows. "Grey Deatherage." Beckett swore and pushed his plate away. He'd lost his appetite for dessert.

Wade looked at him pointedly and motioned for Jaggar to continue.

"First thing I can say for certain, is that Grey lived in that house for many years. He…" Jaggar swallowed audibly, his throat clicking dryly. "He, ah, dated Ella's grandmother first and believes he fathered both her children. He then had, ah, relationships with those children. No offspring ever resulted from his relationship with Patricia Carmi, but Linda Carmi had one child who he believed was his. Shay Carmi, Ella's older sister."

Beckett looked around the table and could tell most of them already had heard this information. Trevor looked murderous, Ella queasy, but Dahlia's hand over her mouth and Mac's slow head-shake spoke volumes.

Crew spoke up. "Flowers in the Attic, *shiften*-style."

Mac snorted. "Sorry your granddad is such a dick, Ella."

Ella turned her head away and dropped both hands to her belly. Trevor rubbed the back of her neck and she shot him a grateful look.

Jaggar's two-toned face went stony, but he pushed on. "Judging from Linda Carmi's disappearance from Serenity during that pregnancy, until she got sick and had to return, we are guessing Grey's attentions were unwelcome. We've put out an APB for him, but Chicago PD has already been looking for him, and unable to find him for months, since he stopped showing up to work."

He picked up some papers on the table and riffled through them, found what he was looking for, then went on.

"From what I've been able to piece together, Grey and the angel who fathered the one true mates…" He broke off and looked through his papers again. "The angel- we know him as Azerbaizan- but Grey calls him Azer, they were friends. Grey might even have known about his plan to father the one true mates before he did it. Grey may have had some say in the making of the pendants and what kind of powers they would have. We're theorizing that's why the angel started with Linda Carmi, because of the connection she and Grey had. We also think Grey didn't know this, maybe still doesn't know it."

Jaggar looked around the table at the stunned expressions, then spoke in a rush. "He also might have at least one of those pendants and he seems to think it has the ability to summon Khain."

Beckett snorted. Wouldn't that be a kick in the pants. Summon Khain and then what? Kill him? Imprison him? Could that possibly be something that all the one true mates together could do? He remembered the ripped-up forest and thrown trees outside.

Jaggar waited until Wade was able to quell the outbursts that had erupted in response to what he had said, then continued. "His notes are rambling and incoherent, clearly the work of a crazy male, but it seems that Azerbaizan told him even he couldn't control what the pendants did, only that they would complement the one true mate's individual powers and possibly serve as beacons of some sort, but Grey didn't believe him." Jaggar's voice lowered and his eyes dropped to the table. "Besides that, everything I was able to translate leads me to believe that Grey has been working directly against our core mission for thirty or forty years now, and that he may be responsible for some of the acts we have attributed to Khain in the past."

The table erupted in talk again and Beckett pushed his hat up on his head, rubbing the scar over his right ear. It wasn't something he did often, but this conversation had him remembering that night so many years ago when he'd lost his father and brother. He'd seen Grey that day, been abused by him.

Wade held up his hands. "Everybody quiet down. We need to talk this out, and you all need to be aware of exactly what we're up against here. If Jaggar is right, and I've no reason to believe that he is not, it could mean that Grey has suddenly become even more dangerous to us than Khain is."

Trevor dropped a hand heavily to the table. "What do you mean, against our mission? Our only mission is to protect the humans from Khain and get rid of him if we can. That mission?"

Jaggar nodded, his voice sick. "I'll need to translate more of the languages to be sure, but it seems that Grey believes if Khain dies, Rhen dies, and therefore his main goal for the last thirty years has been to keep Khain alive, protect and help him."

Beckett swallowed over the lump in his throat. Rhen was their *deae*, their goddess, the being who had created all *shiften* as warriors in the fight against Khain. Her body currently resided under the police department of Serenity, too weak from the act of creation for her spirit to command.

"Protect how?" Beckett asked, suspicion leveling him.

"By killing anybody who has the power to harm him. By running interference between us and him. By trying to disrupt the very concept of us finding mates again."

Everybody at the table looked dumbfounded. Trevor finally spoke. "But why?"

Wade sighed heavily. "I do believe that Grey is insane, as Jaggar has said. I could go so far as to say he is moonstruck beyond hope of return. And if he believes that killing Khain will also kill Rhen, then he will never allow it, because threaded through his writings and ramblings is evidence that he is in love with Rhen, as much as the angel Azer is."

Nobody at the table had anything to say to that. Beckett

felt sick to his stomach. A *wolfen* in love with their goddess? A moonstruck *wolfen*? Which meant he was so crazy he could not be made right again, could not be cured with a run or a healing touch. No, Grey was not just a *wolfen*, Grey was a *Citlali*. The most powerful of all *wolven*, with powers the rest of them did not have, like the ability to stop other *wolfen* with just a touch, bind them from moving or breathing.

Beckett seethed. He had always thought Grey was dangerous, but this proved it. For some reason, Wade was staring at him. Beckett met his eyes questioningly.

"Beckett, most of the people at this table don't know the story of how you lost your father and brother." His voice was gentle, but it did nothing to untwist the knife in Beckett's chest. "Are you able to share that story? It could be important."

It took Beckett a moment to realize why Wade wanted him to tell everyone how his father and brother had been killed. And when he understood, he couldn't say a word. His throat closed and utter rage pulsed through him. Grey couldn't have been responsible for that.

He pushed away from the table, refusing Crew's hand of support, fleeing from the cabin, from the question that made him want to rip off his clothes, shift, and run until he dropped.

CHAPTER 6

Cerise sat just outside the closet, watching as Kaci's chest rose and fell evenly. Kaci had fallen asleep a few hours before, still sitting up in the corner, staring at the little TV.

Cerise had laid her down, turned off the TV, put their only blanket under her head, and covered her with Myles's old sweatshirts, what they both used as blankets. They had no bed. They slept on the floor every night, what did it matter if it was half-in, half-out of the closet?

Cerise wanted to sleep, but she was too keyed up. Their entire future rested on what happened in the morning. She stood and looked at the window, noting the utter blackness of the night. Morning would not be coming for hours yet.

She walked to the door and eased it open, heading out into the trailer to try to make a decision. On the other side of the trailer, in the only other bedroom, she could hear Myles snoring. She tiptoed close and peeked in, counting empty beer cans. Fifteen empties and two jars of moonshine. Perfect.

She gazed at his wrinkled, sour face. *Just die already.* Guilt filled her at the thought. She shouldn't think that about her own father, but she beat it back. She'd suffered more at his hands than she'd ever gained. Negative thoughts were a natural consequence of that.

Cerise left the doorway to his room and stared at the front door, trying to make her decision, then passed it by. She went back into the room with Kaci and dug her book out of their hidey-hole. She stood next to the window and tried to read by moonlight, but her legs kept wanting to walk, her toes to tap, her body to move. Finally, she gave up reading. She was too antsy to sleep or even stay still.

Again, she gazed outside. She should ride Zeus one last time, because after tomorrow, she might never see him again. She looked around the room, knowing there was no paper to leave a note for Kaci. She wasn't sure Kaci could read anyway, because she'd been so resistant to learning. Not that Cerise was any good at teaching something she'd only recently pieced together herself.

Instead, she dug through the bag they were taking with them and found Kaci's old stuffed animal that had been in her hand when Myles had first brought her to the car, when he'd stolen her away from her real parents. Fittingly, it was a stuffed horse, the body brown, the mane white. Zeus was the opposite, with a light tan body and a dark brown mane. They still didn't know where he'd come from. He just showed up one day, woefully underweight for a horse, and providing Kaci and Cerise with a project they sorely needed. An object for their love and attention that let them forget about the negligence and abuse they normally suffered.

Cerise stared at the frayed toy, at its threadbare skin and cotton popping out in places. She tucked it into Kaci's hand and hoped if Kaci woke up, she would understand that Cerise would be back soon and would not worry.

Cerise headed outside through the back door, hooked an apple out of the shed, and stood in the backyard, watching the forest behind it for some sign of Zeus. He normally stayed close by. Movement caught her eye and she turned that way, seeing Zeus clomp toward her, head raising and lowering. He stayed quiet, knowing better than to whinny or neigh this close to the trailer. Myles would chase him away if he ever saw him, or maybe shoot him with buckshot for fun, because Myles was an asshole.

Cerise held the apple out to Zeus, then patted his neck and flank as she whispered to him. "We're leaving soon, Zeus. I wish we knew who you belonged to, so we could get you back to him or her. We're going to miss you so much."

Tears threatened but she held them back, remembering that day they'd first seen him, a little over a year ago, pacing them in the forest, watching them with wary eyes. He'd been scrawny and thirsty. They never did know where he came from, but he'd let them ride on his back and listened when they told him not to come too close to the trailer. They filled the trough for him in the woods to drink water from, even in the winter and stole hay from the neighbor's fenced pasture to feed him.

"What do you say, Zeus? Are you up for one last ride?" Her whisper carried in the cold night air.

Zeus nickered softly, pushing his velvety nose against her.

Cerise bit her lip hard. He'd been a lifesaver, literally, pulling Kaci back from the brink of depression after Sandra had disappeared and Myles had been quicker with his fists than usual. Cerise had done her best to take the blows so Kaci didn't get many, but Cerise had been still recovering from her long illness, and was not always able to move fast enough. When Zeus showed up, Kaci had smiled again, laughed again. Healed at least a little.

Cerise grabbed his mane with one hand and swung herself up, a move she was extremely proud of and had spent weeks perfecting. She leaned forward. "One last ride," she whispered into his ear.

Zeus took off at once, into the trees. Cerise closed her eyes, feeling the wind whip through her hair, letting her fear about what would come fall away, letting Zeus pick the path they took. Everything would work out. It had to. California was Kaci's future, and maybe Cerise's also.

Cerise kept her eyes closed even when Zeus burst out of the forest to cross a meadow. She could tell he had because the wind grew colder and the scent of evergreen fell away. She opened her eyes and looked around, wondering why Zeus hadn't circled around and re-entered another trail. Normally he preferred to stay in the woods, and so did she.

Too late, she realized where Zeus was headed. To the house with the blue and white mailbox that looked like a barn. The house with the tunnel.

Zeus slowed and Cerise sat up straighter, watching the house as they neared it. No lights were on, it looked as empty as it had been the last time they'd been there. Her thoughts flew to the man at the end of the tunnel they'd found in the basement. The man she'd thought about every day since then.

What was his name? What did he do? Was he a nice man? A trustworthy man? Or a man like Myles? She winced. No way, he couldn't be that bad.

Zeus stopped in front of the gate and stomped his foot

as if to say, *see, I brought you here. I know this is where you wanted to go.*

Cerise stared at the house for a long time before she slipped off Zeus's back and walked down the driveway exactly as she had before. *Stupid!*

She continued to yell at herself, but still her feet did not stop. She found the window she had broken before, still stuffed with cardboard exactly as she'd left it. With luck, the owner wouldn't discover it until summer.

Without thinking, she dropped to her knees, pushed the cardboard out, opened the window, and slid into the basement.

***

Stupid!

Cerise stood in the tunnels, staring at the door that led to the man she couldn't stop thinking about. She'd opened the door once, but stood outside as his scent, that strong, clean outdoorsy man scent had washed over her. Was she really going to do this?

You're never going to see him again.

But you're risking everything. If you get caught, Kaci is doomed.

Still, she couldn't stop herself. She pushed her eye up close to the little plastic square again, waited for the beep, then entered his basement and made her way up the stairs, as if in a dream.

Once inside the kitchen, she turned to the living room. Immediately she noticed that the large picture of the city was gone, the one she'd been so fascinated with. Only an empty spot where it had been stared at her.

Without knowing exactly how she got there, she stopped in front of the empty square of wall and touched it, running her fingers over the inert tan paint, realizing she'd been looking forward to seeing that picture again. She wanted to go to whatever city was depicted in it, for real. Wanted to see those skyscrapers, maybe go in an elevator to the top floor. All new experiences for her. She wanted to *live*, not just exist any longer.

She wondered about the man, upstairs sleeping. She could feel him so clearly, almost outline his body in her mind. Who had he given the picture to? A woman? Why? Had he been the photographer? Had he been in a plane?

Again, her awareness of him peaked. She could feel him, like a pulse in her own body. He called to her, and she was unable to resist. Her feet carried her to the stairs, unconsciously avoiding all the squeaks she'd triggered last time.

At the top, she froze as a noise came from his bedroom. A light moan. Like he was in pain. Another nightmare? The thought of him hurting bothered her.

She made her way to his room on trembling feet, barely able to believe she was there again. She was an intruder. But then she saw him and her thoughts fell away. He looked exactly as he had the last time. Strong. Handsome. Kind? Was she imagining that? How could a person look kind in their sleep? Again, a camouflage cap sat on the pillow next to him, and she smiled gently at the sight of it. The room smelled like beer, though, and she frowned at that.

His hands fisted on the sheet and pulled at it, raising it to chest level. He spoke, his voice a low rasp. "No, not him! Please."

Cerise went to the bed quickly, and touched his elbow, holding her fingers there. Immediately, his face relaxed, and the sheet dropped to his body again.

She stared at his lips, red, and thick, with a cupid's bow rounding the top one, and wondered what it was like to kiss a man. *This* man.

She bent over him, that strange state of surreal-ness forcing her hand, making her barely able to think about everything that was so wrong about what she was doing, and pressed her lips to his.

Her body responded at once with hyperawareness, the nerve endings in her face singing at his nearness. His lips were firm, and his scent filled her nose. She wanted so much more and almost hoped he would wake up.

When he didn't, she stood and turned to leave. She would almost certainly never see him again, and the thought made her heart hurt in ways she didn't understand.

But.

Kaci was more important.

CHAPTER 7

*C*erise hurried out the door of the empty house, looking for Zeus, noticing the faintest streaks of light crossing the sky. Sunrise would be coming in less than an hour. She needed to get home quickly. Zeus was twenty feet away, eating grass from a hole he'd pawed in the snow at the bottom of a ditch. He turned to her as soon as she thought his name. *Good boy.* She would miss him so much.

A low rumbling caught her ear as she pulled herself up onto his back. She sat very high on Zeus, swiveling her head, unable to reconcile the sound with anything she had heard before. It sounded like a monster lizard crossing a meadow would, dragging a stomach as big as a house over the ground.

She slid back to the ground for a moment and stood still, her hand on Zeus's flank. Under her feet, the ground was shaking. Something heavy was coming from the direction of home. Cerise frowned, knowing it wasn't an animal. She was now able to hear the rumbling of machinery. She climbed back on Zeus. "That way, Zeus. I want to know what it is." Worry plagued the back of her mind, but she wasn't exactly sure why.

They paralleled the forest they normally would ride through, Zeus trotting along the edge of the empty country road, towards the noise. When Cerise finally saw what it was, she was relieved for only a moment. A tractor of some sort, bigger than one she had ever seen, with three wheels on each side, and taking up the entire road. No one would be able to pass. The closer it got, the more she could feel the ground shake, even from atop the horse.

"Into the forest, Zeus, I want to get ho-"

Cerise's eyes went wide. What if that monster machine had woken Kaci? Or worse, Myles! She leaned over Zeus, her body tight with fear, and spoke determinedly into his ear, "Zeus, faster than you've ever gone, you have to get me home right now. Kaci needs me."

As if he understood, Zeus sped up, entering the forest, then following a familiar path that would get her home in record time, but still, she knew it would not be fast enough.

***

Cerise slid off Zeus as soon as they entered the back yard, the tiny trailer sitting there, surrounded by trees, looking completely harmless. "Zeus, you should go," she said quietly, already walking.

Cerise entered slowly through the back door, ignoring the pang that always filled her chest when she did so, ignoring also the tangle of electrical wires that she had to step over.

How many times had she hoped someone would come to the trailer and arrest Myles for stealing electricity?

Cerise listened/felt the trailer. Two bodies, awake, both in Myles's room. Her heart dropped to her stomach and adrenaline spurted into her veins. Her fault! All her fault!

She walked that way swiftly, her eyes on the closed door past the kitchen, her hand retrieving a fireplace poker from its holder. She took the last few steps to the door, lifting the poker to her shoulder and choking up on it like a baseball player, a memory sliding through her mind. Kaci had loved the movie, A League of Their Own, but one day she'd left it on the floor after watching it and somehow crawled over it, cracking it in half with her knee. Kaci had cried herself to sleep, but had become fastidious about returning the DVDs to their cases after that. That movie, watched only a few times, was the sum total of Cerise's knowledge of baseball.

A muffled noise escaped the room. A gasp? A scream stopped by a grasping hand? Cerise's steps never wavered. No matter what she found, she would be dealing death when she got in there. Not the kind of thing she could hurry for. She needed to go in under control of herself.

Step. Step. Would Kaci recover? Had Cerise made the biggest mistake of her life all for nothing? She'd seen him. So what? So absolutely nothing. If Kaci's innocence was gone forever, she would never forgive herself for it.

Cerise let go of the poker with her left hand to push the door open.

Myles was sprawled atop his filthy mattress, Kaci pulled on top of him, one of his hands covering her mouth and the entire lower half of her delicate face. They were both fully clothed, and Cerise's heart unclenched slightly at the sight.

But Myles's zipper was down, and he was shoving Kaci's hand inside that disgusting opening.

"Let go of her." Cerise's voice sounded deadly, even to her own ears. She would swing no matter what, but she wanted Kaci clear first. Myles tightened his hold on Kaci, raising red, runny eyes to Cerise. He sneered at her and she saw murder in his gaze. That made two of them.

Kaci cried out as Myles's hand tightened on her wrist for a moment, then he sneered and pushed her away from him. Her feet tangled together and she fell into the wall. Myles stood, his head lowered like a bull about to charge, eyeing Cerise like she was the red cape.

Cerise's eyes never left Myles's face. "Get out of here, Kaci," she said, not bothering to tell her to leave the trailer, to run, to get away. It didn't matter if Kaci did or not. If Myles won the battle that was about to be fought, he would catch her no matter where she went. Catch her and continue what he had started. If Cerise won, they could still escape. Together.

Cerise gripped the cold steel tighter in both hands and watched for Myles's next move.

He took another step and raised his chin. "Come on, then," he said, spreading his hands wide.

For the first time, indecision filled Cerise. Should she make the first move, or should she wait for him to come to her?

No, if he decided to charge her, she might not get the poker down fast enough. So she moved in, feinted left, then went right with all her power and strength. Only a little surprised, he got a hand up between them. The poker sliced the back of his arm and a flap of skin opened, blood spraying across her face. She didn't acknowledge it, already pulling back for another swing.

He lunged, grabbed the poker and twisted it out of her hand, throwing it against the wall. Cerise shrieked, then attacked him with her nails and her teeth, letting the image of little Kaci trapped in his arms with her hand being forced onto his disgusting body fuel her rage. She had no chance of winning and she knew that, unless she tore out his throat, and the way she felt, she might be able to do just that.

Instead, he got a hand on her throat and slammed her against the wall, then swung her body in a wide arc against another wall, where she hit the side of her head. Blackness threatened.

She'd lost. Kaci was doomed.

I'm so sorry, Lemon. My fault, my fault.

"Let her go," Kaci's soft voice said from the doorway. Cerise rolled her eyes to Kaci, screaming inside her head. *No! Run!*

Myles gaped at Kaci, his mouth open, his hold on Cerise's neck slackening. He'd never heard Kaci speak before. He didn't think she was able to.

Kaci had them all fooled.

Cerise tried to hold on, but blackness danced around the edges of her vision. Her eyes rolled, trying to see Kaci clearly.

Kaci held the gun with the blue-swirled grip. She stood in the shooting stance they'd seen on TV thousands of times, her eyes narrowed, the gun looking too big for her small hands.

"I said. Let. Her. Go. Or die."

Myles snorted. "So, the little freak could talk all along, hey? That's some secret. Hold on there, missy. You'll be singing the rest of your secrets in just a second." He turned back to Cerise and his grip tightened as he slammed her against the wall again. Blackness took her and she felt pressure on her jaw as her legs gave out. Oxygen, she needed oxygen, now!

Boom. The insistent sound of the gun going off pulled her back to reality, as Myles's hands on her throat loosened once more and blood and flesh bathed her face and chest.

Myles, minus half of his head, fell to the ground, pulling her down with him. She yanked backwards, barely maneuvering her neck out of his slackening hands to avoid falling on the mess that used to be him.

Dead.

But Kaci had been the one who killed him.

Innocence lost, but not in the way she had first thought. And it was all Cerise's fault.

***

Cerise's hands hung loosely in her lap, her fingers twitching as she fought with herself not to push Zeus to his limit, not to lean over his neck, tell him to just go, to just take them anywhere, and she closed her eyes and waited for whatever fate was bringing them next.

She knew if they galloped along this country road, they would be remembered. Two girls, in clothes that were too big for them, neither wearing coats, one holding a faded green canvas bag, the other with wet hair in this cold, both riding bareback on a horse at a gallop? It would definitely raise eyebrows.

She looked around in the morning sunshine at the empty road beside them, wondering if the horror of Myles's death was stamped on their faces.

Could people see that she'd pitched a gun into a creek not even half an hour ago? A gun that had just killed a man?

What about her promise to herself to come back and take the blame for his death once she had Kaci safely ensconced with her real parents? Could anyone read that vow in the set of her body and face?

A car noise rumbled in the distance, coming toward them from behind a hill, and Cerise stiffened. It was a black Jeep, an older man with silver hair staring at them as they passed, his eyes taking in everything. Cerise looked away, hoping Kaci did too. She held her breath until the sound of the Jeep faded from the way they had come.

Moments later- or maybe hours- Cerise had no concept of time in her numb brain, Kaci spoke from behind her. "Look." Cerise raised her head, unable to think, unable to feel.

A pasture to their right, with six horses, all staring at them. Up ahead, Cerise spied a gate. It was perfect, and aside from *killing* Myles instead of leaving him sleeping off a bender, their plan was going perfectly.

"Stop," Cerise said to Zeus. She slid off, took the canvas bag full of their clothes and money from Kaci and motioned for her to get down. She nodded at Kaci. "Say goodbye."

Cerise turned away, not wanting to see Kaci's tears spill. She could still hear her, though. Kaci's voice thick, she said, "You'll have a family now, Zeus. Thank you for everything." Kissing sounds, then a strangled sigh. Cerise's heart clenched painfully. Kaci had loved the horse more than she'd loved Myles. So far, she'd barely responded to the fact that she'd killed a man.

Cerise clamped her tongue between her teeth. Too much. She couldn't take any more pain that day, any more surprises. It was still morning, though, and many hours of pain could await them.

The gate opened easily and Cerise led Zeus through it with apples. The other horses ran away, causing Kaci to frown.

"He'll be fine," Cerise said having no idea if he would be

or not. "They will come back." Another presumption on her part. As long as someone fed and watered Zeus, and treated him well, Cerise was happy.

She closed the gate and began to walk towards town.

After a long while, she said, "We're doing it, Lemon. We have to be strong, because we are on our own." Her words were more to herself than to her sister.

Kaci ran to catch up with her. "We always have been."

CHAPTER 8

*B*eckett woke up slowly, smacking his lips together, like he'd just put on Chapstick. He cracked his eyes open and looked around the room, grabbing his cap and putting it on his head first thing, like he always did, effectively hiding his scar. He sat up and groaned, holding his head in his hands. "Hair of the dog that bit me on the ass," he joked to himself but the words fell flat in the empty room.

He ignored his pounding head and stood up, looking at the alarm clock. He'd slept through it, if he'd set it at all. After leaving Crew and Dahlia's place, running like a coward from his friends, he'd gone straight to the liquor store and bought enough liquor to drink himself into a stupor. Alone. On his couch, staring at the empty spot on his wall and trying not to think about that night when he'd lost what had been left of his family. He was surprised he'd even ended up in his bed, rather than sprawled out on his living room floor.

Beckett headed out to the hallway. Fuck if he was going to work. He didn't care what was going on. They'd have to save the world without him today. He would do something else. Anything else. By himself. Crew would be busy with his new mate. A pang of guilt hit him. Saving the world meant keeping his best friend's new mate safe. Shaking his head, Beckett remembered that poor forest floor, ripped apart and burned, that tree flung a half mile away by some invisible force. She could take care of herself.

A scent that didn't belong in his home reached him, the realization freezing his muscles. Beckett stopped midstride on his way to the bathroom and flared his nostrils.

A light and airy scent, sweet like red licorice coated with sugar, so candied his mouth began to water.

She'd been there!

Beckett frowned. Not sure why he associated the scent with a she, but still, he knew exactly who he was thinking of, the girl from his dreams. The one he'd begun dreaming about just over a month ago, right around the time he was supposed to have met his one true mate, according to Crew. Could he somehow be traveling in his sleep, like Crew used to, and his waking self didn't remember that his dreaming self *had* met his one true mate? No, that didn't make a lick of sense.

He stayed where he was, letting the scent come to him, trying to call to his mind the image of her. He got only an impression though: long hair, light-colored, wide-set eyes, sweet expression. Innocent. *Mine.*

Beckett frowned again. If that was really her scent, had she been in his house? He prowled through each upstairs room, then headed downstairs, checking to see if any of his windows were open. They were all unlocked, even his front door was, but none stood open, so the smell was coming from inside the house.

Beckett turned in a circle in his living room, knowing if she had been there, she was gone now. He returned to his room and pulled on a dark, long-sleeved shirt and dark pants, then shoved his feet into his work boots. Work clothes, even though he had no intention of going in. He was sick of being a good soldier, even though he hadn't decided what else to do. He had no options, really, being a good soldier was in his blood, was his fate.

He made his way downstairs, ignoring the pain in his chest that still lingered from the night before. Something he'd had years of practice doing.

At the bottom step, on a whim, he dropped his nose to the railing and scented deeply. She had been here. Hours ago. His nostrils quivered as he tried to pick more information from the scent. Human or *shiften* or one true mate? He couldn't tell. Only that her scent was luscious, like nothing he'd ever smelled before. His body stiffened with all the best kinds of tension. He wanted her, and he'd never seen her face or heard her voice. It was like voodoo, or a love spell he couldn't fight; didn't want to fight.

Beckett shook his head, indecision filling him. Was this where it began? Would he meet his one true mate today? When he found her, would they go live out at Trevor's property with the rest of them? He laughed lightly. A freak commune if he'd ever heard of one. No way was he ever doing that.

He rubbed a hand over his mouth and stared around his living room. What to do first? His eye fell on the blank space on the wall that he'd taken Crew's present from. He reached it in two steps, then touched it lightly, then pressed his face almost against it. She'd *touched* the wall here. But why? He leaned close to catch more of her scent. Sweet. Divine.

Desperate to know more, he got down on his hands and knees and put his nose to the ground, aching to determine exactly what else she had done in his house.

He rose, walked through the room into the kitchen, turned in a circle, then dropped to the floor and smelled the linoleum. Yes, even the outline of her shoes called to him, old canvas, overlaid with her sweet scent. He stood, knowing exactly where he was going.

A few minutes later, in his basement, he looked around at nothing but old shit that he'd never gotten rid of. Years of accumulation since he'd come from Kentucky to Illinois. Why would she come down here?

He noticed another scent. One that was older and hard to distinguish from the smell of the basement, but he knew it was there, just the same. His eyes locked on a spilled container of old DVDs he no longer needed in the digital age, Beckett kicked off his boots and stripped bare, then stood back in his mind to let his wolf come forward.

His eyes rolled in his head and his back bowed as his body fell forward and began the change. Pain ripped through him with the shift, but so did pleasure, the unique pleasure of allowing his stronger physical nature to best his stronger intellectual nature. His wolf growled as soon as it could, not liking to be inside and hating the liquor he'd drank the night before, blunting both their senses. *Sorry, big guy. I needed it.*

Fully shifted, primally different but also the same, Beckett ran his tongue out over his lips for a moment, then prowled straight to the box of DVDs, taking air in through his nose in short little puffs, letting the scents roll around in the chambers there, teasing more information out of them. A girl and a woman, no relation. The girl pre-pubescent, human, hurting, weak physically but not mentally, emotional torture stunting her physical and psychological growth. She had been there more than one moon-cycle ago.

The woman, strong. Warrior strong, but indecisive. Her emotions had roiled both times she'd been inside his house, instinct driving her but her conscious mind fighting it tooth and nail. He could smell both the blackish-green, viscous texture of the thoughts, and the smoother, cooler, redder scent of her instinct, but not what either had contained, only that both had been strong enough to leave an imprint behind.

Beckett left the DVDs and cased the room, checking every corner, discovering where the two females had entered. When done, he returned to his clothes. His wolf's eyes gazed up the stairs to where he knew the exit from the house was, but Beckett easily moved forward and caged him. He'd had so much experience over the last decades that it was easy.

Human once more, ignoring the loss he felt at the transition, Beckett pulled his clothes on, his mind turning over everything his wolf had discerned. She'd been in his house twice, yet somehow he'd never known, not even scenting her the first time, or maybe scenting it and dismissing it for some reason? His wolf had discovered something else, too. She'd touched him. On his mouth. With her own lips. Meaning she'd kissed him, only a few hours ago. His tongue snaked out, trying to taste her on his lips.

Beckett didn't try to puzzle that out. She must have had her reasons. It didn't bother him one bit, in fact, he would give anything to experience it again with this mysterious female. Awake, asleep; he'd take whatever he could get.

None of what happened before mattered. Only what he

did now was important. His eyes fell on the retina scanner on the wall, and that feeling that something momentous was happening to him deepened. His heart picked up speed in his chest. Maybe Crew *had* been right after all. Time to follow the female and find out exactly what was going on here.

He wondered for a moment how she'd gotten the door open, then dismissed the thought. He wasn't good at puzzles, didn't enjoy them. He craved action, and that was available for the taking. He moved in front of the scanner, triggering it, then slipped into the corridor beyond. He rarely used the tunnels, hating being closed in, and preferring to drive everywhere. His preferences immediately ceased to matter because he knew immediately she had been there. The sweet licorice smell assailed him, stronger in this enclosed space, soothing him like a lover's caress.

His mind empty and serene for the first time in weeks, he turned right and followed the scent.

***

Beckett stopped at the edge of the forest, his mind spinning in a way he wasn't used to. He was by nature a grunt, a foot soldier, a worker-bee doing what he was told to do by someone smarter and higher up the feeding chain than him. But now, a seemingly unsolvable puzzle lay before him, and he was loath to give it up to anyone else. The unknown female had entered the tunnels through a patrol officer's house, one she'd broken into first, then returned that same way, and ridden a horse through here.

Why?

He took one step into the cool evergreens, not feeling the frigid air against his skin, even though he had no jacket, no hat or gloves. His mind burned with a craving to solve this mystery, warming him from the inside out.

He turned his face to the sky, taking the scent of pine resin, wood smoke, and frozen earth into his lungs deeply. His wolf loved it, wanting out and Beckett almost gave in. He'd lived as a wolf for three weeks once before, using the transition to blunt his immense grief. The idea beckoned and maybe would have won if the licorice smell of the female didn't beckon stronger. He picked up speed, jogging to follow it.

His phone rang in his back pocket and he ignored it, briefly considering pitching it into the woods, but killing the idea when a new scent reached him.

Death.

Not hers.

He shook himself, still not knowing who *she* was. His jog quickened to a run as he followed the well-worn path through the forest, ending at a small clearing that marched directly to a trailer, one that was old and ramshackle, with the roof sagging on one side, extension cords snaking through the yard, and blue tarps covering two windows. He stared at the metal home, realizing the scents of blood and gunpowder were coming from inside. He hadn't brought his gun, but it might not matter. He had better weapons.

Beckett unleashed the animal inside him for the second time that morning, and dropped to the snowy ground, watching the trailer carefully as his body completed the shift. Blues muted to grays and grays faded to tan, while the orange extension cords on the ground became yellow. Colors and the urgency of his thoughts and emotions were the only things that faded as he shifted. Scents, sounds, primal needs, and the slightest shift in the atmosphere exploded in vibrancy.

The fact that he was able to shift at all meant no humans could possibly be staring out the window.

No live ones.

CHAPTER 9

*B*eckett circled the perimeter of the trailer once, ensuring to himself that nothing moved or breathed inside, then he returned to the rear yard, ignoring a scent that screamed at him. Later. Inside first. Back at the building, he stood on his hind legs, and tore away one of the tarps. He leapt inside, neatly clearing the window and landing in a tiny living room with attached kitchen.

She had been here. Lived here. Her scent was everywhere, but so was stale beer, strong moonshine, and hand-rolled cigarettes. He turned right, toward the smell of blood, ignoring everything else.

The door of a small room stood open. Beckett lumbered toward it, his wolf so large he took up most of the hallway, his back much higher than the knob of the door. In his peripheral vision, the black socks his wolf wore swung into view every time he took a step. The hated black socks that branded him as the subject of the Saving the Savior prophecy, that had both ensured him a spot on the KSRT, and killed his father and brother. Beckett often wondered if he would have been able to do something to stop their deaths, that question one he could only drink into blackness for a short while.

He crossed the threshold, his nose interpreting the story even before his eyes saw the dead human. The girl, the pre-pubescent one from his basement, had stood right here in the doorway and fired the gun. He nosed closer to the dead body, marking every blood spurt and splatter, then catching the scent of the woman, then her blood. He picked his way carefully over the scene until he could do what he intended, something very unusual for a wolf, especially one his size. He raised up onto his hind legs to get his nose closer to a spot on the wall, to be certain of what he suspected.

Yes. No. The scent of her blood from a small spot on the wall provided him confirmation of his theory, and more mystery. Everything in the room told a clear story, except for the mysterious, slight scent in her blood, one he almost recognized by name, but his wolf told him was poison, name or not.

Beckett dropped back to four legs and backed away, placing his paws carefully, sparing the dead human not so much as a glance. This was a justified shooting if he'd ever seen one. Imagining what the human, who reeked of binges and sour rage, had done induced an urge in Beckett to lift his leg and piss on the body. He restrained himself.

He crossed the room, back into the rest of the trailer, following the scent that most interested him now, the light, sweet scent of the woman that made his mouth water.

On the other side of the living area, he found one more room and pushed his way inside. Again, the room told a story.

The bitter scents of years-old fear, despair, and despondency that made Beckett shake his head in as much muted empathy as his prowling wolf could manage. But the redolent, wholesome scents of love, togetherness, and dreams soothed him.

Again, he nosed along the floor of the room, until he smelled something that caught his attention: himself.

He pushed his way into the closet and, using his teeth, pulled a sweatshirt off a TV no bigger than a toaster. Behind it was a stack of DVDs, and at the very top of the stack, one of his DVDs, taken from his house.

Beckett sneezed at the riddle, backing out of the closet. He would be heading in to work today after all. He dropped his nose to the ground again and followed the most recent scents of the girl and the woman who had spent many unhappy years in that room, puzzling out their last steps. They had left by the front door, hours ago. He would follow, but first, he had one more scent to check, and a phone call to make.

He leapt back out the window, dismayed to find a breeze had picked up, which could make tracking the twosome impossible. He would still try.

The scent he had ignored earlier called to him, and he dropped his nose to the ground to follow, skirting a sad-looking shed built from metal roofing, to the farthest western corner of the yard, just before the forest started.

He rubbed his muzzle against the snow, then against the dirt below, trying to catch the scant scent that was left.

A decaying body lay below him. A woman, buried in a shallow grave for no more than a year. The dead man inside had been the one who buried her.

Beckett headed back to his clothes, then swung left as another scent called to him. He entered the forest swiftly, his paws making no noise as he trod on the groundcover of needles there. When he found what his nose told him was there, he sat back on his haunches and stared for a full minute, canting his head first to one side, then the other, then he crept forward and took an identifying sniff of one of the orange mushrooms flecked with white. Poison! Just one of these mushrooms could put a full-grown man into liver failure. But there were at least twenty growing between the roots of the tree.

Beckett sat back again, taking in the plot of mushrooms as a whole. It extended around the base of the tree, its edges an obvious square, making it look as if they had not grown haphazardly there, as mushrooms did in the wild, but rather as if they had been cultivated, like in a garden.

The mystery surpassed anything he could puzzle out in animal or human form, so Beckett headed for his clothes. He would call in the detectives, and let them do their job.

When he reached his clothes, his phone was ringing already. He shifted as quickly as nature let him, then knelt naked in the snow and fished his phone out of his pants pocket, his senses on high alert.

If it would have been anyone else, he would have ignored it, but it was Crew.

"Crew," he said warmly into the phone.

Crew's harried voice put Beck on alert immediately. "They need you, Beck, at Clear Sky Lake. Me, Trevor, and Graeme are locked down here at the house, in case this is a trap to lure us away from our mates, but it's not. It's for real."

"What's for real?" Beckett said, but the urgency in Crew's tone told him more than he wanted to know.

"The *Vahiy*. The signs leading up to it. Khain just tripped one of them somehow. He's trying to force it to happen."

Beckett swallowed hard. The *Vahiy*. The end times. Also

known as the DOR: The Day of Reckoning, or the Death of Rhen. No one knew what it meant, but all *shiften* universally feared that day. Would they cease to exist? Drop in their tracks as their connection to Rhen was cut off? Or maybe they would lose their ability to shift. Or, somehow worse, would Khain become so strong they could not hope to fight him?

Fear mobilized him, making him forget for only a moment what he had just discovered. "Where do they need me?"

"At Clear Sky Lake. It's on fire. We've set up a command post here, but Wade and everyone else are at the lake."

Beckett frowned. "Everybody?"

Crew grunted, then moved away from the phone and said something to someone else in the room. It sounded like *another one?*

Beckett waited until he had Crew's attention again. "Crew, what if this *is* a trap. What if he's going to hit somewhere else while we're all out at the lake?"

"Doesn't matter, Beck, you gotta go. Remember the 777 signs? The one about a lake fire says this: *Shiften hesitate, shiften fail. The demon gets the upper hand, his fire raging into a firenado that marches his plot forward.* Meaning if he has his way and this sign gets out of control, it leads right to the next sign. We've got to stop it."

Beckett's hand tightened on the phone. Firenado? Never heard of it, but it didn't sound good. "What's the next sign?"

"It's in flowery language, almost like propaganda, but Sebastian thinks it means Serenity burns to the ground, but it might go farther. We're getting reports of more lakes on fire, one in Mississippi, one in Oregon, a few further south." He stopped and spoke again to someone else in the house, then when he returned to Beckett, his voice was tighter than ever. "Beck, we aren't sure how he's doing it, and if we can't figure out how to stop it, he could burn every major city in the entire country down, at least every one that's built on a waterway."

Beckett knew that was almost all of them. *Fuck.*

"I'll be out there in twenty, Crew."

He would call in what he'd found here, but he wouldn't be able to search for (his mate?) the two girls who were probably scared out of their minds. He'd have to tell patrol to take it easy on them if they were found.

CHAPTER 10

*G*rey Deatherage trod down the last three steps that led into his sanctuary, chanting meaningless words with each step like offerings to the gods.

"Horrors. Hostages. Hounds."

He reached the bottom, the cold concrete floor so much like the tunnels at every police station he'd ever worked at. But none of his fellow officers knew about this tunnel, and if he continued to receive Rhen's favor, they never would.

He strode along the cramped, dank corridor, ignoring the spirits that pushed at him from all sides.

"Triple H. Mudge. Mudged. Mudger."

His voice was soft, echoing almost not at all, as his footsteps were louder and covered it.

At the end of the tunnel, he pushed open the door to his inner sanctum, the only place he felt safe. It was not locked, had no cause to be. The door at street level was hidden and locked to his satisfaction.

Grey swung the door shut behind him and stood still for a moment in the complete and utter darkness, taking stock of the large room with his acute senses. Behind and above him, the faint call of an ambulance siren swelled and waned, and a single horn honked once, sharply.

In front of him, the room opened like a cavern and the spirits pressed in on him more, welcoming him home, wanting to talk with him. He could handle them, and he knew they would keep out anyone bent on finding his secrets.

He crouched and felt to the right of him for the electric lantern he knew was there. He picked it up and lit it with a lighter from his pocket, then strode to the very center of the large open room that held only one chair and an end table next to it. He only came here for his most important work and he didn't need more.

Above him, footsteps sounded dully, as the humans went about their business. None of them knew of the room below their feet. This room that was supposed to have been filled in completely, bulldozed to hell, like it had never existed.

Grey sat in the La-Z-Boy and flipped his feet up with the lever on his right side. Relaxation always helped when trying to communicate with angels.

Just one angel, actually. Azerbaizan, that son of a bitch who had not answered him in years. Grey could feel the bodiless dickstand was still alive, so he kept trying. Could an angel even die? Maybe.

Grey relaxed, starting with his scalp muscles and working down to his toes. He took deep even breaths and let the spirits pull at him, their fingers ruffling his hair and moving his clothing slightly, but doing no more than that. He could not help them and they could not harm him.

Grey imagined Azer's presence, his being made of light and fight and fire, and fixed it firmly in his mind, seeking him out, asking for him, commanding him to answer.

Azerbaizan, you shimmery bastard, answer my call. Light damn you, talk to me!

Nothing.

Grey took another deep breath and sent out his feelers. He had nowhere to direct his thoughts, nothing to focus his request on. But Azer was not dead, he knew it. He could feel Azer's presence, like a light flickering in the darkness, he just could not feel where the light was, how it was, if it was hurt or contained in some manner. Could he be asleep or unconscious like the actual Light? Maybe. Perhaps fathering the one true mates had weakened him to the point where he could no longer communicate.

The last time they had conversed, Azer's plan was to harvest materials from The Haven, to be combined with materials from Khain's home, the *Pravus*, to form into objects of power which he would leave with the women he bedded. Pendants that would remind them of who their children really were, and would also help the children communicate with their father as they grew, so he could shape them, guide them, help them develop their powers, and prepare them for their lives as half-angels fated to mate with *shiften*. Any who did not have that preparation would enter adulthood weaker than they should be, possibly unaware of their powers, more prone to losing their minds to what humans would call insanity, what *shiften* would call being moonstruck, but in reality it would be a desperate incongruity between what their souls knew to be true about themselves and how society shaped them to behave.

The pendants had been Grey's idea. Which Azer swiftly forgot. Flighty cocksucker only remembered what he wanted to.

Frustration bubbled within Grey, ruining his concentration. He gritted his teeth and willed it back. Did he dare try to contact Rhen?

A deep swell of longing filled his chest, longing to feel her presence, to hear her voice, to know how she was. But if he did that, she might tell someone where he was. Someone meaning Wade, that asshole, and Wade would come looking for him, bringing his troop of thankfully incompetent circus puppies with him.

Grey shot out of the chair, almost knocking it over in his anger. He was stuck, with no possible plan of action.

As much as he liked to take potshots at the KSRT, the truth was, they had pulled off a coup, entering and exiting the *Pravus* like it was a coffee shop, with no loss of life and a victory that would go down in *shiften* history as the beginning of the end for Khain, unless Grey was able to stop it.

Three one true mates had been found and now they had a *dragen* on their side. Last he'd heard, Troy and Trent, the two non-shifting *wolven*, had been inducted into the KSRT, and they worried him more than any of the other members. They had no prophecy, either of them, but because they were non-shifting, they saw and intuited things the others did not. If either of them scented him, he was almost certain they would know instantly of his betrayal. Which is why he had disappeared. *One of the reasons* he had disappeared.

Grey paced, his strides long and purposeful as he circled the room just out of the reach of the flickering light.

Khain could not be on the losing side of this battle, but Grey did not know how to make sure of that. Khain had been winning for so long, his move to kill all the *shiften* females a stroke of genius that Grey had been certain would decimate the spirit of the *shiften*, leaving them no choice but to mate with humans and wait for their line to weaken to the point where Khain could do as he willed. Grey himself had never found a *wolven* female to mate, so the act had not affected him in quite the same way as it did his brethren.

Those had been the early days, when Grey had not quite realized what a *shiften* victory over Khain would mean, so he had not argued against Azer's plan when he first heard of it, had in fact helped him put it into motion.

And now, it would destroy everything, unless he was able to derail it somehow. So, what to do now? How to continue to move his own plan forward?

An idea shot through him like a spear and Grey changed direction mid-stride, sprinting for the center of the room. He lifted the kerosene lantern off the table and tore away its false bottom. Out tumbled three bundles of cloth that wrapped his most precious possessions within them.

The answer had to lie with them. He did not know exactly how to use them, or even if he could, since they did not belong to him, but he knew they were filled with great power, greater power than even Azer had ever predicted or intended. Now to decide which one to–

A light glowed from within one. All thoughts were ripped from Grey's mind and his fingers convulsed, then straightened, relaxing almost to the point of dropping the three bundles. He forced his muscles to respond to his commands again, carefully putting the other two bundles down slowly, then unwrapping the one that was glowing, being careful not to touch it.

He didn't know what the glowing meant, but he suspect-ed the pendant could hurt him in some way in this state.

With shaking fingers, he used the cloth and the chain to which the pendant was attached to maneuver it onto the table, so that he could stare at it, trying to discern its secrets.

A snarling wolf with amber-colored eyes stared up at him. The glowing came from the eyes of the wolf, pulsing lightly, the yellow glow washing over the body of the wolf and casting a relief he had never noticed before. With each pulse, pulse, pulse of its eyes, the yellow glow made the feet of the wolf appear to be a different color than the rest of the wolf.

Grey dropped to his knees and stared at the piece, seeing in his imagination the angel on the other side, but discarding it as not important. The wolf was what was important, and why it was glowing.

As Grey changed his position in relation to the wolf, re-alization plowed through him. He knew which female this particular pendant belonged to, remembered taking it from her family home years ago, and now, fortuitously, he knew who her mate was.

He stared at the phenomenon, the glowing light casting the shadows on the wolf that were not otherwise there, the boots that identified this wolf as one of only a handful, and only one of them was in the KSRT.

He still did not know why the wolf's eyes were glowing, but his path was now clear.

Finish his business with Beckett Oswego.

Ensure Beckett never found his mate, or his mate nev-er found him. Either would work. Both would be better. He knew where Beckett was, so that's where he would start.

But what to do with the pendant? Bring it with him? It

was dangerous to him, he knew that, but– his phone rang, cutting off his thoughts.

"Deatherage," he barked into it, his eyes still on the pendant on the table.

"Chief," a raspy voice said. Old habits died hard.

Grey's mind spun. More coincidence. He did not know what he was about to discover, but he knew it would uphold his cause, cement his decision. A gift from the gods, maybe from Rhen herself, sparking his path like a lighted arrow.

He could barely speak. "Go," he finally choked out.

"Pekin. Myles Pekin. He's finally surfaced."

With stunning clarity, Grey finally knew exactly where Myles and Sandra had run to, and knew that he could now take out both birds with one stone. Further confirmation of the rightness of his course of action.

"In Serenity?" His words echoed through the large empty chamber, almost mocking him and how he hadn't been able to find them, had never thought to look for them there. Of course they were there. Rhen favored him no more than anyone else. *No! That was not true!*

The voice on the other end of the phone said nothing for a moment, and Grey pulled his attention back to the cold silence he could read immediately. *If you knew, then why have I been typing this name into the system every night for years?*

"Yeah, Serenity," the voice said carefully, keeping the accusation out of his tone. "But there's one hitch. He's dead."

"Curiouser," Grey said, not surprised at all. "Liver failure?" Myles favored the moonshine, anything to blunt the pain of his failings.

"No, he was shot."

"His wife do it?"

"No, suspect unknown. The wife is dead, too, probably for at least a year, and buried in the backyard."

"Tsk, tsk. Not a proper burial, was it?"

Again, that slow, heavy moment before his contact spoke again. "Okay, yeah, well anyway, you wanted to know if I ever saw his name on the wire, and there it is."

"Certainly, you did a stellar job. And now there's only a bit of your assignment left."

Another hesitation. Grey didn't say a word, knowing the wolf would realize his place if he just thought about it long enough.

"And what is that?"

"I know who did it. I need you to convince Serenity PD to find them and deal with them properly, until I can get there." Then what? Break them out? He couldn't kill them. An idea bloomed in his mind, something about jail assassinations. Probably beyond his ability to order, but he did have associates.

His contact became all business. "Name? Description?"

"Cerise Pekin and Kaci Pekin. His daughters. Cerise is 25, but looks younger. Her hair is probably long and was strawberry blonde the last time I saw it. She is light-skinned and approximately five foot, five inches tall, with hazel eyes. Kaci is 12, and tiny for her age. She's painfully thin and doesn't speak, with rusty red hair and freckles all over her face. They say she's mute, but I'm not sure if I believe it. Both will probably be wearing shoddy, shabby clothes. You can't let their looks fool you, though, both girls are incredibly dangerous and mentally unstable, especially the older one."

He hadn't seen either in years, not since the last time Cerise had tried to steal Kaci away, causing Myles and Sandra to run from his displeasure, but he *felt* those descriptions still fit them. "Check the bus stations, hitchhikers on the major highways going west, maybe even the train stations. They'll be trying to escape. When they're found, do not keep them in a holding cell, they need to go straight to jail." *If* they were found. They'd hitchhiked last time, and if they were more successful this time, they could be out of Illinois already.

"Not the 12 year old? Especially if she's tiny."

"Yes, the 12 year old. Straight to juvenile hall. She's dangerous, would cut off her own mother's head for burning cookies. Don't fucking question me."

The male on the other end sighed. "Yes, Chief."

"Good wolf. Do it right and you won't hear from me again. Fuck it up and you'll be wiping my ass for the next decade."

"Yes, Chief."

Grey hung up the phone. End times called for dirty, desperate measures.

He checked the time. He could be in Serenity in three hours, less if traffic was light, which it never was. Still, just in time for Beckett to come home from work.

A bullet to the head from his own second story window as he trudged to his front door would deal with him nicely.

Then Cerise Pekin could rot in jail and no one would ever even miss her.

CHAPTER 11

*C*erise curled the money in her fist, fear spiking through her. They had enough money, but they still weren't going to be able to escape. She could read it in the bored, seen-this-shit-before expression of the woman behind the desk. From behind, Kaci crowded close to her, practically burying her face in Cerise's back. Cerise could feel her panic, and was trying not to give in to panic herself. There were just *so many* people at the bus station!

The line behind them was hostile, she could feel their accusing stares on her back, hear two women whispering about her. "Please," she said to the ticket-seller. "We have to get to California. My-our… our mom is dying." They'd already killed someone that morning, then walked for six hours to get to the bus terminal. She didn't have any energy left to worry about the lie.

The woman cracked her gum, then rolled her eyes. "I told

you, if you don't have I.D., I can't sell you a ticket. It's the law." She leaned forward, her face set. "I can't break the law for you, honey. I'd lose my job."

Cerise's palms began to sweat, wetting their money. The train station was miles away and she didn't think Kaci could take one more step. And what if they got there and couldn't get on the train without I.D. either? They were completely out of options. Except hitchhiking. She'd promised Kaci…

A male voice from the line behind them yelled, "Buy a ticket or move!" and the ticket-seller rolled her eyes again, lifting one hand, pointing to Cerise's left. "I can't help you, honey. Just move on."

Cerise stuffed their money into the pocket of her jeans, then shuffled to the left, trying to hold herself together, to think of some other option.

Kaci clutched at Cerise's shirt, her head still down, her slim frame trembling. Was she crying? The nondescript music filtering through the terminal stopped and a clunk sounded, coming from everywhere. Cerise glanced at the ceiling, as Kaci jumped against her. A male voice came through one of the speakers Cerise had spied. "Bus 215 to Indianapolis boarding at Gate 2A."

With the announcement, a stream of people rose from their chairs, crossing the room directly behind and in front of Cerise and Kaci, trapping them where they stood. Smells of cigarette smoke, unwashed bodies, and some sort of pungent, garlicky food assailed Cerise. Someone's bag shoved her in the side, almost knocking her to the ground, forcing a cry from Kaci.

Cerise pulled at Kaci. "Come on, let's get out of the way." Kaci wouldn't even lift her head and look around. Neither of them had ever been in a room with so many people before.

Even when they'd tried to escape Myles and Sandra the other times, they'd never dealt with anything like this.

Cerise pulled Kaci to the closest wall, where only one other person was standing, and one sitting, both men, which put Cerise automatically on her guard. The one standing was staring at the corkboard that covered the wall, reading the notices there. The one sitting wore layers and layers of dirty clothes even shabbier than what Cerise and Kaci wore, with what looked like mud on his face and in his beard. Around him were worn plastic bags stuffed with clothes. Cerise could smell him. Dirt and body odor. Lovely.

She wondered if he were homeless, sleeping here on the floor at the bus station. What if she and Kaci were forced to sleep there tonight? What would they do if they could never get to California?

The male on the floor smiled brightly at her, revealing only one tooth in that smile. Cerise watched him suspiciously, sensing he wanted something.

"Got some money, sweet girl?" he crooned, when he caught her eye. "I haven't eaten in days."

Kaci kept her head buried in Cerise's back, still refusing to even look around. Cerise was torn, her eyes flying away from the man on the ground. She had money, but she needed it to take care of her and Kaci! But they had both eaten rice and beans the night before and they even had some cans of food in their bag. So, technically they were better off than-

One of the notices caught her eye and she shuffled closer to it to get a better look, reading it in her painstakingly slow manner, especially the words she'd never seen before.

Need a ride to Spokane.

And below that:

Hippie van headed to Seattle!

Excitement seized her. They could find a ride, pay someone to drive them the entire way there! If they had enough money. Her eyes searched the papers on the wall to see how much a ride all the way to California would cost.

Something touched her ankle, and she almost screamed out loud. She pulled her foot back and looked down.

The homeless man had crawled over to her. "Girl! I'm hungry. I know you ain't gonna let me starve. Watchoo got? Coins? Anything."

Cerise dug in her pocket, deep down past the bills and found a handful of coins. "Here," she whispered, dropping them in his hand. He smiled brilliantly again and scuttled back to where he'd been.

The other man who had been perusing the board inched closer to her. "You shouldn't encourage them."

Cerise glanced at him. Tall, young, clean face, nice clothes. She wanted to ask him for help but something inside her kept her mouth frozen. Self-reliance. It was the only way. Her only chance. She and Kaci were completely on their own and they couldn't trust anyone, especially not any men. She nodded sharply and pressed closer to the board, reading as fast as she could.

She found one!

Ride offered to Los Angeles, California 2-28.

I am heading to Los Angeles on Friday and have room for two passengers and some cargo in the car. All I ask is $100 for gas and some help with the driving. Text me.

Cerise read over the message again, the noises of people laughing, coughing, talking, and yelling from all around them fading as she concentrated. She wasn't entirely sure what day it was, but she had $100. They could make it without hitchhiking! She couldn't drive, but maybe if she gave the person more than $100 that would be ok? She reached in the bag for their pen and her encyclopedia, copying the phone number given down on the inside cover, then looking around for pay phones. She didn't see any, but they had to be around, they always were in the movies she and Kaci watched.

Something brushed her ankle again and Cerise looked down. The homeless man was back, but he wasn't looking at her. He had his dirty hand clutched around Kaci's slim calf. "How about you, sweet? You got any money? I could use a footlong." He nodded to the Subway in the corner of the terminal.

Kaci kicked out with her leg, whimpering, finally forced to look around, to open herself up to their situation. The man's grip seemed to tighten.

"Let go of her," Cerise ordered, pulling on Kaci's arm in the opposite direction. She looked around, but the man who'd told her not to encourage him had disappeared. They were the only people close by. Across the terminal, she spotted two security officers bent over a desk. She bit her lip and dropped her gaze back to the homeless man.

He still had ahold of Kaci. "Come on sweet, give old Bourbon a dollar. You can spare some. You get a allowance, yeah?"

Kaci whimpered again and threw Cerise a helpless look. Cerise gathered her under the arm and yanked her out of Bourbon's grip, but her shoe came off in his fingers. He snatched it up like she'd wrapped it in a box and handed it to him. Another announcement came over the loudspeaker and suddenly the corridor was filled with people again, people intent on their destination, not caring about anyone but themselves. Kaci took a wobbly step backwards as someone cut between her and Cerise, then a flood of people followed that first person and they were cut off. Cerise pulled her bag closer to her side, snatched her sister's shoe out of Bourbon's hands, and tried to find Kaci. She couldn't see her anywhere. "Kaci," she called. No answer. "Kaci!" she yelled, trying not to give in to fresh panic. Nothing. Kaci was short and thin and physically weak. Only a girl…

Cerise pushed her way through the streaming crowd of people. "Kaci, I'm here, come to me, Kaci!"

A scream ripped through the room. Cerise turned toward it. Kaci had somehow been pushed by the crowd almost to the doors that led outside. Cerise caught her terrified glance and tried to warn her to stop screaming, but Kaci didn't seem to be able to.

By the time Cerise reached her, security was there, too.

***

"Please," Cerise told the security officers. They were sitting in a back room, both of them in hard plastic chairs, and two security guards leaned against the desk opposite them. "She doesn't speak. She never has. She's not able to talk to you."

They exchanged glances, one of them tall, one short, both with expressions that said they didn't believe, didn't care.

Cerise tried again. "Are we in trouble? She was just scared. She won't do it again, but we have a-a friend to meet."

The tall one took a clipboard off the table. "Just give me your name, miss. We'll let you go when we finish our report."

Cerise's heartbeat sped up. Lie? Tell the truth? There was no way anyone had found Myles's body already. No one ever went out to their trailer. They had no visitors.

Another security guard entered the room and handed the

tall one a piece of paper, giving Cerise another moment to try to decide. She hugged a still-shaking Kaci close to her, Cerise Pekin on her tongue. She would tell the truth.

The eyebrows of the tall guard shot up and he looked at Cerise suspiciously, then handed the piece of paper he'd just received to his partner, as the new guard left the room. Cerise's mouth went dry as the short guard eyeballed her and Kaci again, eyes narrowed.

"Cerise Pekin?" tall guard said slowly.

Cerise couldn't answer. It was over already. They'd been caught so quickly. But how? And what would happen to Kaci now?

CHAPTER 12

erise walked dully into the foreboding jail building as a female guard held her arm and the shackles on her wrists bit into her skin, but all she could hear was Kaci's screams as she was physically wrestled away from Cerise, hours before, when the sun still shone. Now it was dark, and bitterly cold.

The cops had shown up to the bus station, and she and Kaci had ultimately had no choice but to go with them. They hadn't been handcuffed, but they'd both been searched for weapons, their money taken from Cerise's pockets and put in a tan envelope Cerise somehow knew she would never see again.

Would she ever see her sister again? Kaci might not be any blood relation, but Cerise considered them closer than sisters. They loved each other with a fierceness that couldn't be garnered by anything other than walking through hell together. But Cerise had failed Kaci. And it had all started with her trip on Zeus in the dark morning hours, her trip to that unknown man's house. She began to hate him a little bit in her mind, even though he'd done nothing to her, but her only alternative was hating herself, and she still needed herself, still had to think of a way out of this. A way back to Kaci.

She'd tried desperately to explain that she and Kaci couldn't be separated, that Kaci wouldn't be able to handle it, but the cop had shaken his head and said there was nothing that could be done. He'd seemed harried, overworked, in a hurry to get rid of her, speeding through her fingerprinting and arrest. She still didn't know how they'd found Myles's body so quickly, and no one had asked her any questions about it. She'd watched enough cop movies to know someone was supposed to interrogate her, but no one had. They'd ripped her and Kaci apart, ignoring Kaci's screams and handing her over to a stern-looking officer who had taken her to another part of the building.

Cerise had held her breath as the two officers had discussed Kaci's destination.

"*Chief says juvie.*"

"*Juvie won't take her, they're overflowing, say she's too young, anyway.*"

"*How old is she?*"

"*I don't know. The sheet says twelve, but that has to be wrong, she doesn't look older than nine or ten, and they don't like to take them that young at juvie anyway.*"

"*He doesn't want her in foster care, says she's dangerous.*"

"*Interim home, then.*"

"*Got it.*"

Cerise turned to her left, to the guard who had her by the elbow. "Where's the interim home?"

The guard grunted and threw her a dismissive glance. "In the door, that's it. Stand in front of the desk."

Cerise blew out a breath, frustrated. She tried again, at the desk, where another female guard stood and asked her questions.

"Name."

"Cerise Pekin. Where's the interim home in Serenity?"

The guard stared at her, a sneer on her face, handing Cerise a pen to sign the paper in front of her

"Please tell me," Cerise said, just as she captured the pen, holding back her tears. She was in jail. Tears were to inmates like blood was to sharks, she imagined. Knew, from her short stay here before. Desperation and determination filled her in equal measures and her mind flexed, giving that short flex/push sensation she'd noticed before. She frowned, as did the guard in front of her, but the guard also spoke, almost reluctantly.

"5150 Northrock Blvd."

Relief filled Cerise and she attempted a smile. "Thank you."

The guard sneered again, but only half-heartedly. She opened her mouth to say something, then closed it, then turned and gathered up Cerise's linens. "These are yours." She nodded to the other guard and Cerise was on the move again, through a locked gate, into a small room for a body cavity search and to change her clothes into plain, grey prison garb. She didn't mind the clothes so much, but the atmosphere was stifling, the guards were surly and bitter and the walls themselves were drab and pressed in on her. Out of that room, they were buzzed into another locked gate, then she was led down a dark corridor into an open, dark bay.

Snores and whispers and hostility filled the room, along

with beds. Rows and rows of beds, three bunks high. Kaci's screams in Cerise's head were finally replaced by something. Dread. She'd been to prison before, for three nights, and had been in three fights that time, one for each night. She knew by experience that keeping her head down didn't keep her out of trouble.

The guard spoke to Cerise, her voice a curious mixture of nearly bridled anger and boredom. "Lights out was at nine. All inmates must be in their bunks and all talking ceases by ten. If you are still talking after ten you'll get a written warning. You don't want a second. Everything else will be explained to you in the morning."

The guard stopped near a bed that had one bunk empty, the bottom one. Cerise rolled out her mattress, covered it with her sheet, blanket, and pillow, feeling the eyes of the women around her on her back. She remembered this. And she also knew exactly what was coming as soon as the guard was far enough away.

Cerise finished laying out her bed, then sat down, waiting, leaning forward at the end of her bunk, her back against the bunk above her. She risked a kick in the back of the head, but she thought she could dodge it. Being trapped in the bunk would be worse.

A woman peeked down at her from above. Cerise let her look. "Hey, fish, what's your name?" the woman finally whispered.

"Cerise."

"Cerise, huh, ain't you pretty, little miss fancy pants, with all that red hair?"

Cerise frowned. Her hair was poorly cut with the only pair of scissors they had, blunt safety scissors. She did it herself whenever it got so long it irritated her, but she knew the line in the back looked jagged and hacked. And her hair would never be red by any stretch of the imagination, maybe strawberry blonde, but mostly Cerise just thought it plain.

"What'd you do, fancy-pants?"

"Nothing."

Another woman's face peeked over, from the very top bunk, and the three women in the bunks across from them all picked up their heads in interest, the woman on the middle bunk and the top bunk leaning on their elbows, while the woman on the bottom swung her feet and body out and sat like Cerise was.

Cerise let awareness flood out of her, trying to track the emotions of everyone at once. So far, no aggression from any of them. Maybe she would sleep tonight. She was bone-weary after not sleeping the night before, but even if her bunkmates let her sleep, would her guilt?

The woman above her laughed. "Nothing, huh, I've never heard that one before."

Cerise stared at the floor, waiting, her body tense, primed for whatever would come to her. If they would just leave her alone, she could start working on a plan to get out of here.

A small voice tried to tell her she would never get out. She was at the mercy of the courts, the cops, the jail. She had no friends, no knowledge of what to do next. She'd been offered a phone call and hadn't taken it. The only people she knew in the world, besides Kaci, were Myles and Sandra. Myles was dead, and Sandra had disappeared a long time ago.

"Seriously, what'd you do?" the woman asked again. "Why are you in here?"

The woman on the very top bunk above her spoke to her. "Just tell her. Cici got a thing 'bout knowing what everyone did to get in here."

Cici nodded emphatically. "That's right, I got a thing, now fucking *tell me.*"

Cerise looked up, then, meeting Cici's gaze. She had a broad face and almond eyes, with strange black markings above her brows. Cerise wasn't sure if they were makeup or tattoos. "What did *you* do to get in here?" she whispered.

Wrong answer shot through her mind as Cici's eyes widened, then lost their humanity, going from curious to murderous in a split second. Cerise tensed to spring to her feet, too late. Cici had already caught her in the back of the head with a bare foot or ankle. It should have hurt Cici more than it did Cerise, but Cerise's head was still battered, her skin split and swelling on the right side, hidden by her hair.

Cici jumped out of the bed with deadly efficiency and hooked an arm around Cerise's throat, pulling her to the ground.

"Oh shit, here we go," the woman on the top bunk said, rising up on her hands and knees to look over the sea of beds.

Cerise's head bounced off the floor, making her vision swim. She got her hands up, trying to push CiCi off her, but Cici had already twisted and latched on to her, both her hands around Cerise's throat.

Play dead, something inside her urged. P*ass out and she'll let go.* Cerise gritted her lips and fitted her own hands around Cici's throat. *Fuck. That. Noise.*

She snarled silently, even as her lungs screamed for air already, tightening her own fingers on Cici's throat as Cici stared down at her, her mouth in a deadly grimace.

Decades of pain, anger, and un-acted-on retribution gave Cerise strength, the image she had of Kaci wordlessly screaming as she was pulled away from Cerise fueling a slick hatred of anybody who dared give her shit right now. She was DONE.

Stop it, you flaming bitch! I didn't do shit to you. Take your fucking hands off me! Cerise screamed, but only in her mind. From her mouth, barely a whisper escaped. Her mind *flexed* like it had before, and a mental *push* escaped her body like a physical thing, stronger than she'd ever felt before, focused on Cici's flat eyes.

Cici's eyes widened for just a split second before both her pupils blew at once, expanding until no iris was visible. Her lids slid shut and she collapsed onto Cerise. Cerise twisted on the concrete floor, guiding Cici's body to Cerise's left so her dead weight wouldn't slam into Cerise's face. Instead, it slammed onto the floor with a sickening thudding sound.

Cerise sucked in a breath, then pulled her hands back to her temples, as pain rippled through head and neck and her vision went blurry. The beginnings of a migraine? No, it was ebbing already.

"What did you do to her?" the woman from the top bunk said in a clear voice sure to bring guards. Dimly, Cerise could hear all the women jump down from their beds, feel them pushing past Cerise to get to Cici.

"Guard, guard! Cici's ears are bleeding! We need the nurse, now!"

Cerise tried to open her eyes, tried to look to her left, but heartache rocked her. The day had gone from any-thing-is-possible, to can't-get-worse, and there were still a few hours left.

***

Cerise pressed her lids together slowly, consciousness

returning to her in a rush, not daring to open her eyes yet, hoping that everything she remembered had been a bad dream. How bad had the day been for her to be wishing she were home, at Myles's mercy? She tested the earlier pain in her head by moving slowly to the left, the soft beep beep of medical equipment floating into her awareness. The pain was gone. She blinked and opened her eyes slightly, enough that she could see fluorescent lights set into a white ceiling. By the weight on her wrists, she knew she was handcuffed to a bed. Still in jail, then. Lucky her.

She let her head fall to the right so she could gaze that way, hopefully without revealing she was awake. In the bed next to her, Cici reclined, her eyes closed, tacky-looking blood drying in her hair, clear tubes in her nostrils and colored wires snaking from her chest to a machine. *You did that,* her mind whispered to her. You *pushed* her too hard. Cerise frowned internally at the voice, trying to remember exactly what had happened just before Cici had keeled over. Cerise *had* done something. That strange, rippling flex her brain executed. She'd felt it before, but never had she done something like *that* to anyone before. That hard. That strong. She thought back, trying to remember other times she'd felt that flex, that push from her brain to another, and what the outcome had been.

A few examples came forward in her memory, to be examined by her. Several years ago, before Sandra had left them, before Cerise had even been sick, it had happened. Sandra had been angry at Myles about something, had been looking for someone to take it out on. Cerise had been in the kitchen, making Kaci some rice when Sandra had strode in, hand-rolled cigarette jutting from the corner of her mouth, rage and smoke circling her head like a cloud, muttering curses.

Cerise should have dropped everything and fled the room, but she hadn't. Sandra had honed in on her, like a torpedo on a target, reaching her before Cerise could even pick up the bowl and turn away from the counter. Sandra had grabbed her by the back of her head and slammed her face into the counter. Cerise could have fought back, but she knew if she did, Kaci would be targeted to take an even greater onslaught of random violence. So she'd tried to cushion her face's landing with her hands and spoken in her mind again. *Please Momma, no more. I hate it when you hit me.*

And for once, Sandra had let her go. She'd backed up a step and stared at Cerise, looking dazed. Cerise had gathered up her bowl and spoon and rushed from the room, away from Sandra's immediate field of vision, not thinking farther than escaping the immediate threat. But now she thought of it, turning the experience over in her mind. Had that *push* come out of her? She thought it had. And had Sandra ever hit her again?

Other times? Yes. One recently. That man whose house she had broken into. The big one with the handsome grin. Cerise nibbled on the inside of her lip, trying to remember every detail. The first time she'd gone to his house, when he'd woken and spoken to her. She'd touched him, then sent the *push* out at him, desperate not to be caught there.

Oh! And what about not even an hour ago? The guard at the front who'd told her where the interim home was-

A female voice spoke from somewhere in the room, cutting off her thoughts. "She only needs one guard, in my opinion. Her head injury is pretty serious. If she wakes up, she won't be in any condition to escape."

The unseen woman changed position, her voice coming clearer and louder, like she had just faced Cerise. "I don't think the other one needs to go. She's got a head injury, too, but it looks old. She might have passed out from the fear." She paused and listened. "I know, we don't want to ask for two ambulances, but I don't think she needs to go to the hospital." Irritation crept into her voice. "Ok, I'll call you back."

Cerise let her eyes fall completely closed and tried to keep her breathing even as footsteps approached her bed, not sure what her plan should be.

"Don't bother faking, Pekin. I'm not stupid."

Cerise blinked and opened her eyes fully, meeting the nurse's gaze. Her skin was a chocolate brown, her hair a beautiful natural afro, and she looked tough, her expression skeptical, but open and slightly amused.

"I'm sorry, I wasn't trying to fake," Cerise said to her.

The nurse hooked a thumb toward Cici. "What'd you do to her?"

Cerise pressed her lips together. Crap. "I don't know. She had me pinned down, then she just collapsed. Maybe she had a stroke."

The nurse's face didn't change expression. "That's not what her friends said. They said you were on top of her and slammed her head into the ground."

Cerise's eyes widened and the nurse's amusement faded, leaving only the skepticism. "Don't worry, I don't believe them, anyway."

"Why?"

The nurse shrugged. "She doesn't have any bumps on her head. A stroke won't make blood come out of your ears, though." She leaned forward. "Did you choke her?"

Cerise's eyes widened again. How to answer that without getting in more trouble?

The nurse's expression changed again, this time

favoring amusement. "You got that innocent look down, missy. Someone got your number, anyway."

She took ahold of Cerise's wrist, feeling the pulse there. Cerise pressed her hand up, so the backs of her fingers were grazing the woman's arm, touching as much as she was being touched, feeling instinctually that it would help what she was trying to do.

Flex. Push. "I'm sicker than you first thought. I need to go to the hospital, too."

CHAPTER 13

Over here! Move it, cop, faster unless you want this place to fry!"

Beckett put all his weight into the hose, hauling it inch by agonizing inch away from the fire truck. His clothes were ruined, covered with water and foam and even burnt in a few places. The fire department and the police department were all stretched thin, skeleton crews protecting the city and every available body called in from days off and specialty details.

Behind him, the lake, big enough that the other side couldn't be seen even when it wasn't on fire, continued to burn. They'd put out the edges, but nothing had touched the middle. This close to the lake, night was hot as a literal hell would be, the constant flames searing away the cold.

On the other side of the truck, he heard Wade arguing with the fire chief about what they should do next.

"Fuck this working the edges, Chief. You have to hit it from the center. Bring in the helicopters. Fires are popping up at lakes all over the country, and unless we figure out what works, and soon, we're going to be wiped out. The whole city!"

Beckett hauled on the heavy hose, knowing Wade was right, they were masturbating out here, doing what they were doing, if not for their own enjoyment, then just to keep themselves busy. They'd barely made a dent in the fire, and they'd been out at the lake for hours, skirting its edges, trying water, chemicals, and foam, even though they were worried about the environmental impact. This lake was the main reservoir for water for the entire county.

The *bearen* chief's voice did not hold the same urgency as Wade's did. He almost sounded bored. *Fucking bears.* "Oh right, and how many years have you spent fighting fires, *Deputy*?" He sneered the last word.

Wade's voice became even tighter. "Fuck, Chief, I know you got a problem with me, but can't you get over it long enough to work together on this? You trying to burn down the city, you overgrown squirrel?"

Beckett grinned, against the phenomenally heavy fire hose he clutched to his chest. *Call him another name. That'll convince him.*

Ten feet away from him, Bruin rushed over, grabbed a length of hose, and began to pull. He looked as bedraggled as Beckett felt, his hair wet and plastered to his head, his clothes dripping. Finally, with the two of them working together, it moved a few feet. "How much does this fucker weigh, Bruin?" Beckett forced out as he dug his feet in and pushed/pulled for all he was worth.

Bruin's gaze followed the length of the hose. "One hundred foot hose, filled with water, nine hundred pounds or so."

Beckett felt like dropping it. "Nine *hundred* you say?"

Mac came up on Beckett's other side, grabbing more hose. "Put your back into it, hardhead," he grunted to Beckett.

Beckett ignored him. More headway. Maybe that *bearen* ordering Beckett around would shut up, finally.

A *bearen* in full fire gear rushed past Beckett, ducked under the hose, then caught Bruin with his shoulder in an obvious body-check. Mac dropped his length of hose and stared after him. "Hey, you dick, come back here and try that again!"

Beckett grunted as the weight increased. "Mac, a little help."

Mac glared after the offending *bearen* until Bruin spoke. "No worries, bro, they don't bother me."

Mac flipped the bird at the *bearen's* back, then picked up the hose again. With volleys of grunts and heaves, the three of them messily maneuvered the hose to where the *bearen* had wanted it. They dropped it.

Beckett looked to Bruin. "What was that about, you piss somebody off?"

Bruin shrugged. Mac answered for him. "All of them apparently. I heard a different acorn-head call him a traitor earlier." He faced Bruin. "What's up, bro? Spill."

Bruin shrugged again. "They think I think I'm better than them. They don't think I should be carrying a gun or hanging out with wolves."

Mac faced Beckett, his face a parody of surprise. He hooked a thumb at Bruin. "You hear that? Them bears are some judgmental berry-eaters, aren't they?"

Beckett just stared at Mac, not taking the bait. He buffed his nails on his ruined shirt and stared out at the flaming lake as hot air hit him in the face. He hoped that the breeze they'd been dealing with all day wasn't turning into an actual wind.

Because that's what it felt like. He'd learned what a firenado was, a whirlwind induced of fire and caused by rising heat and high winds. He'd also learned that what the signs said could come next would be an actual fire tornado, when a wildfire created an actual cloud that spawned a real tornado, which was a thousand times more dangerous and could easily flatten a path through a city, while starting the rest of it on fire. That's why they were all out here, every last male, busting their asses.

Bruin stared at Wade and the fire chief still arguing over the fire. "Well, something has to put it out and not ruin our water for life!" Wade shouted.

"Baking soda," Bruin whispered.

"What?" Beckett said, edging closer to him.

"I think baking soda will work," Bruin said. "I even ordered a couple truckloads after Mac told me about the *Vahiy* signs. They are mounded in piles behind my house."

"You gotta tell your chief," Mac said.

Bruin shook his head sadly. "He doesn't listen to me. Never has. Thinks I'm useless and stupid."

Mac's face twisted in anger. "Well, he's gonna listen to me. Anything's worth a fucking try."

***

Hours later, Beckett was released from the scene. The fire was almost completely out, Bruin's suggestion working like gangbusters. They'd already spread the word to all the other afflicted counties, and more were reporting success.

As he strode away from the scene, his mind immediately went to what he'd dealt with that morning. He dug out his phone and began making his calls, the first one to Detective

DuPage, the one he'd left in charge of the scene at the trailer. Beckett had no real authority over DuPage, but as a member of the KSRT, he received respect and allowances from everyone on the force.

"DuPage."

"This is Oswego. You still out there?"

"Nah, we wrapped up thirty minutes ago. I'm at the station working on my report."

"What do you know?"

"The dead male, his name is Myles Pekin. A moonshiner who had been on that plot of land for a few years now. He came from New Mexico and bought the place with cash. It already had the trailer on it. The woman buried in the back yard is probably his common-law wife, Sandra Cook."

"Could you do a tox-screen on her?" Beckett asked, thinking of the mushrooms in the forest.

"We can try. But we know what killed her."

"What?"

"A blow to the back of the head."

Beckett whistled, low and long. "What about the other woman and the girl that lived in the trailer? Any word on them?"

"They were found at the bus station this morning."

Excitement whirled in Beckett's chest, much like he imagined a firenado would bounce around in a forest. "You have them at the station?"

"Ah, hold on." Beckett pressed the phone to his ear as he walked. He'd parked his truck over a mile away, not wanting it covered in soot and ash. DuPage came back on the line. "Says here the older one was taken to county and the younger one to the interim home."

Excitement turned to dread, then bitter anger. "What?

You know as well as I do that was self-defense. Why did they go to lockup?"

"Calm down, Beck, I didn't have anything to do with it. Word came down from somewhere else they were to go to lockup. Someone up the ladder. "

"Who?"

Beckett heard computer keys clacking, even over the sound of his own heart pulsing in his ears, as DuPage looked through the digital file. "It doesn't specify. Just says Chief. Doesn't say which chief from where."

Beckett swore. If she were his mate, he was going to ream someone a new asshole for that call. Maybe even if she weren't. "How long ago?"

"Ah, looks like she went at about eight or nine."

"Thanks," Beckett said, about to hang up, when DuPage's voice stopped him.

"Wait, a note just came in on her file. She's headed to the hospital. For a-a head injury." His voice dropped an octave. "She was attacked by a bunkmate."

Beckett swore again, and picked up his pace. "Thanks, I'm out," he said, hanging up the phone and jamming it in his pocket, then stopping himself. He needed a change of clothes. He'd head straight over there and Rhen help this mysterious chief if she was hurt badly.

He reached his truck, rooted in the back for clothes, then snarled when he found nothing but a towel.

He'd grab a change of clothes at the hospital, then go find-

He realized that he hadn't even gotten her name.

CHAPTER 14

erise stared at another ceiling, her anxiety skyrocketing, handcuffs pinning her to another bed.

"Uh, can I get a drink of water?" she called to the prison guard blocking the entrance to her hospital room.

"Wait till the nurse comes back," he grunted.

She pressed her lips together and looked around the room for the fiftieth time, then settled on the ceiling again. *Pushing* the nurse wouldn't do any good, she needed to *push* the guard or she would never get out of here. She didn't know what exactly *pushing* was, or how long she'd been able to do it, or what its limits were, but she'd seen its effects clearly on the nurse in the prison. As soon as she'd said, *I need to go to the hospital, too,* the nurse had frowned, then pulled Cerise's lower eyelid down and stared at whatever she saw there, and said, "You're sicker than I thought, you need to go to the hospital, too."

It had almost fallen apart when the ambulance had shown up to take both her and Cici to the hospital, and the paramedic had asked what was wrong with Cerise. The nurse had looked him in the eye and said, "She's sicker than I thought, she needs to go to the hospital, too." Cerise had panicked for a moment, even her untrained ears telling her that wasn't an actual diagnosis, but then the nurse had shoved two charts into the paramedic's arms and shooed him toward Cerise's bed with her hands. The paramedic had set his lips and done what he was told, which was take Cerise to the Emergency Room, where she still hadn't been seen by a doctor.

It was a busy night, lots of firefighters kept walking by her room, the smell of chemicals and fire drifting in to her every time one passed. Somewhere down the corridors she could hear men talking loudly, urgently.

What if I can push the guard without touching him? She thought maybe she could, at least a little, but somehow knew whatever strange power her brain had was stronger when she touched someone. What if all she was able to do without touching him was make him suspicious?

She stared at the ceiling, wondering if she were really going to try. If she didn't, she would be taken back to the jail and hopefully not be in any more trouble than she already was. She'd get a chance to talk with a lawyer, maybe get to tell her story to someone, maybe be able to convince someone to let her out? And how long would that take? How much damage would be done to Kaci in the meantime? Kaci, who was completely innocent in all of this. Kaci, who'd never been apart from Cerise for more than a few days, and all of those days had been spectacularly awful for her.

But if she could get this guard to come over to her, maybe, somehow, she could get out of the hospital. This ability of hers that she'd discovered was an absolute game changer for them. She could *push* someone into giving them a ride to California. It wouldn't even matter if he or she was a person they ordinarily wouldn't want to get in a car with. She'd already proven she could protect herself with it.

A pang of guilt hit her as she wondered again how Cici was. *She shouldn't have tried to strangle you.* Cerise knew that, but still, she didn't want to hurt people, didn't want to force anyone to do something they didn't want to do. She knew the pain of that.

But what choice did she have? *None.*

She opened her mouth to call to the guard, planning to try to *push* him to come closer to her, close enough that she could touch him, then she could tell him to unlock her handcuffs. Before she could say a word, a male voice spoke at her doorway.

One she'd heard before.

"Hey, Corporal, why don't you take a break, I need to talk to her in private."

She whipped her head up, not daring to believe her ears.

The guard nodded, falling over himself to move out of the new guy's way. "Yes, sir. I'll be at the nurse's station. Yell for me when you're done."

The man from the house she'd broken into strode into the room, his eyes locked on hers, the look on his face one she couldn't quite puzzle out. He looked almost… hungry.

He was wearing blue scrubs that barely fit his wide chest, the camouflage hat she'd seen on his pillow now perched on his head. He brought the smell of old fire from the hallway in with him. She searched his chest for a nametag, but found none.

She stared at him, waiting for the first words out of his

mouth, wondering what they would be. Did he know she'd been to his house not once, but twice? Was she about to get yelled at? Threatened? Beaten? She tried to think back, to remember what she'd said to him when she *pushed* him. She thought maybe it had been to forget about her.

She tried to shrink away from him as he got closer, still unable to read the look on his face. Her mind tensed in fear, but her body stayed calm, like it knew something she didn't. Her shoulders were still knotted from the earlier fight, but the rest of her body was relaxed. He reached her and put his hand on the bedrail, only a few inches from her hand, and her first instinct was to reach up and touch his fingers, but she stayed herself, wanting to hear what he would say first. Wanting to read his emotional weather.

He smiled then, a grin that would have made her knees weak if she'd been standing. A grin that made her heart quicken and everything in the room blur but his face. "Hey there, darlin'," he said, his voice a country drawl she found delicious, even through her fear. "They treatin' you right in here?"

Cerise felt her lips part and her eyes go wide. She didn't know what to make of him. Two words escaped her lips before she had a chance to think about them. "I'm scared."

His face twisted with compassion and something stronger. "Don't be," he said, then reached down to grasp her hand softly, something like expectation on his face.

Cerise curled her fingers around his, not thinking. *Flex. Push.* She held back the flex, tried to control its strength, keep it under control. Power rippled out of her, she could feel it go, like actual muscle contractions, or tears falling from her eyes. She tried to pay more attention to it, but lost it when she spoke, her awareness of it dissolving as she used a different part of her brain. "Get me out of these handcuffs," she whispered to him, her muscles finally tensing. "I have to go find my sister. She's in real trouble and I need your help."

The man frowned and stared at her for a second. Cerise had a moment to wonder if she'd been imagining the *push* before, grasping at insane straws, but then his eyes unfocused slightly. He let go of her hand, turned to the table next to her and rummaged through it.

"What are you looking for?" she asked, still whispering.

"Something to spring the lock on those cuffs, I don't have a handcuff key on me."

Oh. Right. Smart. She pushed up on her elbows to watch, her gaze pulling back to the door every time someone passed, fearful thoughts running through her head, until one grabbed her attention. *He's going to get in trouble. He's going to lose his job.*

Cerise bit her lip. She hadn't even considered that. She wouldn't be able to make up for this one. She couldn't pay back something like that.

He stood up straight, holding up his hand, a tiny silver piece of metal glinting in it. A paperclip. "This'll work."

He maneuvered one end of the paperclip to stand straight out, then bent over the cuffs holding her right hand to the bed and it sprang open almost at once.

The word *stop* was on her tongue, but she didn't say it. She had to choose between Kaci and this man. Maybe if she came back here after she'd gotten Kaci to her parents, said she'd held a gun to this man's head, then maybe he wouldn't get in trouble.

Her mind grabbed onto the idea with strong hands, convincing her it could work, had to work.

She would figure out the details later.

**

Beckett skirted the hospital bed and bent over the second pair of handcuffs securing the woman to the bed. He'd felt no visceral reaction when he'd touched her, and he knew from talking with Crew, Graeme, and Trevor, that if she was his one true mate, he would have known the first time he touched her. Strangely, he felt no disappointment, only anticipation and determination. She might not be his one true mate, but she was still special to him. He would discover exactly how and why.

Within seconds, he had her unlocked. She sat up, rubbing her wrists and fixing him with a curious stare. He smiled at her, his heart strangely full and satisfied, an emotion he didn't know if he'd ever experienced before. She looked so lovely, so sweet, so innocent. He took a deep breath, pulling in her delicious licorice scent. He was so glad to have found her, and so glad she seemed to not be badly injured, that he was having a hard time focusing on what he had planned when he'd first entered the room.

His mind serene for the first time in weeks, maybe years, he took a step back and waited for her next move. He felt good just being in the room with her, just standing near her. Questions ran deep in the back of his mind, like *who are you*, and *why were you in my house*, but he didn't ask them. They didn't seem important.

Oh! He'd almost forgotten. "You have to go find your sister. She's in real trouble and you need my help. Wait here."

She raised a hand and started to say something, but he was already moving out the door. He hooked a right in the hallway and found the same scrubs cart that he had taken the scrubs he was wearing from. He ran his fingers along the women's sizes, grabbing an extra small, small, and medium size of a pastel purple scrubs pair. He had little idea how sizes for women worked. He turned back toward the room, then thought better of it and returned to the cart, grabbing a large also. She was not tall or big, but he'd learned over the years with women he'd brought home or bought presents for that not only were women weird about sizes, but sizes were never consistent across brands. He briefly considered wheeling the entire cart into the room, then shook his head and ran back to the room, where she had climbed back into the bed and covered herself with a blanket. When she saw him, the relief on her face was obvious.

"You came back," she said, swinging her legs onto the floor and throwing the blanket to the side.

"You have to go find your sister, but you can't do it in those clothes. Here." He thrust an armload of scrubs at her, and turned around, pulling the curtain so she could get dressed in private, then stood at the door to guard it.

Within a moment, she said, "I'm done."

He turned and pulled the curtain open, wanting to just stand and stare at her, she was that lovely in the purple. But she was trembling, her eyes darting from him to the door behind him, like she was terrified.

He frowned, wanting to fix it for her, still not even knowing her name, but feeling a profound connection with her that made his heart hurt in a way he hadn't felt in years.

He held out his hand. "You have to go find your sister. She's in real trouble and you need my help." The words sounded strange to him, but he didn't stop to think about why. They had to be acted on because they created an unbearable tension inside him that he somehow knew would only ease when the concepts were finished.

She clasped her hands to her chest and stared at his hand, not taking it. He dropped it to his side.

"Let's go."

CHAPTER 15

Cerise modified her pace so she was a step behind the doctor, or whatever he was, her head down, eyes on the floor in front of her feet. There was no way they were getting out of there without being stopped. Their plan, or lack of a plan, was going to do nothing more than get her thrown right back in jail, tacking on attempted escape to murder. The black hole that was her life threatened to swallow her whole, but she put one foot in front of the other, taking each moment as it came.

A female rushed past her and Cerise pulled closer to her doctor, blindly following his lead. He worked there, so he knew how to get them out with the least amount of human contact, she hoped. He took a sharp right, then pushed a door open. Frigid air hit her in the chest, and she'd never been so glad to feel it. They were outside!

"My truck is this way," he said, his strides so long and purposeful she had to run to keep up.

"What's your name?" she asked him, finally daring to look up. The few people walking though the parking lot weren't paying them any attention.

He slowed a little and flashed her that grin again, that thousand-watt one that made her heart flutter. "Beckett," he said. "Beckett Oswego."

She smiled back, in spite of herself, almost believing they could pull this off, that he was helping her of his own free will, that the world would treat her and Kaci well for once.

He strode between a truck and a car, then pulled open the passenger door to the truck. She stopped in her tracks and stared for just a second. The truck was green and huge, lifted high off the ground, with tires that almost reached her waist. *No doctor in any movie she'd ever seen drove a truck like this.*

She remembered herself and hurried forward, grabbing onto the handle of the door and a handle just behind the seat, raising her foot so high to reach inside the cab that she wasn't sure if she would make it, then hoisting herself inside quickly, mostly with her arms, not wanting Beckett to help her.

He checked to be sure her feet and hands were clear, then slammed the door and hurried to the other side. He climbed in, then looked at her. "Where to?"

"The interim home," she said hesitantly, trying to remember the address she'd been given.

"Right," he said and twisted his key in the ignition, backing expertly out of the stall, and heading decisively out of the parking lot. She thought she heard tires squeal. The clock on his dash said 2:14 in the morning. No wonder exhaustion was starting to catch up with her.

"You know where it is?"

"5150 Northrock Blvd."

She nodded even though he wasn't looking at her. "What is it?"

"The interim home? It's kind of a halfway house. A place for runaways to go when they can't or won't go home but don't have anywhere else to stay. Sometimes, when there is crowding at juvenile hall, they will send non-violent offenders to the interim home instead, since they do have basic security."

Cerise swallowed, liking the way he sounded, the cadence of his speech and the deepness of his voice, and feeling hope at his words. He had a slight accent that went well with his open face and easy grin. "What kind of security?"

Beckett shrugged, maneuvering his truck onto a main road. "People work there who do checks on the residents at night, and they provide structure during the day, maybe give them rides to school and work, some tutoring, that kind of thing. It's supposed to only be a temporary place to stay for kids who have nowhere else to go."

Cerise nodded. She could get Kaci out of there, somehow.

Beckett glanced at her. "What's your name?"

Cerise stared at him, indecisive. Tell him the truth? Lie to him? "Cerise," she finally said, feeling as shy as Kaci for a moment.

He grinned, making Cerise want to grin back. "Cerise, that's beautiful. What does it mean?"

She frowned. "Mean?"

"Yeah, does it mean anything? Do you know what it's from? It's an unusual name."

She shook her head. She had no idea.

He nodded slightly, his lips curling in a teasing manner. "Beckett means beehive. And no, my parents weren't beekeepers, so don't ask."

Cerise clamped her lips together to avoid laughing. It didn't seem right, considering the circumstances, but Beckett's manner was so light, almost teasing; he was so easy to talk to…

A cop car sped past them, lights on, no siren, in the direction that they had come from and Cerise shrank in her seat, then swallowed hard. Definitely no laughing. Even if she hadn't been a criminal before, she was now, and was she ruining this nice man's life? If ever a situation called for dour seriousness, this was it.

"How old are you, Cerise?" Beckett asked, his voice twisted somehow, expectant.

Cerise waited until her heartbeat slowed a little, watching the streetlights speed past them in the dark, then answered, not sure if she was telling the truth or not, ashamed to not even know. "23."

Why had his face fallen when she said that? Had he wanted her to be a certain age for some reason? Cerise had no experience dealing with men of any kind, except alcoholic, abusive, baby-stealing fathers, but still, she couldn't think of one reason why Beckett would care how old she was. Unless he wanted to… date her? But 23 was over 18. "How old are you?"

"30."

Her eyes traced his strong profile with new respect, and new awareness. So young to be a doctor. She frowned at the camouflage cap. She'd never seen a doctor wear a baseball cap in a movie, either. She knew movies couldn't possibly mirror real life exactly, but she'd also seen with her own eyes that they did a good job of reflecting much of it. She opened her mouth to ask him exactly what he did, but he slowed, then turned the wheel sharply, driving down an incline into the parking lot of what looked like a house to her. Two-story, big, but nothing like the jail she'd been in.

"No, Beckett, not here in the parking lot," she breathed, her fingers tightening on the door handle, her eyes searching for cameras and guards. She put her hand on his arm and *pushed* him lightly, the flexing in her mind rather pleasant now that she was knew what she was doing. Kind of. "Can you go out of the parking lot and find a place to park about a block away? Then wait for me while I get my sister?"

His brows furrowed as he spun the wheel, making the big truck turn in a tight circle and throwing Cerise against her door.

"Go out of the parking lot and find a place to park a block away. Wait for Cerise to get her sister," he muttered. She studied him, looking for any sign that he was in pain; that she was hurting or distressing him, but already his forehead was smoothing out and that quarter-grin he always seemed to sport returning. *If only she were a normal person who had met him in a different life!* College or something. Or at a coffee shop. She could fall for him in a heartbeat.

No. She looked out the windshield and scolded herself. No matter how cute he was, or how nice he seemed, all men had a dark side. She'd never met one who hadn't. *You've met almost exactly zero men,* the snide voice of her mother that took up so much time in her head said, *so don't think you know shit about men.* She shook her head, ignoring the voice. Self-reliance was paramount. She was the only person she could count on. Her, and Kaci.

While he was driving, he pulled a phone out of his pocket and maneuvered it with one hand, holding it to his mouth like he was going to speak into it.

Her hand shot to his forearm. "What are you doing?" she asked, trying to keep panic out of her voice.

"I'm going to call my boss, tell him—"

"No!" She *pushed*, maybe too hard, but Beckett didn't wince. "Don't call him, please. This is our little secret for now, ok?"

"Ok."

Phone back in pocket. No argument. Cerise breathed a sigh of relief, sagging in her seat.

Beckett pulled to the side of the road. Cerise looked around, realizing he'd done exactly as she'd asked. They were on a residential street a block away from the interim home. He turned off his truck, then smiled at her. She opened her door, looked back at him, wanting to *push* him again, to make him promise he wouldn't go anywhere. *You can push him too much. He's stronger than most, so he can take a lot, but you still must be wary. You'll either hurt him, or hasten the time when he becomes immune to your ability, as your mate must be.* Cerise frowned at the words, or rather the feeling that had pulsed through her that had imparted the words. It had been universes different than the voice of her mother, more like a knowing. But how could she know such a complex thing about a power she'd just discovered she had and a man she'd only just met? And mate? She didn't have time to puzzle that word out, she had to get Kaci.

She shot Beckett one last look, then slid out of his truck onto the ground. She had to trust him. Not easy, but there were no other choices available.

***

Beckett twisted in his seat so he could watch Cerise run

back the way they had come. She looked adorable in those scrubs. He ran his hands over his chest. Much better than he did. He looked like a first-class rube, especially wearing his work boots and cap with the scrubs. He needed something dark with plenty of pockets for weapons and tools. Something that made him look like the badass he was.

Beckett frowned as tension tightened him from the inside. He wished she had let him help her get her sister. He hooked an arm over the back of his seat and looked over his shoulder again to see if she was returning yet, then faced forward and frowned deeper. Had he really just popped her handcuffs and led her out of the hospital? He had thought calling Wade and telling him would be a good idea, but only for a second. Cerise was right, keeping it a secret was a better idea. If she had been his one true mate, all of this would be excusable. Wade would have popped her cuffs himself and led her out the front door and into Beckett's arms. But she wasn't old enough to be his one true mate, and although he enjoyed touching her, he hadn't felt that first sledgehammer of desire, as Crew had called it when he'd explained it, meaning she wasn't his one true mate. So none of what he had done was excusable.

Images danced through Beckett's brain. Cell doors slamming. His badge and gun stripped from him. *Wolven* went to jail when they broke human laws sometimes. Or worse, *Citlali* could bind their shifting ability for good, leaving them as weak and vulnerable as any human. Luckily, that only happened with Rhen's support, and Rhen was a soft touch for her *shiften*. For anyone really, sometimes even Khain, it seemed.

So why had he done it? Because she'd asked? Beckett knew he was impulsive, even hotheaded sometimes, and he definitely felt a connection with her, one stronger than he'd ever felt in his life. He wanted her. Plain and simple. Human or not. But that didn't explain what he'd done. Maybe because he knew she was innocent? She hadn't shot the gun, was being slammed against the wall when the other girl had done it to save her life. But still, he had to follow the rules, and normally he did. So why not this evening? Maybe she actually was his mate, somehow? *Mine!* The impulse to protect her, to take her in his arms, to *claim* her roared strong inside for a moment and he felt his fangs lengthen. He clamped control around his wolf, dismissing the thought, the instinct, as best he could. Something told him if she saw him like that, under the influence of any instinct that would make him react violently to innocent males around him like he'd seen his pack-mates do with a new mate, she'd ghost on him before he knew what was happening. But… she *wasn't* his mate. So why was he feeling this way?

He sighed and dropped his head onto the seat behind him. Everything had seemed to make so much sense when she'd been there with him in his truck, seemed to be the only possible option, but now, nothing made sense to him anymore.

He looked through the rear window of the truck again, hearing a dog bark, loud in the sleeping neighborhood. It stopped and he tried to relax in his seat. Cerise would be back soon. Then his inner tension would ease.

A small white sign in the grass between the road and the sidewalk ten feet ahead of him caught his eye. He got out of his truck to check it out. He could tell immediately what it said, but it made no sense. It only had one word on it, professionally printed.

Werewolves

Beckett tapped the brim of his cap with two fingers, then

looked around. Twenty feet away, he saw another sign. He jogged to it.

are

Twenty feet past that one he spied another.

sexy

Beckett grinned. Was that the end of the signs? Nope, at least one more. He jogged over.

fuckers

Beckett laughed out loud, pulling the last sign out of the ground and looking it over for identifying markers. Nothing.

He pushed it back into the grass. Let some uptight biddies call it in to the station in the morning. Give them something to talk about for weeks.

He played the message over in his head, wondering who had crafted it. *Werewolves are sexy fuckers.* He didn't know about the rest of them, but the message fit him just fine.

Wondering if Cerise thought so, he headed back to his truck to wait for her and the sweet calmness she brought with her.

CHAPTER 16

Cerise walked quickly across the grass that led to the interim home, feeling clumsy in her prison-issue boots, so different than the light canvas tennies she usually wore. The boots had no holes in them, so technically they were superior, but she hadn't gotten used to their weight yet.

Her gaze crawled over the interim home as she tried to work out what to do. No bars marred the windows, but she did see motion lights near the corners. The house was down in a severe dip on the corner and hidden almost completely from the traffic driving by, and if she approached from the side maybe she could get up to the wall along the back without triggering any motion lights. Myles had put motion lights up at their place, but she and Kaci knew all of the blind spots by heart.

She headed straight for the side wall of the place, running

her fingers along the chain-link fence of the dark house directly next to the interim home, then almost shrieked as a dog rushed out a doggy door in the wall of that house and began to bark at her. Cerise froze, then ran down the hill that led to the interim home, feeling like every person in the neighborhood would soon be peeking out windows, trying to figure out what was going on. On instinct, she *pushed*, the flex in her mind rippling outward toward the dog. *Stop barking!* She put a hand to her temple, as a dull ache started then stopped there, but breathed easier immediately when the jarring noise stopped and the night became quiet once more. Could she control animals too?

Cerise frowned, crouching slightly, knowing she needed to move quickly, but sudden realization flooded her, pinning her in place for just a moment. Zeus had always listened to her, never to Kaci. She had no idea how to command a horse with reins and a saddle and whip (yuck), but Zeus had always seemed to read her mind to some degree, knowing when she wanted to go faster or slower, or even backwards. She'd known she had a knack with horses from the first day he'd shown up in their yard, hungry, thirsty, but obviously seeking human contact. Had she been *pushing* him all along, and not knowing it?

The dog barked once, a warning bark, then made a small noise that sounded like it was about to start growling. Cerise scrambled up the hill. She needed to touch it. *Pushing* from afar just wasn't as good.

It was medium-sized, black, with dark, liquid eyes and a tail held straight out, only wagging at the tip. It's ears were laid back, but twitching, much like Zeus's did when he was on high alert. She didn't know enough about dogs to interpret any of that, but she knew she had to move quickly.

"Hey, boy," she said in a soft voice. "I won't hurt you. I won't come in your yard." She put her hand up, over the plane of the fence, fear spurting through her when his teeth appeared and he crouched slightly. She *pushed* immediately, before she got any closer. *Don't bite me. Stay calm, don't bark. I'm friendly.* The dog's ears relaxed and his face opened, while his tail and back end began to wiggle broadly.

Cerise felt like sagging in relief, but instead, she moved her hand to his head to pet him. He jumped on the fence to get closer to her, making it jingle. Cerise jerked her head up, searching windows in all the houses nearby for signs that anyone was watching. She didn't see any. Now what to tell this dog…?

She thought for a moment, briefly wondering if she told it not to bark again, if she would be hurting it somehow, maybe making it not be able to bark ever again in its life? No time to worry about that. Just give it finite instructions.

Rubbing its head, she spoke softly to it. "Go inside, go to sleep. Stay asleep until morning… unless the house catches on fire or something bad, then wake up your owners and get out."

The dog dropped to the ground and stared at her as if confused for a moment, then it turned and went inside.

Cerise winced. That was a messed up command if she'd ever heard one. Straight and to the point next time.

She whirled, desperate now to get to Kaci, but how? She ran to the interim home, hugging the wall, glad for the solid-colored scrubs she wore. She turned the corner of the wall, staying below the sensors of the motion lights, then turned the corner and tiptoed to the first window.

Cerise peeked inside and could see the dim shapes of bunk beds, and an open door leading to a hallway. A bright light shone from some room at the front of the building.

Cerise swore lightly, then moved on to the next window. She would never find Kaci this way! The next window showed the exact same thing as the first. It was so dark, Cerise couldn't even tell if anyone was in the beds.

Did she dare walk around to the front and talk to whoever was working there? *Push* them into getting her sister? What if there were two of them? Could she *push* two people at the same time?

Wait. What if she *pushed* Kaci? Cerise had a second to wonder if she ever had without realizing it, before the brilliance of the thought hit her. But how could she target Kaci if she didn't know where she was in the house? The few times she'd done it, she'd been facing or touching the person. Except for the dog, she hadn't been able to see him the first time.

But she'd always been able to tell, somehow, where people were inside a house, like their blood was full of metal and she was a magnet, easily able to feel their fields or auras or whatever it was she felt. Cerise pressed her back against the brick wall and *felt* inside the house. In the two rooms she was between, five kids slept, none of them Kaci. She had no idea how she knew that, but it was as obvious to her as the white snow under her boots.

She sent her feelers out farther, finding Kaci in a room on the second floor. Shit. She *pushed* with her mind, lightly, feeling the pulse of energy head out and up. *Kaci, wake up and come to the window.* Would it go through the wall? She could only hope.

Almost immediately she was rewarded by a noise above her. Hardly daring to hope, Cerise shot forward, up the hill slightly to get past the overhang of the second floor, then turned and looked at the windows up there. Kaci's face, small and impossibly sad, was there.

Cerise felt a cry of relief bubble up within her and she tamped it into submission. Not the place or time. "Kaci! Down here!"

Kaci's eyes went wide when she saw Cerise. She leaned forward against the screen of the window. "How'd you get out of jail?"

"Never mind. You have to get down here, right now." Cerise already had a plan, but she would almost certainly have to *push* Kaci again to get her to do it, which felt wrong somehow, to *push* someone she loved. But they didn't have time for anything else.

Kaci surprised her, by punching out the screen and starting to climb out the window without a second thought, making Cerise wonder if she had *pushed* her without realizing it.

Someone spoke from behind Kaci, making Kaci glance over her shoulder. She didn't say a word when she faced forward again, but her face was tight and she moved quicker.

"To the tree, Kaci, see it?" Cerise called in a whisper that seemed as loud as a shout.

Dismayed to see Kaci was in bare feet and pajamas that looked like single-color long underwear, Cerise briefly considered telling her to go back and get her clothes, but scrapped the idea when someone stuck their head out the window. Another girl, younger than Kaci was. She only watched Kaci scramble across the slanted overhang, though, didn't raise an alarm.

When Kaci reached the tree that Cerise had indicated, the one that was a good ten feet taller than the building, and was completely trimmed on the side facing the building, she looked behind her once, then leaned forward and put both hands on its trunk.

Cerise shook her head in wonderment, then ran to get underneath her. Kaci had never been what Cerise would call brave in most situations, but her actions tonight were courageous as hell. Cerise hoped the interim home hadn't been as awful as her experiences in foster care had been.

Cerise danced below Kaci with her arms out, wondering if she could catch her if the girl fell. She needn't have worried. Kaci stretched her body, found footing on a branch just beneath her, and scrambled quickly down the tree. Kaci had always been good at tree climbing. In the summer, they sometimes spent hours surveying the forest from the boughs so high up, no one could hear them or see them.

Kaci reached the ground and Cerise gathered her into a bear hug.

"Are we on the run?" Kaci whispered into her neck, her voice small.

Cerise grabbed her hand. "We are. Can you make it through the snow? We only have a block to go." As she spoke, she began to run, pulling Kaci with her. Cerise would carry her if she had to, Kaci was small for her age, but Kaci had been through worse than walking on the frozen ground in her bare feet.

Within moments, they made it up the hill and down the block, never sparing even a second to look back at the interim home.

***

Beckett cast another glance over his shoulder and frowned. Cerise was coming, but she did have a young girl with her. The girl he had scented at their home, he was sure.

They were coming fast and the girl looked to be barefoot. Another escape. Shit.

But when Cerise ripped the passenger door open and tried to push the girl up into the seat, his mind smoothed out slightly. It was worth it, although he briefly lamented the fact that the little sister would be coming with them. He'd rather be alone with Cerise, if he were going to risk everything he had for her. He twisted in his seat to face them, trying to hide his sudden irritation. He didn't like kids. Didn't understand them. Thought they were irritating and annoying. And huge liabilities.

This one looked at him with eyes as big as dinner plates, freckles covering her cheeks, forehead, and chin, then put her hands out, pushing against the seat and resisting Cerise with all her might. The girl was painfully thin and small, all knees and elbows and terrified eyes, but she fought like Cerise was pushing her into hell, succeeding in staying out of the truck.

"Lemon, he's going to help us," Cerise grunted, lifting *Lemon* and trying to push her up onto the seat. The girl would have none of it, and Beckett could smell the fear coming off of her in waves, even though he normally wasn't great at scenting emotions in his human form. Her fear was of *him*, making him do a double take. He wasn't scary. What had her so spooked? Oh. He remembered exactly what she'd been through that day. The day before and the day before, too, probably. He wiped the irritation out of his mind and tried to look welcoming.

The girl didn't say a word, she just twisted in Cerise's arms and tried to climb over her shoulder. Cerise looked down the street, her expression frightened, then lowered the girl to the ground gently and took her by the hand to the back of Beckett's truck. Beckett didn't watch them. He could hear their frantic, whispered conversation easily, although they probably thought he couldn't.

"He's not going to hurt us, I promise. He's a nice guy," Cerise said.

The girl's voice was almost a whimper. "How do you know?"

"He saved me. Got me out of handcuffs and took me out of the hospital."

The girl didn't say anything for a minute, and Beckett could almost hear Cerise looking up and down the road again. All dark still, no cars, no sound of sirens.

The girl's voice was softer still. "You were in the hospital?"

"I can't explain it now, Kaci, but I promise you, I know this guy won't hurt us. His name is Beckett. He's a doctor, sworn to help people, not hurt them." She stopped for a minute as if grasping for something else to say, then told Kaci, "His name means beehive."

Kaci's voice raised only slightly, and her words shook, whether with cold or fear, he didn't know. "Let's try the train, Cerise. I can walk there. I'm not cold at all. Just me and you."

"Kaci, no, we-" Cerise broke off and ran the five feet up to the open passenger door. "Beckett, do we need I.D. to ride on a train?"

Beckett nodded. "Since 9/11, you need a passport and a Social Security card just to take out a library book."

Cerise frowned at him like she hadn't understood anything he'd just said, then she turned slowly back to Kaci and disappeared from his sight.

"We can't go on the train, Kaci. It's go with Beckett to California, or hitchhike. Do you want to risk being caught by the cops again?"

Beckett's hands tightened on the steering wheel. No way

was he letting these two out of his sight. He'd never met anyone who needed a friend more than they did. He glanced back at them once, wondering what kind of run-ins they'd had with police that would make Cerise's voice twist the way it had when she'd said *cops*. Not good ones. Damn, that complicated his position a little, unless he continued to let them believe he was a doctor.

Even in the dim light of a nearby streetlight, Beckett could tell Kaci's lips were trembling, her eyes tearing. This little girl might turn out to be an annoying mystery, but for now, Beckett's heart broke at how terrified she was. Of him. Of everything.

He didn't know what most kids needed, didn't care, but something about this one plucked at his heartstrings and he thought he might know what she needed. He'd had a dog as a pet once when he'd been young, before his father and brother had died, a tiny little thing that had been abused. He'd found her in the alley behind their house, fur matted, blood on one flank. She'd been a nervous thing, always running from him, until he'd started to share his lunch with her. His father had taken one look at her and declared her old and said she wouldn't live more than a year, and he'd been right, but during that year Beckett had spoiled her rotten. She'd slept on his bed, always got at least a quarter of anything he was eating, and he wouldn't let anyone say a harsh word to her, or she would run away and not come back for days, until he lured her with food again. She had never completely been at ease with the world, never been able to handle anyone in the house raising their voice, and Beckett had been the only one who could pet her. That's what this little bitty slip of a girl would respond to, he knew it, suddenly. Being spoiled rotten.

He rooted fiercely for her to get in the truck, already

trying to think of ways to ease her mind, prove he could be trusted, spoil her.

He listened hard, waiting for her decision, wondering what Cerise would do if she still balked.

But when Kaci spoke, her voice had changed slightly. Some of the fear had leaked out, and a bit of wonder had replaced it. "Cerise, he sounds like Luke and Bo Duke."

Beckett grinned, knowing he'd found his ace. She liked country boys? That was a role he could play to perfection.

CHAPTER 17

Cerise's eyes shot open and she sat bolt upright in the truck, the towel she'd been using as a pillow against the window falling to the floor. Kaci whimpered and put her arm over her face, still sleeping, her head in Cerise's lap.

Cerise blinked hard at the highway flying past them, trying to figure out where they were. The sun was coming up behind them, which meant it was close to 7:00 in the morning and she'd been asleep for almost four hours.

But she'd forgotten to *push* Beckett the night before when he'd asked where they were headed to and she'd tentatively said Las Vegas, Nevada, not knowing why she'd lied. His reaction had been so normal, so accepting, she'd never even thought of doing it. Plus she'd put Kaci in the middle of the bench seat, meaning she'd have to reach around Kaci to touch Beckett. Stupid!

What had he said? He'd grinned and told her, "I'm owed time off at work and I've got a full tank of gas. A road trip sounds like just what I've been hankering for."

She'd frowned at him, noticing at once that his Southern accent had deepened considerably. But when she saw Kaci watching him carefully, measuring his words in that quiet way of hers, she'd gone with it, wondering if he'd somehow heard what Kaci had said about him sounding like the boys from the Dukes of Hazzard TV show.

Now suspicion crept in. What exactly did he want from them? Or was it as simple as the fact that her *push* had some sort of residual? Once she told him to do something once with a *push*, could she give him more commands and he'd follow even without one? That didn't seem right, somehow.

She spoke quietly, not wanting to wake Kaci. "Where are we?"

He responded just as quietly, his tone soft. "Should be seeing signs for Des Moine exits any minute here."

She gaped at him. "Des Moine, Iowa?"

He grinned, quickening her heartbeat. God, he was handsome, and the stubble on his cheeks and chin made him even more so in this early morning light. "'Course, darlin'. Gotta go through Iowa to get to Nevada."

She didn't speak for a long time, her hands twirling in Kaci's rusty red hair. They'd made it out of Illinois. They were on their way to California. Could be there by tomorrow if they didn't stop. She might possibly be able to pull this off, to find Kaci's real family, to get her to someone who would love her and care for her and give her the life she deserved.

Cerise knew someone had to answer for the laws she'd broken and Myles's death, but it would not be Kaci.

She snuck a glance at Beckett. He'd driven all night, not

even stopping to go to the bathroom, she didn't think, unless she'd missed it. For them. Because she'd asked him to. Maybe she hadn't been just trying to convince Kaci that he was a good guy last night. Maybe she'd been right and he actually *was*.

She faced forward again, warning herself not to get too comfortable. Because maybe he wanted something from them, or was just under her influence.

He yawned, causing her to turn to him again.

"You tired?" she asked, wondering if she could *push* him not to need sleep. She wouldn't do such a thing, but couldn't help but consider the limits of this strange power she had. And the repercussions.

He cast her a sideways smile, then nodded at Kaci's sleeping form. "Tired *and* hungry. What do you say we get some breakfast when li'l bit wakes up."

"Her name is Kaci."

He nodded. "Kaci. Got it."

Kaci stirred, then pushed herself into a sitting position, blinking owlishly at the highway they were on and pushing her hair out of her face.

"Mornin', Kaci," Beckett said in a normal voice, his Southern accent thicker than it had been a second ago. "Fancy some chow?"

Kaci didn't answer, but she did look at him. Cerise wished she could see Kaci's expression instead of just the back of her head.

Cerise spoke to Beckett. "We, ah, we don't have any money. Ours was—" What could she say? Stolen? In fact, it was at the police station, inventoried in a tan envelope.

"I'll spot you both," Beckett said simply.

Cerise frowned. "What do you get out of this?"

Beckett looked at her for a moment, then shrugged. "Nothing. I'll get to sleep at night, I guess. I never met nobody who could use help like you two could and I'm not gonna let you starve."

Cerise pressed her lips together. She didn't want to be pitied, but in reality, she couldn't afford not to accept his help. Couldn't afford not to be extremely grateful for it. They wouldn't make it to California without him.

She pulled Kaci into her arms and spoke fiercely, getting it out of the way. "I'm not going to, you know, *do* anything for your help. Kaci neither."

Beckett's face tightened with anger that terrified her until she realized it wasn't directed at them. "Good. I'd destroy anyone who tried to make you *do something* in exchange for a simple kindness. You don't owe me *nothing*."

Cerise felt tears float to her eyes unbidden and she forced them back. She'd never had anyone be *kind* to her before.

From this new perspective, with Kaci pulled into her arms, she could see much of Kaci's face, see that she was now staring at Beckett with something like awe.

That makes two of us, Lemon.

***

Beckett swallowed the rage that coursed through him when he thought about what kind of a life these girls must have lived. He didn't want to scare either of them. If Myles Pekin, or anyone who had ever hurt them, had been in front of him right then, he would have taught them a life-lesson, though, one that left them unable to ever hurt females again.

He calmed himself so he could speak, then nodded at the rest stop sign that flashed by them and turned his country roots up to full blast. "What do ya say, li'l bit? Breakfast time? Fast food? Fancy food? What ya got a hankerin' for?"

He could feel the weight of Kaci's stare on him, but she didn't say a word.

"She doesn't talk," Cerise said.

Beckett flashed her a look. He'd clearly heard her talking at the back of his truck while they debated going with him. Cerise shook her head sharply. Oh, maybe she didn't talk to strangers? Or men? Anger coursed through him again and he cut it short.

Cerise chose her words carefully. "She doesn't…"

Beckett raised a hand. "You don't have to explain it to me. No one in this truck has to do anything they don't want to, including talk." He winked at Kaci, but she didn't respond. A desire to see her smile bloomed in his chest, surprising him with its ferocity. He wanted to tease a bit of happiness out of her, almost as much as he wanted to convince her big sister to trust him. Something told him doing the former might help the latter, but that didn't matter as much to him as doing it for its own sake. Little girls should smile, should laugh, should be *happy*. He might not know shit about kids, but he knew that much.

He looked at Cerise. "Any ideas? We can stop anywhere. McDonalds, Subway, a sit-down restaurant. Anything you want."

Kaci twisted in her seat and moved her mouth to Cerise's ear. Whispering.

"McDonalds," Cerise said.

"Perfect." Beckett hit his blinker and edged to the right to take the next exit.

Within a few moments, he found a McDonalds to pull into, sneaking glances at Kaci. Her eyes ate up her face, like everything was brand new to her. Cerise wore a similar expression and Beckett noticed her knuckles were white, clasped tightly in her lap. How much of this *was* a fresh experience? They couldn't possibly have never been to a McDonalds before, could they?

He parked close to the building, making a note to get gas before they started driving again, then turned off the truck, then looked at Kaci and Cerise. "Maybe we should buy Kaci some shoes first."

Cerise swung her face towards him, indecision and panic on her face. "Oh no, you don't have to do that. We-ah, she'll be fine."

Beckett thought she was probably right, except… "They might not let her in." He nodded to the No Shoes, No Shirt, No Service sign on the door.

Cerise looked for only a second. "Really?" She nibbled on her lower lip, and Beckett thought she couldn't look more adorable. He also couldn't decide what was bothering her more. Taking more of his money? He didn't care. He had very little to spend it on, except his one hobby, and the only baby he was interested in, his truck.

He opened his mouth to tell her that, then closed it again. Maybe it would be better to ease her in to letting him spend money on them. It would take a while to get to Las Vegas, and if they weren't on a time crunch, he would stretch it out as long as possible. He was in no hurry to get rid of them. "Maybe if you carry her, it will be ok." She was small enough.

Cerise nodded eagerly, then exited the truck, turning back for Kaci, who seemed to float into her arms, her eyes glued onto the fast food restaurant. Once inside, Beckett pointed out the bathrooms. "Don't let her stand on the floor in there. It can get downright grimy."

Cerise nodded quickly, and within a few moments, they were all back at the front. Beckett led them to a table in the back where they wouldn't get too much attention. "Anything you want," he said. "Just tell me and I'll get it for you."

Cerise and Kaci slid into the booth, and Cerise's eyes met his. She shook her head slightly, looking completely overwhelmed. Beckett watched her for a moment before he realized what was wrong. "I'll surprise you."

He came back five minutes later, holding three bags and two drink carriers filled with soda, milk, coffee, and orange juices balanced directly in the middle. He'd ordered three of everything on the breakfast menu, plus one of all the drinks.

He ripped open the bags and spread them across the table, the greasy scent of fried hash browns making him lick his lips. He took out two Big Breakfast platters and placed one in front of Cerise and one in front of Kaci. Kaci looked from him to the Styrofoam cover on the platter, then back to him again, her eyes wide. He nodded and gave her an encouraging smile, ripping the lid off and pulling her fork out of its plastic sleeve to hand it to her.

"There's so much food," Cerise said in an awed voice.

"'Merica," Beckett grunted, then shoved an entire hash brown in his mouth and washed it down with some soda. "Go easy if you're not used to it. It's pretty greasy." He tipped another wink at Kaci. "Just the way McDonalds should be."

Kaci only stared, then darted her hand forward to take her fork, then cut into a pancake and delicately placed it in her mouth. Her eyes opened wide in pleasure and she chewed quickly, made another mouthful disappear, then stabbed her fork into the eggs.

Beckett nodded at her and pushed a drink toward her. "Try the soda, li'l bit," he said, watching her closely. As she took a sip, her eyes crossed, then sank closed as the bolus of sugar hit her tongue. A whimper of bliss escaped her throat. He'd bet a year's salary she'd never tasted soda before. She could use a little fattening up, but he'd be sure to talk to her about the dangers of too much, eventually. He frowned at the thought, wondering when he'd turned into a lecturing old man.

Cerise started on her meal, more hesitantly than Kaci had, but soon she also discovered the relative joy of fast food.

Beckett grinned at both of them, pushing food toward them, encouraging them to try at least a bite of everything on the table. "It ain't worth a plugged nickel when it comes to nutrition, but it sure tastes good."

CHAPTER 18

*G*rey hunkered, completely still, in Beckett's bedroom, Beckett's stink coming at him from all directions. His eyes were trained out the window, watching for Beckett's easily-distinguishable truck, his mind focused 100% on the task at hand, finishing what he'd started so many years ago. When the first rays of the morning sun filtered over the eastern horizon, he finally gave up. Beckett wasn't coming home.

Grey relaxed, dropping to his ass on the bedroom floor and leaning against the wall, then pulling out his phone, but before he turned it on, he lolled his head, thinking hard, replaying the prophecy that had ultimately led him to be there, hunting Beckett.

The booted wolf, a tempest in the storm, saves the Savior in the final hour. The Demon cries.

When he'd first heard that prophecy, Trevor Burbank had

already been identified as the most probable *Savior*, from the *Savior Prophecy*, and Grey couldn't touch him without revealing his plans, his treachery as most would see it. He'd made some attempts on Trevor's life in a roundabout fashion, binding him, trying to convince him to kill himself, but it hadn't worked. So when he'd heard of the booted-wolf prophecy, he'd latched onto it, determined to discover who the booted wolf was. If he could get rid of the booted wolf, killing Burbank would not be necessary. If the booted wolf wasn't around to save the savior, Burbank would die somehow, probably at the hands of Khain, in the final hour, which Grey interpreted to mean the last battle, the one that determined if Khain lived, or Rhen lived.

Grey's purpose was simple. Make sure they both lived. Forestall the final hour, forever. If he had to dismantle the KSRT, indeed, the entire *shiften* populace to do it, he would.

It had been simple to decide which booted wolf, of the only five or so he knew existed, was the one the prophecy referred to. Beckett Oswego's *renqua* was a circle with three wavy lives projecting out from it in a circle, rather like an abstract rendition of a hurricane as seen from above, *a tempest in the storm.*

Unfortunately, *wolven* were single-minded, and he'd found none he dared try to bend to his ideals, so he worked mostly alone, or with humans, or with a few select half-breeds. Which meant his plans had to be sneaky, roundabout, under the radar.

He'd manage it somehow. Take out the one true mates. Take out the savior. Take out the booted wolf. All he needed was to break one cog in the wheel, throw something important off, and history would sway in the direction he required. He knew it.

When he'd gotten into Serenity the night before, Cerise Pekin had just been delivered to the jail, and Kaci Pekin was already settled into the interim home. Which was almost perfect. Before he went out to search for Beckett, though, he needed to make sure they were both still there. He called his contact, not waiting for the male to finish saying hello before he barked out his demands. "Report."

"Ah, Chief, you're not going to like this."

Grey shook his head. He knew exactly what he was about to hear, and the dolt was right, he didn't like it one bit. "Tell me."

"Cerise Pekin got into a fight and was transferred to the hospital late last night. Apparently she walked out of there, escaped somehow, and hasn't been seen since."

"And Kaci Pekin?"

"Also gone in the middle of the night. Slipped out of her bed and crawled out the window."

Grey clenched his fingers into his palms, but his voice never belied his anger. "I want to be told immediately if they are found."

"Yes, Chief." The male sounded eager, and surprised to be let off without an ass-chewing. Grey would deal with him later.

He hung up, trying to decide his next move, then realized he had to know if Cerise and Kaci were with Beckett or not. He called the number to the KSRT office. It rang and rang. Twelve rings. Twenty. Just when Grey was about to give up, a harried voice answered. "What?"

Grey didn't recognize it. He kept his voice neutral, and tried to smooth its normal rasp enough that he wasn't immediately identifiable. "I need to speak to Beckett Oswego. It's an emergency. Is he there?"

"Ain't no one here," the voice growled. "We got our own emergencies to deal with."

Gently, almost delicately, Grey removed the phone from his ear and pressed the end call button. A dead end.

He stood and paced. If the KSRT had figured out Cerise was a one true mate, she wouldn't have had to escape, she'd have been freed by Wade or one of the other Hardy Boys.

So that meant they were both on the run, the only question was if they had connected with Beckett first, which Grey knew could have happened, somehow, being led by a divine hand. He knew exactly where the girls were headed, so that was no problem. He could meet them there, but if Oswego was with them, Grey would need help. He could handle Oswego on his own, but one thing he'd realized from his many conversations with Azer before the angel had disappeared, was not only would the males be drawn to their mates to such a degree that they'd be twice as dangerous if their mate was in danger, but the one true mates' powers would also be strengthened and more focused when they were together with their mate, making them dangerous in a way Grey couldn't possibly predict.

He needed help. He raised his phone again and paged through his contacts until he found the name he was looking for: Bane. He called the number.

"Yeah, what?" The voice was high, open, excited. Not Bane. "Zane, it's Grey, get me your brother."

"You got something for us, boss? We got a job? I was just telling Bane we hadn't heard from you in a-"

Grey cut him off. "Just get me Bane, now!"

Nothing. Grey could imagine Zane's hurt look as he held the phone away from his ear and went to find Bane. But trying to talk to Zane was an exercise in futility. He might as well be explaining his plans to an inanimate object for all Zane would underst-

Grey's thoughts cut off mercilessly as he realized something important. Inanimate objects sometimes spoke volumes.

Bane came on the line, speaking with his usual plodding deliberateness, wasting not one more syllable than was necessary. "'Lo?"

"I got a job for you. Get ready for a road trip," Grey said, his mind already at his Lambo. "I gotta call you back to give you the details."

He hung up without waiting for an answer, stood, then took a tube of his own creation out of his pocket, and sprayed the concoction on his face and body, plus some in the air for good measure, then more over all the spots he'd touched and sat on. If Beckett did come in anytime soon, he would be able to tell someone had been in the house, but he wouldn't be able to identify who. He'd think it was a *foxen*, as this particular mixture had *foxen* scent mixed with masking agents, like wintergreen, camphor, and eucalyptus. He worked quickly, his mind humming with excitement.

Once out of the house, he covered the ground to his Lamborghini quickly. It was parked a half mile away, off the road a bit, between a farmer's stack of hay bales on one side and a hill on the other. When he reached it, he stopped for a minute, frowning. That wasn't his sleek, black, Lamborghini 350 GT. He put a hand to his forehead, then patted his goatee, remembering. The Lambo was in storage. He couldn't drive that thing with every cop in the country looking for him. Which, if they weren't now, they would be soon. He'd taken this silver mini-mom-van from a supermarket parking lot, swapped the plates with another silver mom-van just that morning, like he always did when he needed something to drive.

His mind for details was going, as it probably had to, in order to make room for his genius. He was the only *wolven* in existence who had the foresight to realize what a huge mistake the rest of them were making. *Genius.*

He slid open the side door and fished under the fabric covering of the child safety seat that was installed in the back seat, complete with crumbs and remnants of baby puke. He pulled out what he'd hidden there, slowly, testing it with his fingers. The wrapped pendant that belonged to Cerise Pekin.

Carefully, he unwrapped it. It wasn't glowing, which was good. It gave him the courage to attempt the crazy idea he'd thought of while on the phone. Quickly, before he talked himself out of it, he stripped off his glove and wrapped his bare fingers around it.

"Mudge, Mudger, Mound, Hound, Hive, Hell," he muttered, his brain feeling cracked open and examined. His thoughts pushed around in his head, motivated by the energy coursing through him from the pendant, energy that did not belong to him, that he had no right to try to harness. He focused anyway, trying to ask his question.

"Mudge Mudge she?" he said, his fingers swelling and cracking open in tiny spider webs, plasma leaking out.

He pressed his eyes shut and tried again. "Mudge-mudge. No, *where. Where is* she?"

The pendant seemed to pulse in his hand. *Cheat!* it screamed at him. Traitor! it crooned, turning deadly. But it knew where she was, he could tell. If he could just hold on…

Images shuddered past his closed eyes. I-80. Thunderclouds. The people of Iowa welcome you. Nebraska, the good life. Snow. A green pickup truck. Red hair. *Oswego.* Grand Island. Hilton.

Grey forced his fingers open, letting the pendant fall to the ground, as his body did, too.

***

Grey woke slowly, trying to open his eyes, but unable to. They felt strangely swollen, like he'd been stung by a dozen bees on his face. He pressed his fingers to his overripe skin and pulled his eyes manually open, cracking the seal of yuck that had sewn them shut. He forced himself into a sitting position, shivering violently. The day was overcast, socked in almost, so he couldn't tell what time it was, but common sense told him he'd been there for hours, unconscious in the snow.

The pendant!

He searched for it, his fingers finally grazing it in three inches of powder. He pulled his hand back and stuck his fingers in his mouth, realizing his lips were swollen, too, his entire face, maybe. He found the cloth he had wrapped the pendant in and picked it up with that, desperate not to touch its cool surface again. It had hurt him.

But he knew what route to take. If he and his team got lucky, maybe they could catch up to them before California, ensure no one else got involved.

He placed the wrapped pendant back in the folds of the child safety seat, then closed the door and opened the driver's door, about to slide behind the wheel, but something stopped him. A scent on the wind.

He lifted his swollen face and flared his nostrils. Was it what he thought it had been? He strode to the front of the minivan, then climbed on the hood, then up the windshield as high as he dared, trying to gain high ground, pressing his face to the sky again, and flaring his nostrils.

Yes. Myles Pekin lived nearby. Less than two miles away. Or had, when he'd been alive, betrayed by his sour scent, which was a fixture on the wind.

Grey grinned and hopped to the ground. Coincidence always meant that The Light or Rhen or Khain or an angel was at work, molding the futures of the humans and the *shiften*, shaping their paths, lighting their way. What greater coincidence could there possibly be than Myles and Sandra Pekin fleeing Grey in New Mexico and settling in Serenity, less than two miles from Cerise Pekin's fated mate.

Although a lesser wolf might have argued this particular coincidence worked against Grey's plans and not for them, Grey knew different. Someone was helping him. Someone wanted him to succeed.

Rhen? Possibly. He stood stock-still and drew lines in the murky sand of his mind until he convinced himself of more than that. Possibly turned to almost definitely. Almost definitely morphed into certainly. *He was untouchable.*

He got in his mom-van and backed out, turning right on the road, seeking the highway.

Nebraska or bust.

CHAPTER 19

Cerise surveyed the miles slipping past them with heavy-lidded eyes, feigning drowsiness so Beckett wouldn't talk to her or ask her questions. Kaci didn't have to pretend, she was asleep, her head on Cerise's shoulder. Cerise shifted to get more comfortable and pulled Kaci's head into her lap, as much as their seatbelts would allow, then allowed her body to relax again, trying to seem on the verge of resting, feeling guilty even as she did so. Beckett hadn't slept at all, and he was starting to look tired.

He swayed in his seat slightly, tapping his fingers and thumbs to the music on the radio, possibly trying to keep himself awake. The singer's voice on the radio was deep and throaty, vibrating country in a way that fascinated Cerise. She and Kaci never had music to listen to, never had radio of any sort, only able to listen to movie credit intros, or the occasional snatch of song in one of the shows they snuck at night. Only now did she realize what they'd been missing.

She picked apart the lyrics, loving them, loving everything about the song, loving especially when Beckett sang along, softly, so as not to wake Kaci. She watched his profile as he sang, finding it even more interesting than the highway and the other cars. His strong jaw, full lips, the stubble growing on his chin. Her eyes traced his tattoos that wound down both muscular arms and she bit her lip to keep from asking him about them. She never would have thought tattoos would look good, be *sexy*, but his were. She wanted to trace each one of them with her forefinger, find the starting and ending places, feel the texture and temperature of his skin under them.

Cerise tore her eyes away from him, back onto the road, onto Kaci's hair, anything to stop her thoughts in their tracks. She was ruining his *life*, using him for her own ends against his conscious will, she had no right to think those kinds of thoughts about him. But she couldn't keep her eyes away; they returned to him, almost lovingly.

He sang along with the music.
I met a girl
She made me smile, she made me wait
She crossed the street, she crossed my heart
She fixed her dress, she bit her lip, she lit me up
I met a girl with crazy shoes and baby blues
The way she moves is changing my whole world
I met a girl

He glanced in Cerise's direction and she let her eyes drop shut, her heart rate speeding up. If only he wasn't so *nice*, so *kind*, she might have found it easier to stop looking at him, but he was. Kaci had insisted on drinking all of the soda that was left, then asked to stop four times in their first hour and a half of driving. Cerise had gotten frustrated with her, but Beckett had only grinned and said, "Li'l bit has a li'l bladder. It's not her fault," then found the closest bathroom each time.

She hadn't explained *anything* about why she'd been handcuffed to the bed the night before, why she'd had to break Kaci out of the interim home, or how they'd ended up with no money and no shoes, trying to make their way across the country, and he hadn't asked. She didn't think it was because she had *pushed* him either. She could sense his genuine curiosity, but also his marked restraint. He didn't want to make her uncomfortable.

Cerise chanced a slit in her eyelids. He was facing forward again. She shifted her head position so she could gaze out the window. She'd never had anyone care about her comfort before, except Kaci. It felt good to have this big, strong man taking care of them both. She felt *safe* with him. *Dangerous,* her mind tried to whisper. She didn't fight it, but she didn't encourage it, either. She would just have to wait and see if Beckett was for real or not.

A green sign ahead caught her attention and she sat up, frowning at it, trying to read it in her plodding manner before it disappeared.

"Welcome to Nebraska?" she said, the incredulity in her voice making Kaci shift and mutter. "We're in Nebraska already?" It was one thing to calculate how long it would take to cross a state while staring at the sterile page on a map, another to experience it in real time. The last time she had been in a car for more than a few minutes, had been years ago, after she'd tried to steal Kaci away from Myles and Sandra the second time, and they'd gotten her out of the police holding cell, then driven for two days to their new home in Illinois.

Cerise and Kaci had been in the back of the truck, forced to lie down the entire time under blankets, threatened with a beating if anyone saw their heads pop up.

Beckett chuckled. "Sure are."

Cerise peered at the sky, not liking the darkness of the clouds, and the way errant snowflakes were starting to whiz past them. "Looks like a storm."

Beckett changed the radio station, finding an all-weather one. The announcer droned on about winds and snow and eighteen inches overnight in a bored voice.

Cerise swallowed hard, realizing she hadn't thought about what they would do if they had to stop, then realizing the storm wouldn't be the only thing that would force them to. Beckett needed to sleep.

"Eighteen inches. That sounds bad," she said. "Will we be able to drive in it?"

"We gotta stop this evening anyway so I can rest." He glanced at her. "Unless you want to drive for a bit."

Drive? "I-I." She tripped over her words, then finished lamely, "I don't know how."

Beckett looked at her appraisingly for a moment, then said, "Oh." He patted the dashboard of the truck. "Cooter's got snow tires, and they'll plow and de-ice, so we can keep going for a while, but we should decide on a city to stop in for the night. I'm partial to Hiltons, myself. I'll bet we can find a pool for li'l bit to play in."

Cooter? She almost laughed that his truck had that name, Kaci would love it, but then she picked apart the rest of what he had said. Hotel. Stop for the night. Pool. She was in way over her head and there was no way out but through.

***

Beckett could feel Cerise's sudden agitation and it bothered him immensely. It was like every new development floored her, made her have to rethink her plan over again. Like she'd never traveled, never been in a car, never been to a McDonalds, never stayed in a hotel. What kind of a life had she lived?

He'd seen a documentary once, called *True Stories of Feral Children*, which had documented nine children who had little to no contact with human society, no awareness of social cues, and no ability to speak a language. Trent had insisted on watching it in the break room one day at work, because one of the children had been lost in the forest and raised by wolves. Beckett had scoffed at first, but then been fascinated by the stories. Three of them had been from the United States, one abandoned in the woods by kidnappers, the other two victims of mentally ill parents. Cerise and Kaci were obviously not *that* bad off, but Beckett had been in their home, and he had smelled that Myles Pekin had certainly been an alcoholic and a drug addict. It wasn't hard to draw parallels between the stories.

What he wouldn't give to know her, to learn her story. And Kaci's, too. But he would have to be careful. She didn't trust him, neither of them did. He was surprised they were in his truck at all, regardless of how few choices they'd had.

He decided to risk a question, just to let her know he was open to talking. He felt certain she would deflect it, and then he would talk about himself. *Lie about yourself?* Eh, he would just steer clear of what he did. Let her think he was a doctor for a little while longer. He'd never said that he was, she'd assumed it.

She was in your house.

The thought hit him between the eyes. She *had* been.

He'd almost forgotten in the wake of everything that had happened since he'd woken up in his own bed, her scent in his nose, yesterday morning. He frowned, remembering that his first thought when he'd scented her had been about Crew telling him he'd already met his one true mate. He snuck a look at her. She was looking out the window, chewing on one fingernail, one hand on Kaci's back, her long strawberry blonde hair looking adorably messy around her shoulders.

Could she be his one true mate? And why wasn't he thinking clearly around her? Why could he not seem to connect thoughts and occurrences in a coherent manner when she was around? Did something about her mess with his memories? *Could* he possibly have met her six weeks ago, then forgotten?

Hope surged in his chest. If she were his mate, everything would make sense somehow. He'd be forgiven for breaking her out of-

Beckett shook his head, as fat snowflakes began to fall outside the truck, making him flip on his wipers. *Another* thing he'd forgotten. He was now—he looked at the clock— six hours late for work and he hadn't called in to explain why. Wade would have his ass.

He peeked at Cerise again, still looking out the window. She was worth it. Worth all of it. He'd figure it out.

Back to sparking a conversation with her. What could he say that wouldn't put her on the defensive too much?

Where you in my house yesterday? No, too aggressive.

Have we met before? That wouldn't work.

So, I know Kaci killed Myles. I didn't see it, though, I smelled it. Absolutely not.

How about, *want to see me shift? I'm a lot cuddlier in my*

wolf form than I look. Beckett snorted, then saw Cerise look at him from his peripheral vision.

Without thinking, he said, "Tell me about yourself."

The finger she'd been chewing on shook and she shoved her hand under her leg to hide it. "Me? I'm boring."

Beckett nodded, knowing she was anything but. "What are you headed to Las Vegas for?"

She shifted in her seat, then looked out the window for a moment, then back to him. "Kaci's mom is there. She's going home." Her voice wavered.

Beckett nodded again, trying to make sense of that. Wouldn't Kaci's mom be Cerise's mom, too, if Cerise thought they were sisters? But the fear in her voice told him not to ask another question. He wanted to find something to put her at ease. "I could teach you to drive. Want to learn?"

"Really? You would do that?" Her sweet scent flared.

Beckett grinned at her, taking in deep breaths through his nose. He would do anything to excite her like that again. A female had never smelled so good to him. A light flashed in his brain, seeming to say, *she's your mate, dummy.* "Yeah, I would."

She peered out the windshield at the snow, coming down quicker now, the flakes sticking together and trying to cling to the truck before the wind or the wipers flung them away. "Not in the snow."

"Nah, we'll wait till it stops. In the morning, maybe."

She still seemed doubtful. "Not on the highway."

"No, a parking lot. You'll pick it up fast, but you shouldn't drive on the highway till you've had plenty of experience on empty roads."

She peered at him. "Is that… legal?"

"Don't worry, Cerise, as long as you're with me, I'll keep you out of trouble."

CHAPTER 20

*C*erise leaned forward, trying to see out the windshield, but all she could see was a swirling white mess. They would have to stop soon.

"There it is," Beckett said, maneuvering into the exit lane. "Grand Island."

It had taken longer to get there than Beckett had expected because Kaci had woken up with a sore tummy, and they'd had to stop at bathrooms three times in the last two hours. But they'd made it. Beckett had already called ahead and made reservations at a hotel. Cerise swallowed hard, nervous about the arrangements, not sure how he thought they would be sleeping. If she had to, she would *push* him to sleep on the floor, then stay up all night.

Beckett found the hotel easily, parked, and surveyed the Target store next door with satisfaction. "Perfect," he said, then turned the truck off. "I can carry Kaci, if she's ok with it."

Kaci's hand snuck into Cerise's and she squeezed. "I've got her," Cerise said.

Beckett nodded, then jumped out of the truck and rushed around to their side before Cerise could open the door. He pulled it opened, then waited, ready to lend a steady hand as Cerise climbed down. Once Kaci was in her arms, they made their way through the blowing snow to the front door, which slid open automatically when they got close. Cerise held her breath, hoping Kaci wouldn't notice, or she'd want to trigger it again and again, like a toddler who sees an automatic door for the first time. That's what Kaci was, sometimes, when it came to technology. A toddler in a body too big for that age, but too small for the age she really was. Kaci's head was down, laid on Cerise's shoulder, her arms and legs wrapped around Cerise's body. She didn't notice the doors.

They followed Beckett to the front desk where the man there spoke to them all kindly, had Beckett sign something, then gave him three cookies and a small envelope. Kaci's head came up at the smell of the cookies.

Beckett took a cookie out of its wrapper and handed it to Kaci with a smile. Her hand floated up, snatched it, then routed it to her mouth where she took a sniff, then a small bite, her eyes locked on Beckett. Her face twisted in pleasure at the taste, but still she didn't smile back. Beckett didn't seem to mind.

He tried to hand Cerise a cookie, but she waved it off. Her tummy didn't feel great either.

"You want it later?" Beckett asked.

"No."

Beckett made a more-for-me face, pressed the two remaining cookies together in a kind of sandwich, and ate them in two bites. "Mmm," he said, winking at Kaci, who was just finishing hers. She put her head down on Cerise's shoulder slowly, not responding to Beckett, but not turning away from him, either, as Cerise had expected her to.

Beckett held up his envelope. "I have the keys, but I say we head to the store before the snow gets worse. We all need clothes."

Cerise nodded her assent, trying to ignore the guilt that filled her. Was she really going to let him buy them clothes? No choice, Cerise. Just go with it.

Within a few moments, they were at the Target. Beckett led them inside, snagging a cart. "If she gets too heavy, maybe she'll sit in here," he said, indicating the open section of the cart. Cerise checked Kaci's mood, then put her in it when she nodded. She wrapped her arms around her bent knees and tried to look at everything at once, again seeming more like a toddler than her age.

Cerise pushed the cart, following Beckett to the middle of the store. He stopped smack in the middle of multiple displays of cute, colorful clothing around Kaci's size.

"Anything you want, Kaci, what size do you wear?"

Cerise shook her head. "One outfit, that's all we need. And shoes for Kaci."

Beckett flashed the grin that she was beginning to realize meant he was about to charm her into whatever he wanted. "Two," he said. "You both need two outfits, shoes for Kaci, and swimsuits."

Cerise put up her hands, stopped her protest when her gaze landed on Kaci. Kaci was staring at a purple shirt with white ruffles on it, and the raw *want* in her eyes gave Cerise painful pause. She swallowed her guilt and nodded. "You want that shirt, Lemon?"

Kaci climbed over the side of the cart to the floor, drifting to the shirt. Cerise glanced at Beckett, surprised to see him watching Kaci with an expression that looked both sad and thrilled, like he understood their situation somehow.

She gripped the cart handle tighter. Could he possibly?

No. He couldn't.

An hour later the cart was full, Kaci walking alongside in her new purple shoes and purple socks. Beckett had assured Cerise it would be fine if Kaci wore them now as long as they paid before they left. Cerise held Kaci's hand, eyeing everything in the cart. There were two outfits for Beckett, both the same: dark pants with lots of pockets, dark t-shirts and pullover sweaters. Next to them were two outfits for her. A pair of jeans with a simple red top and a pair of leggings with a scooped red top. He'd insisted on getting her a pair of new casual shoes, also picking up two swimsuits, like he'd promised, and buying both of them a light jacket. She'd said they wouldn't need them in Las Vegas, almost letting California slip out, but he'd just grinned at her and said Las Vegas was cool in the winter and if he couldn't spend his money on them, he'd just waste it on the slots when they got there. She couldn't think of an argument for that, so there they were, with two jackets, their hangers hooked over the side of the cart.

Beckett maneuvered them to the grocery section, picking out bottled water, fruit, bags of chips and popcorn, cookies, beef jerky, and something called trail mix. *Road trip food*, he called it.

Kaci's eyes never left him and Cerise wanted to ask her what she was thinking, but she didn't, almost afraid of the answer.

When they finally reached the register, Cerise held her breath. The bill was $492.62. She squeezed her nails into the palm of her free hand at the amount, pressing her lips together to keep another protest pinned inside her. Almost all of the money they had stolen to finance their trip, and Beckett was spending it on them in one trip to the store. He didn't even look like it bothered him at all.

He grabbed up the bags and strode to the front of the store purposefully, glancing back at them a few times as they both walked slowly toward him, like in a dream.

He dropped the bags and fished out their coats, ripping off the tags and handing them over. "It's cold out."

Kaci's was a pastel purple that Cerise had thought wouldn't look right on her, but when she pushed her arms into it and zipped it up, then looked to Cerise for approval, Cerise could only nod and smile. It softened her red hair, her freckled cheeks, made her look even sweeter and more innocent. Younger.

Kaci smiled back at her, then looked to Beckett for just a moment, the smile still on her face.

Beckett grinned and flashed her a thumbs-up. "That coat looks finer on you than a frog's hair split three ways," he drawled.

Cerise giggled, then cut it off when Kaci's eyes went wider and her smile faltered for a moment. Kaci turned and buried her face into Cerise's side, but not before Cerise saw that her cheeks were flushed a bright red. Cerise wondered if Kaci hadn't discovered her first crush.

Me too, Lemon, me too.

The thought scared her so badly she squashed it violently. Life wasn't a game and men couldn't be trusted, no matter how much they bought you and how cute their grins were.

She'd have to work harder to remember that.

***

It only took them a few moments to get back to the hotel. Cerise felt doubly nervous as Beckett led them into an elevator. They'd seen elevators on TV, of course, but neither had ever been on one.

"Press number seven, li'l bit," Beckett told Kaci. She did, running her fingers over the plastic first, then pressing hard enough to light up the number, smiling when it worked. The slight jerk as the elevator began to rise bothered Cerise a little, but Kaci looked positively excited about it. She pulled on Cerise's hand and looked up into her face, smiling so widely that Cerise could see all her even white teeth.

The doors opened and Beckett stepped out, leaving Cerise to pull at Kaci, who obviously didn't want to leave the elevator. Cerise knelt. "Kaci, we can't stay in it," she whispered, leaning close. "Come on, we'll ride it again tomorrow."

Kaci set her face in a mulish expression Cerise had seen a hundred times before and pulled on Cerise until Beckett noticed and returned to them.

"She wants to ride it again?" Beckett asked her. Cerise nodded. "What a fun idea," he declared, getting back in the elevator. Cerise felt tension for a moment, but she relaxed and let herself be pulled back in.

Kaci pressed 14, which was the highest button. When they got there, she watched the doors open and close, then pressed 12, 11, and 10 before Cerise stopped her.

Beckett dropped the bags on the floor next to him, then waved a hand like it was no big deal. "There's two elevators, don't worry about it."

Kaci gave her a look that would have been triumphant if there hadn't been so much pain in it from years of deprivation, then pressed all the remaining buttons. Beckett leaned against the mirrors on the back wall and crossed his big arms over his chest and his right ankle over his left ankle, looking straight ahead with a contented smile on his face, like there was nothing better in the world to do than ride the elevator up and down, stopping at every floor.

On floor nine, when the doors slid open, a man stood there, a frown on his face. He wore a black uniform with a nametag on it and Cerise knew immediately he worked there. She pulled Kaci closer to her, knowing they were about to get in trouble. He stepped inside, looked at the floor lights lit up, all of them again, and frowned, then swung around to face them.

Cerise tensed. Beckett stepped between the man and them. "Sorry, bud," he drawled, his accent the thickest Cerise had heard it. "I ain't never been in no elevator before, I reckon I done gone a smidgen overboard."

The man looked up at Beckett, who stood a full foot taller than him, swallowed, then took a step back. "It's no problem, sir. We like our guests to be happy." Beckett bobbed his head, then leaned against the back wall again.

When the elevator doors slid open on the eighth floor, the man got out, taking quick half-steps, his shoulders bowed as he hurried away.

Cerise breathed a sigh of relief, not daring to look at Kaci, knowing she would probably see that little crush turn into hero worship if she did.

After they'd ridden up and down the elevator from bottom to top to bottom to top again, Kaci finally pressed number seven, then looked back at Beckett as the elevator lowered.

He quirked an eyebrow. "You sure?"

She didn't answer for a minute and Cerise held her breath. When Kaci nodded at Beckett, slowly, but purposefully, Cerise felt like crying. A weight rolled slowly off her chest, the one that had been placed there over the last decade, brick by brick. Cerise had never seen Kaci respond to anyone before. Not Myles or Sandra, not the cops who had picked them up when they'd run away twice, not anyone. Myles had written her off by the time she'd turned three or four, calling her *retarded*, and *too stupid to go to school*, even though Cerise had never gone to school either. Sandra had mostly ignored her.

Kaci squeezed Cerise's fingers, then turned around to face the front of the elevator, leaning bodily against Cerise, waiting for the doors to open.

Cerise felt her own face split into a wide smile, one that nothing could dampen.

Kaci was going to be ok. Cerise, with Beckett's help, would get her home to her parents.

After that, it didn't matter what happened.

CHAPTER 21

*B*eckett strode toward the room, pulling the door key out of his pocket, feeling almost delirious, and completely light, like he could fly. After Kaci had smiled at him, Cerise had lit up like a thousand-watt bulb, meeting eyes with him for just a moment. The first smile he'd seen from either of them that had been for him. Kaci's smile had been sweet and satisfying, like an entire cake baked just for him. Cerise's had been all the icing in all the world, piled on top. And Rhen knew how much he liked the sweet stuff.

Easy there, wolf, he cautioned himself. You got two smiles. That means almost nothing. You've still got to convince them to trust you, to let you in on their secrets, to let you *help* them. Buying a few jackets and shirts was nothing. He wanted to set them up for life, to pull them within his sphere of influence, making sure nothing could ever harm either of them again.

He put the key card in the lock on the door, then thought better of it and moved out of the way, waving Kaci close. He showed her how to operate it, then handed the card to her. Her face lit up immediately and he stepped back to let her mess with it. Within seconds, she had it open, but pulled it closed to do it again, and again.

Beckett leaned against the wall and watched Cerise as she watched Kaci, taking the time to really examine her features. Strawberry blonde hair, mussed from the wind, curling at the ends in a way he hadn't noticed before. Maybe it had gotten wet from the snowflakes as they'd walked back. Gorgeous, perfectly pink lips that made him think of kissing her, smooth skin, a long, slim neck. Her body was hidden in the scrubs she wore, but he could see enough of it to know she had curves in all the right places. His own body responded immediately at his thoughts and he brought the bags in front of him. *Nice job, perv,* he lambasted himself. Way to think about a woman who wants nothing from but your help and friendship. Unless…

He pushed all thoughts away about her being his mate. Even if she was, that meant nothing for now. First gain her trust, then learn her story, then help her out of whatever jam she was in, *then* figure out who she is to you.

Beckett nodded to himself. Good fucking plan. One he would stick to, no matter what.

***

When Kaci finally let them enter, Cerise couldn't stifle her gasp. The room was open, immaculate, with a TV the size of the ones they'd seen in the houses they'd broken into facing the bed. She peeked first inside the bathroom, then past another door that was standing open. It had a second bed.

"Do you two want this room, or that one?" Beckett asked from behind her.

Kaci had already jumped on the one in the room they were in, snuggling into the luxurious pillows, wrapping the blanket around her.

Cerise gave Beckett a shy smile, knowing she'd never be able to repay him for what he was doing for them. "This one."

"It's yours," he said, pushing into the other one to unpack the bags.

Cerise turned to Kaci. "Kaci, take your shoes off on the bed."

Kaci sat up and pulled her feet under her body, holding onto the toes of the new purple shoes with both hands, shaking her head, a nervous expression on her face. Cerise sat next to her. "Lemon, no one is going to take those shoes from you, but you can't wear them on the bed."

Beckett's voice carried from the other room. "Those shoes are brand new. They won't get anything dirty. I say let her keep them on if she wants to."

Kaci shot the open door a look of such relief that Cerise had to shake her head.

"Ok," she conceded. "Beckett's paying, so if he says it's ok…"

Kaci beamed at her, then got up on her knees to whisper in her ear. "Do you think we can watch TV?"

"Um." She turned toward the room Beckett was in. "Can we watch TV?"

Beckett filled the doorframe. "You don't want to go swimming in the pool?"

Cerise looked at Kaci questioningly.

Kaci shook her head, her eyes on the big TV.

Cerise turned back to Beckett, wondering if he'd be upset. He'd bought them both swimsuits. He shrugged. "Go ahead. Maybe tomorrow night we'll hit a pool."

Cerise hid the doubtful expression on her face. By tomorrow they could be in Las Vegas if they drove all day. She would have to decide what to do then. Tell Beckett the truth and ask him (or *push* him) to take them to California? Or strike out without him. Maybe find another board like at the train station, with people offering rides. She knew now that their best chance was with Beckett, but there were so many reasons they shouldn't stay with him, that he shouldn't know where Kaci ended up.

Beckett strode to the TV, fished underneath it, and came out with the remote. He brought it to Kaci and showed her how to use it, then handed it to her.

How did he know that she'd never used a remote before? Was he just guessing? Again, she had that nagging feeling that he knew their story. It felt bad to her, like her own secrets did.

She stood and strode to the far side of the room, pushing aside the curtains, gasping again quietly when she saw the window and the balcony. She'd never been so high up. Kaci would love it. She turned to call her over, but Kaci's eyes were already bright, focused intently on the TV, changing channels so quickly Cerise couldn't follow them. She opened her mouth to tell Kaci not to do that, then closed it. Why shouldn't Kaci do that? She'd never had TV before, only one movie at a time from a DVD on a screen an eighth the size of this one. Let her do what she wanted. Like Beckett had with the elevator. They weren't still riding it, were they? Kaci needed to explore in her own way.

Beckett found a phone next to the bed Kaci was sitting on and picked up the handset. "Who wants room service?"

They were going to eat again?

Kaci reached out her hand slowly and touched Beckett's wrist. When he looked at her, she pointed to herself. Beckett grinned down at Kaci and Cerise saw genuine pleasure on his face at Kaci's response. It made her heart swim and her vision double.

"Li'l bit wants room service, anybody else?"

***

Cerise lifted her head from the pillow and peeked at the clock. 3:13 a.m. She hadn't been sleeping, only going over every instance that she could remember in her life of *pushing* someone, looking at her experiences with new eyes, trying to glean something useful about her mysterious power. She looked at Kaci. Finally asleep, the remote control clutched in her hand, her shoes still on. Cerise got up, muted the TV so she could see by its light, but not hear it, and unlaced her shoes.

Beckett appeared at the still open doorway, filling it completely. "She finally fell asleep?" His voice was soft, but still, Cerise jumped. She'd thought he had gone to sleep hours ago.

"I didn't mean to startle you," he said. "And don't worry, she didn't keep me awake. I'm restless for some reason." He looked toward the door of the room, as if double checking that all the locks were engaged, even though he'd already done that twice.

Cerise couldn't think of one word to say to that. Her heart banged loudly in her chest, and she wondered if he could hear it across the room. She continued to work on Kaci's shoes, pulling them off and placing them next to the bed, so they'd be the first thing she saw in the morning.

"Good night," Beckett said.

She took a deep breath. Stood straight. Faced him. "Good night, Beckett. And… I wanted to say…" How to say thank you to a man who had done so much for them? Especially when she didn't know how much of it was from his own free will, and how much she'd somehow controlled.

"Anytime," he said, then tapped the underside of the brim of his cap with two fingers, and gave her a salute. He pulled the door closed as he left the room.

Cerise walked to it, put her fingers on the lock that would ensure he couldn't get into their room while they slept, pushing it to the right… but without enough force to actually engage it.

She stood there thinking for a long time, then dropped her fingers, leaving the door unlocked.

CHAPTER 22

Cerise woke only a few hours later to the bed she shared with Kaci bouncing as Kaci thrashed about. She felt groggy, realizing in a few moments that she'd slept more deeply than usual, possibly from exhaustion, possibly from sleeping on a bed for the first time in a decade. When Myles and Sandra had fled New Mexico and brought her and Kaci to Illinois, they hadn't bothered to get the girls beds to sleep on. Too busy drinking and drugging and screaming at each other.

Startled, she pushed up onto her knees and looked around. The clock said 6:45. Kaci, still asleep, was whimpering and rolling, her lips pressed together so hard they were thin and white. Cerise had waited for the trauma of the shooting to surface, and here it was.

Cerise lay a hand on her arm. "Shhhh," she said soothingly. "It's a dream, Kaci, just a dream." Kaci didn't quiet. Cerise lay down next to her and pulled Kaci into her arms, running her fingers up her arm. "Shhh, Lemon, you're safe. I'm here." This was a role Cerise had experience with; Kaci had nightmares often.

Kaci didn't quiet, her whimpers becoming louder, her lips thinner. Cerise spoke directly in her ear. "Stop, Kaci, dream about other things, feel better when you wake up. Forget Myles. You had to do what you did. Be strong, sweetheart." Power rippled out of her in tiny doses, straight for Kaci, who quieted immediately. Cerise lifted her head from the pillow and stared into the darkness, eyes wide and horrified, not noticing the streams of diffused light from around the drapes, only feeling the inward tug of her realization.

She had *pushed* Kaci. Without even realizing it, she had *pushed* her. She recognized the feeling of the flex, although at this low of a power level, it had felt like nothing more than a tightening of her mental capacity, like if her brain was a muscle and she had sent an impulse to it only strong enough to make it twitch once, then relax again.

How many times had she done that before? Every time? Kaci had been having nightmares her whole life! She tried to remember what she had said to Kaci during other nightmares and couldn't, tried to remember specific instances, but there was nothing. Could she possibly have hurt Kaci? Affected her in ways she never intended?

She frowned in the dark and let her head drop to the pillow, sleep no longer a possibility, trying to consider every angle of what she had done. If only she knew why and how she had the power, the ability to influence someone's actions! Did anyone else have it? If only she could talk to someone, be positive she was leaving no lasting damage.

Cici's face loomed in her imagination, limp, expressionless, blood leaking out her ears.

Cerise's shoulder muscles tightened in fear and shame. Was she dangerous to people around her?

She ran her fingers through Kaci's red hair, thinking about how small Kaci was for her age, how stunted emotionally, refusing to talk to people. They'd never eaten well, and Kaci had never been treated with anything but violence and disdain by their 'parents'. She'd rarely had an opportunity to be around anyone but Myles and Sandra and Cerise, so her shyness and smallness weren't too surprising.

But what if Cerise had something to do with it, too? What if her *pushes* had changed something in Kaci's brain? Was Cerise just as at fault as Myles and Sandra had been?

She listened for that voice again, the one that had told her not to push Beckett again, but it was silent. She left her mind open, her thoughts whirling. Finally the opposite argument came to her. What if she could help Kaci? What if she could do more than stop Kaci's nightmares? What if she could make her forget about everything that caused the nightmares in the first place? Or at least take away the pain of them? What if she could... *encourage* Kaci to be more emotionally healthy? She stared at the back of Kaci's head. She could try it. Push Kaci right now. Put her hand on her and whisper, *Talk to Beckett tomorrow like you talk to me, like he was your friend.*

She discarded the idea immediately. It didn't feel right to *push* someone she loved, even if it was done with love. Maybe a *shhh, sleep,* was ok, but trying to change Kaci's nature? No way.

Besides, she wanted Kaci and Beckett's relationship to be completely authentic.

As she tried to think about why she would want such a thing, her eyes slipped closed and she fell back asleep.

***

Beckett gasped and sat straight up in the strange bed, tangled in the white sheets, a cry held behind his lips. He'd had the nightmare again, the one that had actually happened. The one where his older brother, Cole, had pushed him out the back door and told him to run, that Cole and their dad would hold the intruders off, give Beckett time to get away. Cole had known he would die that night, Beckett had seen it in his face, and still he'd protected Beckett.

Beckett ran a hand over his face and stared at the ceiling. That made three times this week he'd had the nightmare. After the incident had happened, he'd had the nightmare often, then it had slowed down, coming once a month, once a year, not coming at all for many years, but now it dampened his palms and his forehead in his sleep again. He'd told Wade and Wade had said that whoever had been behind the events of that night was thinking about targeting him again in some way, Wade could feel it, too. That had been before Jaggar's revelation about Grey.

Beckett had responded by openly flaunting his location at all times and leaving his doors and windows wide open at night, until winter came, but still not locking them even then. Let the bastards come. He was no child anymore. He'd come out on top this time, get his revenge.

He stood up and prowled to the door between the two rooms, wanting to open it to make sure Kaci and Cerise were all right, but not quite daring to, knowing such a move could ruin the fragile trust he felt both of them trying to give him, against all their instincts.

He sat on the edge of the bed, clad only in the scrub pants that weren't his, staring at the door, running over everything that had happened in the past two days. The recall still was disjointed in places, not connecting like his memories normally did, especially around the times when he'd taken Cerise out of the hospital and then not called Wade to tell him.

Beckett looked over his shoulder at the clock on the nightstand. 9:10. He was officially going on his second day of not showing up for work. He should call in, at least tell them he was ok. He picked up the hotel phone, held it in his hand for a second, then hung it up, retrieving his cell phone from his pocket, instead. He didn't want anyone to be able to trace where he was. If he was in trouble for helping Cerise get out of the hospital, he didn't need anyone coming to get them, not until he'd gotten her where she needed to be.

He dialed Wade's personal phone number by heart.

"Beckett, where the hell are you?"

Beckett looked at the ceiling. "Nebraska."

Wade's voice was carefully still, betraying nothing of how he felt about Beckett's actions. "She's your one true mate, isn't she?"

Beckett dropped back onto the bed, phone pressed to his ear, glad Wade knew what he had done. Because he would not have been able to explain it without sounding like an idiot. "She might be," he said, having no idea if he really thought so or not. He pictured her face, the bowed lips, soft cheekbones, wide-eyed innocent stare, the way she chewed on her lip when she was nervous. Her determination and grit and self-lessness. She was no party girl, but he could give his heart to her, easily. He wanted her to be his mate more than anything in the world, except maybe getting her successfully across the country, helping her with her plans she was so desperate to fulfill.

Wade began to speak but a knock on the connecting door had Beckett jumping to his feet and hanging up the phone. "Come in."

Cerise pushed the door open, grasping the door jamb, most of her body hidden as she looked at him shyly. "We're awake."

Mine! Every cell in Beckett's body screamed for him to go to her, to gather her in his arms, to plant kisses across her face and collarbone, to swear to her that he would protect her with his life and do anything she needed. He swallowed and tried to get himself under control, not sure where the sudden intensity of the feeling had come from, and knowing if he did any of those things, she would bolt like a rabbit scared from its hiding place by a hungry fox, and she would take Kaci with her.

He grinned, his automatic grin that had charmed hundreds of women in his life. But now only one woman mattered. And he had no idea what she thought of him, if she was attracted to him or felt some inkling of what he was feeling for her. "Breakfast?" he asked.

She looked over her shoulder. "Maybe not just yet. Kaci's tummy is upset again."

Worry coursed through Beckett, a feeling he was unfamiliar with, one he'd taken great pains to avoid in his life. "Is she ok?"

"I think so. We'll be ready to go in ten minutes."

"Let me grab a shower and we'll go."

***

Beckett fiddled with the radio when the news came on,

switching from his customary country station to a today's hits station. The melodic beat from Ed Sheeran's *Shape of You* filled the cab and he turned it up, glancing at Kaci. She perked up immediately and swayed in her seat, her pixie-ish freckled face brightening. They'd had to stop at the bathroom only once, but he could tell by the hand she'd kept pressed to her middle that all the food she'd eaten the day before was not agreeing with her. Cerise too, maybe, as she hadn't asked to eat yet, and they'd been on the road for almost four hours. Beckett's stomach wasn't complaining too loudly. Yet.

Cerise pressed her hands to the dash to look out the window. "Colorado," she breathed, reading the signs. The snow had stopped, the roads were plowed, and they were making great time.

"We made it," Beckett said. "Next state is Utah, then Las Vegas, baby!"

Cerise gave him a funny look at his exuberance and he laughed to himself. She hadn't heard the expression, and now he seemed like a fool.

She turned to Kaci. "You want to eat yet?"

Kaci only stared, then shook her head slowly.

Beckett spoke up. "Sorry, li'l bit. I should have warned you that McDonalds could have that effect on you if you aren't used to it."

Kaci nodded her head. "Totally worth it," she said, and Cerise's mouth dropped open in a perfect O, as the feeling of sweet victory made Beckett sit up taller, grinning like a fool. *She'd spoken to him.*

Determined to act like it was no big deal, he chuckled. "Spoken like a girl after my own heart. Love me some greasy hash browns and gallons of soda."

Kaci grinned at him and he grinned back, locking eyes

with her for just a second, savoring Cerise's stunned expression from next to her.

Kaci bent over. "Bathroom," she said.

Beckett eased into the right lane. He'd been watching the exits the entire morning, making sure he knew exactly which ones had bathrooms. "Hang in there," he drawled. "I'll get you to one fast as a duck on a June bug."

He'd always been one to press home his advantages. Kaci had talked to him, now he just needed to get her to laugh.

CHAPTER 23

Beckett sped into the rest stop, ignoring the spattering of cars already there and the dark SUV following him in, speeding directly to the front of the squat brick building and stopping. He jumped out to run around and reach the passenger door, but Cerise already had it open and was lowering Kaci to the ground. They hurried into the restroom. Beckett closed their door behind them and climbed back behind the wheel.

He parked his truck and got out, pausing a second as he scented *foxen* on the air. He frowned. *Foxen*? *Bearen*? Now he wasn't sure. The strange scent stirred a memory inside him. Suddenly alert, he scanned all the people hurrying to and from their cars in the early afternoon cold, but saw no one who looked suspicious.

He left his truck, then made his way to stand by the entrance to the women's bathroom, some sort of sick anticipation twisting his guts. He'd felt something was off since the night before, and now the feeling grew legs, sprinting around inside him, demanding his attention.

He scanned the parking lot and saw nothing out of the ordinary.

Cerise said something sharply in the bathroom and Beckett twisted toward the sound. As he did, a chunk exploded off the concrete wall behind him with a thick thumping sound, bits of rock flying everywhere, the sound they made when they hit the wall almost musical.

Beckett was in motion before the first bit of falling rock bounced off the ground, launching into a twisting roll that carried him behind the rock wall that hid the open restroom door from the parking lot.

His guns were in his truck. Someone had just shot at him with a rifle with a sound suppressor attached. The shot had been at head level, meaning they weren't messing around. Beckett was in deep shit because whoever it was wanted him dead. By rights, he should be already. He had only one option, and it wasn't waiting around for the cops to show up.

"Cerise!" he shouted, his every sense on high alert. "Stay inside. Don't come out till I come get you! Someone is shooting out here!"

A woman screamed inside the bathroom, but it wasn't Cerise or Kaci. Beckett had to trust that they would do as he'd told them to.

He sprinted out of the protective area, heading for the parking lot, his elbows tucked in, his torso lowered in a bit of a crouch, putting every fiber of muscle he had into moving quickly, hopefully faster than the muzzle of the gun he ran from. No luck there, unless the shooter wasn't a professional.

He'd heard the flat crack of the rifle, way quieter than the boom of a non-suppressed rifle, but not imperceptible, and thought he could pinpoint where it had come from. He was completely exposed moving across the parking lot, using cars for cover when he could. He'd parked in the center row and just reached the driver's side door when he heard the quiet crack of another shot and the twang of it punching through metal somewhere. Beckett ripped his door open, the second shot telling him exactly where the shooter was. Now to go on the offensive.

He fished under the seat, pulling out his concealed carry tote, jamming his keys into the lock. He'd put his duty weapon in there before entering the hospital to find Cerise two nights before. He fished it out, flicked off the safety, then pulled out his secondary, too. No time or need for ammo beyond one extra magazine for each. If he didn't do this right the first time, he'd be dead and completely unable to reload anyway.

He dropped his keys to the floor of his truck and began moving on instinct to the rear of it, gearing up for another all-out sprint. He broke cover and moved fast, bringing his weapons up and firing indiscriminately at the copse of evergreens where he knew the shooter was, the boom of the guns echoing back and forth from the forest on both sides of the rest stop parking lot. From behind him, people shouted and cars slammed to a stop or sped out the exit. He ignored them all, covering ground like it was hot lava about to burn holes in his shoes.

Forty more feet, thirty, then fifteen before he left the parking lot and entered the trees. His eyes scanned behind every thick trunk as he ran and shot, searching out the shooter. If he'd been able to shift, he could have covered the ground in half the time, and flown like an arrow to a bull's-eye directly to the bastard, but the humans everywhere guaranteed that wasn't possible, even if he were hit by a bullet.

As if he'd conjured it, a sharp tug pulled at his upper right arm, dropping it to his side, flopping and useless, his gun tumbling to the ground. He triangulated again, jogged to his left, and squeezed off every round from his other gun in quick succession directly around the tree where he now knew the shooter to be.

The accounting part of his brain told him he was out of bullets, but his fingers didn't get the message. Click. Click. He dry-fired twice, but it didn't matter. He was there, his breath tearing in and out of his lungs, his leg muscles on fire from the all-out sprint. Only twenty feet farther, past the trees, cars whizzed by on the interstate, the drivers oblivious to the life and death struggle about to start.

He dropped his gun and hooked an arm around the neck of the hulking male on the other side of the tree, squeezing hard, trying to snap the asshat's head off his neck. No luck. The guy was as big as he was, bigger maybe, and ready to fight. He smelled like *foxen*, but in a flat, dead way that confused Beckett. He didn't dwell on it, instead using his body's momentum to pull the male backwards off his feet, pile-driving his head into the next massive tree trunk. Even if the male was human, Beckett could hurt him. His human protection drive was inactivated for humans who had tried to hurt *shiften*, or other humans.

Beckett tried to get his other arm up, to twist the male's chin and head, break his neck, but the arm wouldn't work. The male growled at him, trying to gain his footing. Beckett snarled back, knowing he couldn't allow that. This guy was big, and he might have friends around. He called an image of Cerise and Kaci up in his mind, not knowing if the guy was after him or them, but if he was after them, he was *dead*, even if Beckett lost use of both arms.

The trick worked. *Mine!* screamed through his brain, followed swiftly by *protect!* His body surged and his fangs grew in his mouth. All the better to tear out a throat. His right arm worked enough, on sheer willpower alone. He grunted and slammed the male into the tree again, ignoring hands that scrabbled at his arms, then took the male to the ground, aiming his head at a large rock that jutted up from the forest floor.

Crunch. Beckett let the unconscious male slip out of his grasp. From behind him he heard a female scream. He shot a look over his shoulder to the bathrooms. Not a person in sight. They'd all hit the deck, or jumped into their cars, or were hiding inside the building.

Another hulking male who could have been a brother to the one he'd just incapacitated ran out of the women's restroom, Kaci tucked under one arm kicking and screaming, Cerise lying limply over his other shoulder. Knocked out? Beckett's strength surged again and his flat rage turned murderous. That male was about to die.

He sprinted back the way he had come, dismayed to see the male stop at a dark SUV idling at the curb, throw Kaci in an open door, then shift Cerise's weight so he could do the same to her.

Beckett would never make it to them before he drove off with Cerise and Kaci.

If he lost them, he would not survive.

***

Cerise woke in a blur, her head pounding at her temple, unsure who or where she was for a moment. Then it came back to her. Beckett shouting that there was a shooter, telling them to stay in the bathroom. Gunshots. People screaming. Kaci had trembled and whimpered in fear and Cerise had held her as they'd backed into a corner in the smelly bathroom. Footsteps. Someone entering quickly. She prayed it was Beckett even as she knew it wasn't. A man with close-cropped hair and an unkind face, his body massive, reminiscent of Schwarzenegger in every movie she'd ever seen him star in. The guy had seen them and moved straight for them, his blocky face set in a permanent frown. She'd tucked Kaci behind her, put her hands up, palms facing forward, trying to remember how she'd *pushed* Cici, praying the power wouldn't fail her.

But he'd never even tried to grab her, instead swinging at her with his fist, catching her in the left temple. He'd pulled the swing, so as not to kill her, but she was still knocked unconscious.

Cerise cracked her eyes open and saw a terrified Kaci looming over her, cradling her head and rubbing her hair, her lips moving but no sound coming out. They were in the back seat of a large vehicle. Cerise pushed herself up slightly, trying to orient herself, her head pounding worse. How long had she been out?

Not long. They were still in the parking lot. Behind her, she saw Beckett running at a flat sprint, trying to catch them. Tires squealed and the car they were in jumped forward. Cerise forced herself into a sitting position, ignoring Kaci, her eyes only on their abductor who was driving the vehicle, his eyes shooting between the road ahead of him and his rearview mirror. She put her hand on the man's shoulder and *pushed* with everything she had, brain flexing like she was bench pressing twice her body weight. *"Stop the car. Now."*

He tried to twist in his seat to see her, but blood spurted from his nose, and vessels burst in his right eye, making it go red and his face go slack. The car careened forward even faster, the wheel straightening as his hands fell away from it and they headed right for the forest. "Wake up!" Cerise shouted, pushing again, her mind fatiguing noticeably. Kaci screamed in her ear and clutched at her. The man jerked upright in his seat, then slammed on the brakes. The vehicle jumped the curb, but slowed and stopped. Cerise and Kaci were both pitched forward.

The driver's side door was wrenched open and Beckett was there, dragging the big guy out of the car, then slamming him into the door and the concrete again and again. "Get out! Run to my truck!" he yelled and Cerise scrambled to do it.

"Kaci, come on, we gotta go." Kaci followed and they pushed out the side door, then ran to Beckett's truck hand in hand.

When they got there, Cerise lifted Kaci, then snatched the keys off the floor, and climbed in herself, throwing a look at Beckett over her shoulder. He was backing away from the other man, who lay crumpled on the concrete. Beckett looked around at the forest as if scared more attackers were coming, then began to run for them.

Cerise pushed over to the middle seat, dimly aware of Kaci crumpled next to the far door, crying. She stuck the key in the ignition, as she had carefully watched Beckett do since he'd promised to teach her to drive, then twisted it. The truck lurched forward, the engine grinding, then dying. She grimaced and took her hand off the key.

Beckett flung himself into the truck, pulling his door closed, jammed the stick between them to the front, the truck moving smoothly for him. He leaned forward as he drove, his eyes scanning the trees, his hand seeking the radio knob and viciously twisting it off. "There's at least one more of them," he said. "Keep your heads down until we're out of here." Cerise pulled Kaci to her, and they both ducked in the long seat. Beckett moved the stick again, and again, and the engine revved up, spurting them out of the parking lot and back onto the highway.

CHAPTER 24

They drove in complete silence for several minutes, Cerise trying to calm Kaci and herself, until Beckett took out his phone.

"What are you doing?" Cerise snapped, her eyes locked on the phone.

"Calling the police."

Cerise had no choice. She put her arm out and touched Beckett on the wrist. "No police, please," she said, willing to beg, but *pushing* instead. She didn't know what had just happened, but she did know what *would* happen if Beckett called the police.

Instead of his quick and easy agreement, this time he swung his head toward her, his eyebrows drawn. The *push* had been no different than any other she'd tried before, although the flex did feel slow, fatigued. She had a moment of panic, until he put the phone down on his leg and focused on driving again.

His right hand wasn't working well, his fingers unable to curl. She followed that arm up to his shoulder, swearing when she saw all the blood. "You're shot."

Kaci had quieted, but whimpered and peeked around Cerise to see.

Beckett shook his head. "It's not bad. I'll get checked out when we take you to the hospital."

"For what?" Cerise's galloping heart had started to calm, but now it raged inside her chest again.

"You were knocked out. Did he hit you?"

Cerise raised a hand to her temple. "Yeah, but I'm fine."

"You're going to the doctor."

Cerise stared at him, then hardened her voice, ready to *push* him again. "I'm not."

He looked at her and scowled, an expression she'd never seen on his face before. "Don't be stubborn about your health. Look, I know you're on the run, but we can make up a story."

Cerise froze. It was the first time either of them had mentioned it. What had she been hoping? That he'd thought it was some sort of a game that she'd been handcuffed and wearing prison-issue clothing? That he hadn't realized she was an actual prisoner?

Yeah, that's exactly what she had hoped. What must he think of her? Her mind twisted. He thought she was a criminal. And he was right.

He leaned back and lifted his shirt to pull two guns out of his pants. She bit on the inside of her lip and sucked in a breath. He pushed one under the seat, then put the other one down between his legs, fishing a magazine out of his pocket, one-handed.

"Do you know how to shoot a gun?" he asked, his voice deadly serious.

Cerise stared at the gun, unable to comprehend why he would ask that. "No."

"I do," Kaci said, her voice tiny, her sobs tapering off into occasional sniffles.

"I know you do, li'l bit." He seemed to dismiss it. "Any idea why we were attacked back there? Did you recognize those men."

"No," she said again, her voice as small as Kaci's. What did he mean, he knew Kaci did?

"Are you sure?" he asked, his voice hard, his eyes checking the rearview mirror. "I need you to tell me the truth. I can't protect you if I don't know what's going on."

"Beckett, I swear, I've never seen either one of them before, and I can't think of any reason why anyone would want to kidnap me or Kaci." She stopped for a second. "Unless they were police."

Beckett grunted. "They weren't police." He looked sideways at her, then back at the road, then back in the rearview. "Tell me about yourself. About your family. Is anyone mixed up with anything… illegal? Anything that would have people chasing you?"

She looked down at Kaci, then out the window, her mind racing. A friend of Cici's? Improbable. She couldn't think of one reason, but this was a complication she did not need! They had enough problems. "Our, ah, my dad used to make and sell moonshine. We had some guys like that come around the trailer for a while. But that was back before I got sick. And they never had nice cars like that. They always drove old, junky cars. Besides, we didn't take any moonshine from the trailer when we left." She gave Kaci a warning shake of her head. *Let me talk. Don't you say a word.*

"How about money, or drugs?"

Stark fear and guilt pulled at her, making her drop her gaze. She'd stolen money from dozens of farmhouses in their county. But as far as she knew none of them had ever discovered it was her, and none would follow and try to kidnap her, would they? The most she'd taken from one house was $42.

She looked up, catching Beckett watching her. She shook her head, drowning in fear. "No money. No drugs."

***

Beckett kept watch on the road in front of them and behind them, and Cerise, all at the same time. She was lying to him, he knew it. He didn't have to have Troy's nose to figure out what the dark boil of her scent meant.

"Cerise, I want to help you. But those men were out for *blood*. You have to tell me the truth."

She dropped her gaze again and shook her head, frustrating him to the point where he ground his teeth to keep his mouth shut.

Kaci plucked on her sleeve, her sniffles turning into scared sobs again. "Are they gonna kill us?"

Beckett sighed. He was trying to scare Cerise into telling the truth, not scar Kaci for life. "No way, li'l bit, not when I'm around. I'll never let anyone hurt you." He picked up his phone and spoke into it, pulling up the YouTube app, with a search for Taylor Swift already on the screen, then handed it to Kaci. "Open that glove compartment there and fish out the ear buds, that's right, now put them in this hole right here. Good. Now press that big red arrow and put those parts in your ears."

Kaci did as he'd asked, and a smile lit her face, her sniffles quieting again.

Now, back to Cerise. He couldn't be soft with her anymore, they couldn't afford it. Something told him those men were there for him, not her, but if that was the case, why would they have tried to drive off with her and Kaci? "Tell me everything, start with how exactly you ended up in jail, and end with why we are traveling across the country. The truth."

Cerise put her hand on his wrist, her face pinched and drawn. Her hot fingers grazed his skin, shooting desire for her all the way down to his core. "Don't ask any more questions, please. Don't make me answer those. Just help us. Like you said, we need a friend and you're all we've got."

Inside his brain, a knot of tension formed, compelling Beckett to do exactly as she asked. It grew and overlapped, and he felt his questions slip away, his memories of why the questions were important muting themselves, almost like he was drunk. He frowned and fought it. He'd felt the exact same thing a minute ago when she'd touched him. It had made him do exactly as she asked. The other times she'd touched him and told him to do something circled into his brain, like a Ferris wheel of memories. She'd touched him and told him to get her out of the handcuffs. Then touched him and asked him not to call his boss. She'd touched him and told him to leave the interim home parking lot and park down the road and not follow her.

Bits and pieces of memories fell into place, where they should have been, instead of where they been placed and cemented over by whatever she was doing to him.

Her hand was still on his wrist. He stared at it, barely able to breathe as the realizations came to him and he twisted his consciousness out of her control. The effort to do it was monumental.

She spoke, utter shame flashing in her eyes. "Forget you asked me anything."

Beckett's eyes flew wide and he jerked forward in the seat. She'd told him to forget something before. The first time she'd been in his house, six weeks ago. He remembered it clearly now.

He'd been dreaming. The nightmare again. But it cut off mid-sequence, his brother's face fading in the dream landscape of his mind, and an erotic drawing slipped through him instead. He woke by degrees, his cock throbbing in a way he'd never felt before or since, and the scent of his mate filling his nose. Mine! shot through his brain, as he opened his eyes and saw the most beautiful female he'd ever set eyes on. The morning sun from the window cradled her, lighting her hair like a halo, her body like an angel.

"You here to kill me, darlin'?" he drawled, the remnants of the nightmare still on him. He could almost bare his throat to an assassin who looked and smelled like she did. If she would just let him touch her first, he might agree to anything.

"Oh no, no," she said in a sweet velvet voice, curling her hand around his fingers that had ahold of her arm, her face awash in fear. "Go back to sleep. Forget about me, I was never here."

And he had done exactly as she'd ordered.

Beckett's cock throbbed mindlessly to life at the sudden realization and her nearness, and something more.

She was his one true mate, and she was just as powerful as the others.

But a thousand times more lost.

CHAPTER 25

*Y*ou stupid overgrown weasel," Grey snorted, grabbing Zane by the scruff of the neck and throwing him bodily into the back of the mom-van on top of his brother. He got behind the wheel and sped off, ahead of the noise of approaching sirens. He needed to find a deserted pull-off, somewhere that Zane and Bane could shift to heal their battered heads. Both males were groaning, so he had hopes they'd make it out alive. "That redneck kicked your asses. I should fire the both of you."

Grey grinned instead, caressing the bundle in his pocket. Cerise's pendant. He should have known better than to send only two males after Beckett.

He would consider this a practice round. He smiled and both his lips split open. Oops. He craned forward to see his reflection in the rearview mirror. Blood trickled down his face, catching in his dark goatee. He swiped a hand over his head, his shoulder length dark hair coming out in clumps. Gonna be bald soon.

The pendant was doing that to him, like a necklace of kryptonite would harm Superman, but still he couldn't let it go. Since he'd touched it in the field near Beckett's house, it was all he could think about. It was destroying his body, but strengthening his mind. Colors were more vivid, his thoughts made more sense and encompassed concepts he'd never thought of before, and his entire day seemed more alive and interesting. If the pendant were a drug, he'd be hopelessly addicted.

He swung right onto an exit that his bigger, more competent brain told him would be perfect, then immediately right, and right again, following the road to an empty parking lot in front of some sort of an abandoned factory. He drove behind the dilapidated, steel-colored building, finding a perfect spot to park in, an old loading dock area that covered them on three sides. He looked out the back window, noting nothing but open land to the back of them. No humans could see them.

"Ok, Smokey and Dopey, do your thing," he said, pressing the button that would pop the back door. The mom-van had everything.

Zane tumbled out first, landing on the ground with a grunt, then shifting, his monstrous bear letting out a bellow of frustration that made his brother jump. They were half-human, half-*bearen*, although Grey bet they had a bit more *bearen* somewhere down their line. Three-quarters, maybe. They smelled like it.

Both were essentially ostracized from the *bearen* community for not wanting to work as firefighters. *Bearen* were like that. Big, judgmental bastards. All the better for Grey to convince them to work for him. The three of them had a lot of history, and they were loyal, so even though they'd fucked up royally, he wouldn't be firing them.

He watched Bane gingerly hoist himself out the back of the van, then growl as his body expanded to three times its size, fur sprouting, muzzle lengthening, claws sprouting.

He honestly was surprised Beckett had been able to best the two of them. Even in human form, *bearen* were dense, thick, stronger than *wolven*, carrying the mass of their animal in their human muscles. The only explanation was that Beckett had been protecting his mate, or that Cerise had helped him.

He let Zane and Bane snuffle around the loading dock area, his mind in overdrive, a plan forming already. He knew exactly where they were headed. Could get in front of them, meet them there. And then what?

He needed to know what kind of a power Cerise had. Would the pendant tell him? It pulsed in his pocket, a red-black energetic negative. Never. Not on purpose.

Grey watched the bears for a long time, his super-powered mind working, then got out of the van to corral them, grill them about what had happened. There was a good chance that he would be able to control Cerise, no matter what her power was. All he needed to do was get his hands on the little girl. He couldn't hurt her, but Cerise didn't know that.

Grey frowned. Maybe he would need to fly out a few of the humans he sometimes worked with. They could hurt the little girl. And Beckett wouldn't be able to shift with them around, which would be an added bonus. He and Zane and Bane wouldn't be able to, either, but they would have-

Grey stopped mid-stride. He knew Kaci's pedigree. A *bigger* plan bloomed in his mind. If he could pull it off, he could do whatever he wanted to Kaci, with no unfair, internal yoke stopping him. Surely Rhen would approve, if she knew he did it for her.

His plan could work if he were bold and lucky and pulled it off just right. It was risky, but so was opening your eyes in the morning, if you lived right.

Yes. Off to California they would all go.

To invite a demon over for tea and cookies.

CHAPTER 26

Cerise pressed against Kaci, who was pressed against the door of Beckett's truck, her eyes glued to the video playing on the phone Beckett had given her. They were off the highway. Beckett had taken the first possible exit, saying they would take a mix of back roads and Highway 285, in case whoever had attacked them at the rest stop was following them. He kept watching behind them, but so far seemed satisfied no one had kept pace with them.

Beckett dug around behind his seat, pulling out a water bottle he handed to Kaci, then one for her and him, then some bags of snacks. He handed the trail mix to Kaci and kept the beef jerky for himself. Cerise had shaken her head when he'd offered her anything. She was too keyed up to eat.

Something was wrong. *Pushing* him hadn't worked. She could tell, although she had no idea why he hadn't called the police anyway. For the first hour they'd driven after fleeing the rest area, he'd been tightly wound, staring out the windshield with his brows drawn tight over his eyes, his knuckles white on the steering wheel. Eventually, he'd calmed, but she had gone in the other direction, trying to figure out what exactly had happened back there. She was missing something vital, she knew it.

His shoulder had stopped oozing blood, although she didn't like the ragged, bloody, inflamed look of the skin there. Likewise, her head had stopped pounding so bad she could hardly think.

Kaci popped an earbud out of her ear and elbowed her. "Listen," she said, showing her a video, then trying to shove the earbud in her ear. Cerise did it herself. The music was good, light, fast-paced. She popped the earbud out and handed it back to Kaci.

Kaci flipped her finger across the screen to pull up a picture. "That's Jon Bellion," she said, her voice excited. "He's super young, and so talented. He's got *so many* songs." Her fingers flew over a tiny keyboard she had somehow made appear, faster than Cerise could read. A page appeared and Kaci tapped the screen, then read a few sentences about Jon Bellion out loud to Cerise. Cerise grabbed her elbow. "Kaci, you can read."

Kaci shrugged. "You taught me."

Cerise shook her head. "I *tried* to teach you, but you would never pay attention to me. You always whined and said it was too hard. I thought maybe you needed glasses or something." She could feel Beckett paying attention to them, gathering up every word like gold from a mine.

Kaci threw her a look. "It sank in. I got it. I just liked TV better and didn't want to practice. But when you were sick, I practiced then. I read to you sometimes. Over and over again, when I thought you were going to—" Her eyes watered and she looked away. Cerise knew she was going to say, *when you were going to die*. Cerise had thought she was going to die, too, but she hadn't.

The image of Kaci sitting by her bed, reading their only fiction book to her, again and again, floored her. Reading had come so hard to her, but apparently not to Kaci.

Trying to take Kaci's mind off that horrible time in their life, Cerise pointed at a picture on the small screen. A dark haired man with a mischievous smile. "Who's that?"

"That's him! Jon Bellion!" Kaci held the phone up and pushed it into Cerise's face.

"Oh, he's cute," Cerise said, pushing the phone back into Kaci's lap.

A snarling growl ripped through the cab of the truck and Cerise sucked in a breath, whipping her head toward Beckett. His face was twisted in some sort of anger or irritation. The growl had come from him. As she watched, he dropped his lip, covering his canine teeth that suddenly seemed too long, and forcibly smoothed out his expression.

Kaci glanced at him, dismissed him, then shoved the earbud back in her ear and went back to what she had been doing.

Cerise, however, could barely breathe. The cab of the truck had suddenly become too small, the air in it rich and heavy with the clean, evergreen and leather scent of Beckett. She sucked some of it in through her nose, savoring it, her body completely *aware* of him, less than a foot away from her. He was so big. So strong. So powerful and handsome. Her fingers itched to touch him. To graze his forearm, taste-touch the skin and brown hairs there. Her eyes locked in on his lips and she licked her own. She'd kissed him once. She remembered it well. She imagined kissing him again. Would he part his lips? Touch his tongue to hers? She shivered and her eyes slipped closed. She clenched her hands into fists and shoved them into her lap to keep them from straying toward him. What was going on? She'd never felt anything like this before. Her body throbbed like a bruise, one that felt good, one that needed a touch to soothe it.

She sensed Beckett shifting in the seat next to her and she opened her eyes, trying to ignore the incredibly delicious sensation she felt between her legs. A swollen feeling, like all her blood had rushed there. A first-time sensation for her.

Beckett shifted again, then dropped his hand to the zipper of his jeans and adjusted there before returning his hand to the steering wheel. He lifted his face slightly and took a deep breath in through his nose. Cerise's cheeks flamed and she was suddenly certain he could smell her! Smell whatever was happening to her.

He glanced at her and their eyes locked, electricity passing through them. A hot liquid filled her chest and everything blurred but his face and the sensations in her body. The truck no longer existed, nor the road outside. Only him.

He pulled his eyes back to the road, breaking the spell, but his right hand left the steering wheel, headed for her lap. Her eyes widened as she stared at it, not knowing what he was going to do. But he only took her left hand and twined his fingers in it, then rubbed his thumb lightly over her thumb. Cerise almost groaned at the sensation, unable to believe how right it felt, and how every lingering stroke shot through her body straight to her core.

Like a flash, she knew. She was turned on. Sexually excited. Something she'd never experienced before, but of course witnessed in several movies. She'd never understood the shuttered glances, the gasping and panting, the seeming inability of the man and woman to do anything but come together in plaintive kisses and desperate touches.

Now she did. She understood it all. Her breasts were heavy and achy, her nipples hardening like they were screaming for Beckett's touch. She imagined him palming her there, his touch hard and gentle and insistent. She bit her lower lip, wondering if a touch could be both hard and gentle at the same time.

Between her legs throbbed and she shifted, trying to ease it, instead almost groaning as her clothes rubbed against skin that had suddenly become too sensitive.

She curled her fingers around Beckett's, meeting his probing thumb with her own, wanting to stroke him back, even in this tiny way. There was nothing more available to them.

His eyes met hers again, sending another current of awareness through her. A grin curled his mouth and she bit her lip harder, trying to yank back the current of desire that whipped through her, caring about nothing but what it wanted. She couldn't smile, could only stare and try not to moan, alerting the innocent girl next to her that some new twist had entered the relationship between Beckett and Cerise.

Even the attack seemed unimportant at that moment, her mind and body unable to be worried and excited at the same time.

She stared out at the road ahead, not able to imagine how she could make it through the day like this.

***

Beckett untwined his finger's from Cerise's and

downshifted, glad his right arm was still obeying him. He bore right on a lonely exit that would lead them to a field that looked perfect for what he had in mind. He needed to stretch his legs, and he thought it was time for some answers.

He glanced at Cerise, who had stared out the window for hours after their *moment*, stiff and unyielding, her eyes wide, a look of nervous tension on her face. She hadn't been able to sustain it forever, though, and had relaxed fifty or sixty miles later, leaning against Kaci and falling asleep. She looked young, fresh, innocent with her eyes closed, her bowed lips parted slightly, the worry stripped from her by sleep.

He laughed to himself. He'd been worried his uncontrollable snarl when she'd pronounced an unknown male *cute* would scare her, make her look at him with fear in her eyes again. But her scent had said she'd *liked* it. More than liked it. The sweet licorice smell of her had flared, heavy and candied in the small cab, almost dripping from the ceiling, driving him crazy with barely controllable lust to touch her, explore her, *know* her.

And now he'd discovered she felt the same way about him.

He glanced up at the ceiling of the truck and the sky beyond, giving thanks for such a gorgeous, sweet, shy female, wondering why he'd ever wanted anything different, had ever thought he wanted to be forever paired to a female like the raucous and rowdy ones he always met at the bar.

Anticipation filled him. Eagerness to get his female home and safe, to learn her and teach her, an inch at a time, savoring every touch and sigh between them. His cock, which had softened after her scent had finally waned and her fingers had stopped probing his, sprang to life again, thick and rod-like behind his zipper.

He swore at its inopportune and dimwitted readying for something that could not happen. Not now. Not for days, probably. Too much going on, too much at stake, to try to bed her out here. Beckett frowned, realizing he hadn't even considered Khain. Were they in danger from him? That was why Crew and Graeme had both moved onto Trevor's property, huddling together to keep their mates safe.

No, he decided. Khain didn't have any ability to find the one true mates out of thin air. He couldn't hone in on them wherever they were, or he'd have found Cerise already.

The exit dumped them out onto a country road. Beckett drove fast, swinging his head left and right, watching for tails, and the perfect place for what he had in mind.

No tails, flat fields stretching for miles. Perfect.

CHAPTER 27

erise woke up all at once as the truck bounced unsteadily, throwing her head to the side. She straightened in her seat. "Why are we driving into a field?" She whipped her head around. "Are we being chased?" Kaci popped her earbuds out and looked at Beckett nervously.

"No, we're not. I need to stretch my legs. I thought we could take a break here and I've got something I want to show li'l bit."

He drove on, the truck's big wheels chewing up dirt and old snow and the occasional dried cornstalk that stuck up from the ground at odd angles. The sun was close to dropping behind the horizon, and she wondered how warm it would be outside, grateful for the jackets Beckett had bought them.

Beckett finally stopped, turned off the truck, then slid out. "Come on, bring my phone."

"Put on your coat," Cerise told Kaci, grabbing her own

from the seat between them. She hopped down after Kaci, stretching her spine and hips for a moment. Kaci was already headed to the back of the truck after Beckett. Cerise heard him open the camper shell and she hurried back there. She'd seen through the back window that there was some large piece of equipment in the bed of the truck, but hadn't been able to tell what it was.

Beckett had the tailgate down and was pulling out a small, rectangular piece of plastic, only a bit more than an inch thick, but about the size of two dinner plates put together. A thick column ran directly down the center, making her think of the body of a butterfly, with the two pieces of plastic being its wings. As she looked closer, she could see the plastic was really a kind of mesh, and inside the mesh were propellers, like what you would see on a helicopter. "What is it?"

"It's a hover camera." He handed it to Kaci. "Hold it up in the air." Kaci did and Beckett looked at his phone, holding it sideways, pressing buttons with his thumbs. The blades inside the plastic mesh whirred to life, startling Cerise. Kaci only looked thrilled and excited.

"Ok, let go, but let it balance on your fingertips."

Kaci released her grip and the hover camera wobbled for a second, then rose straight into the air. Cerise stared at it for a long time, remembering all the gorgeous pictures from Beckett's house, staring straight down at the ground. So this was how he had taken them.

Beckett flew the hover camera in a circle over their heads, then showed them the phone. A still of the three of them staring up at it was on the screen. He swiped it and looked at Kaci. "You want to try?"

Kaci nodded eagerly, and Beckett showed her how to

maneuver it, lifting his head occasionally to stare down the road in the direction they had come from.

Cerise watched them, Beckett bending to be close to Kaci, Kaci hanging on his every word, her heart strangely full and aching at the same time.

When he handed the controls over to Kaci, she made a few small adjustments, checking the responsiveness of the hover camera, then made it zoom across the field. She whooped and laughed and followed it at an awkward run, her pigeon-toed gait almost tripping her several times.

Beckett came to stand by Cerise. "It's good to hear her laugh," he said. Cerise nodded, watching her. So good.

She turned to Beckett to say something, but he was watching the road behind them again. She looked that way, and realized in the distance, she could see the freeway overpass and the exit they had taken. "Are we being followed?"

He didn't answer for a few moments, then said, "I'm almost certain we are not being followed, but I needed to do this before we stopped for the night. Once we enter a hotel, we will be in much more danger than we would be on the road."

Cerise opened her mouth to say one thing, but something completely different came out. "You aren't a doctor, are you?"

He didn't look at her, just kept his eyes on the overpass, his head raised high, but his expression tightened. "I'm a cop."

Cerise felt her heart triple-time in her chest, causing an actual lance of pain to shoot through it. She pressed a hand to her midsection, because the spike of anxiety made her feel nauseous. She realized that he had stopped in this field not to discern a tail, but rather to talk to her alone.

His gaze finally dropped to her face and his eyes blazed. "You were in my house," he said simply. "Tell me why."

She took a step backwards. "You knew?" She felt betrayed. Like he'd been playing with her the whole time. Her eyes narrowed and anxiety turned to anger. "Is this some kind of game for you?"

He shook his head. "It's not like that."

She didn't believe it. Couldn't believe him. "What else do you know?" she said, spitting the words.

"That Kaci shot that man you were living with, Myles Pekin, and that he's not her father, or your father, either."

Not her father! How many times had she prayed that could possibly be true, that she wasn't related to the monster, even though she never believed it. Cerise tried to talk but all she could do was sputter. She'd been there when Myles and Sandra had stolen Kaci as a baby, but she'd never even considered they might have done the same to her before she could remember it. Her heart broke for her parents. Would she ever find them?

He advanced on her, grabbing her upper arms, his face suddenly wild, his voice barely controlled. "What did he do to you? Tell me. I have to know, before I imagine the worst."

She pulled away from him, rage lending her strength. "You lied to me!"

He shook his head and rapped two fingers against the brim of his cap in emphasis to his one word. "Never." His eyes grew sad. "*You* lied to *me*, but I can understand why you did it."

Guilt and shame filled her, warring with the anger. She had, many times. But the anger won out. She whirled and stormed away from him, not wanting to, but unable to help herself, stark emotion demanding she move, the last vestiges of her pride saying it had to be away from him, who knew so much about her that she would rather bury in an unmarked grave. She ran toward Kaci, yelling before she even got to her. "Kaci, put that down. We're leaving. We're walking. Beckett lied to us."

She grabbed Kaci's arm, pulling it off the phone, which slipped from her fingers and fell in the snow. The hover camera plummeted to the ground. Cerise didn't care, she was raw, bleeding emotion.

Kaci howled in indignation and tried to snatch up the phone, but Cerise pulled harder at her. "Come on, we'll get to California some other way."

Kaci pulled out of her grasp and ran in the other direction, reaching Beckett, who had followed. She ran behind Beckett, grabbing his clothes and burying her face in his back like she used to do to Cerise. "No! I want to stay with Beckett. I love you, Cerise, but... but I love him, too!"

Cerise boiled. Not only had Beckett betrayed her, but Kaci was choosing him over her! "No you don't, Lemon, you just met him. Haven't I told you again and again to never give your heart to the first man who is nice to you!"

Kaci sobbed and threaded her hands around Beckett's waist as Beckett looked on, his face grave. "He's good, Cerise. I can trust him, I know it. Please don't make me leave."

What could she say to that? She turned and stared at the sky, about to walk out of the field herself. But Kaci was her responsibility. She *couldn't* just leave her, even though she knew Beckett would take care of her, would not mistreat her. She knew that if she did leave, or if something happened to her, Kaci would be treated like gold by Beckett. She frowned and fought back tears as she realized if those thoughts were right, then the earlier thoughts she'd had about him were wrong, fueled by anger and guilt.

Her shoulders sagged. Behind her, Beckett spoke softly to Kaci. She looked and saw him kneeling at her level, holding one of her hands. He kissed the back of it and waited for her to respond. She nodded and he wiped her tears away with the pad of his thumb, then stood and retrieved the phone and the hover camera.

Her heart hurt.

He watched until Kaci got the hover camera in the air again, following it with only a portion of her earlier enthusiasm, then walked to Cerise.

Warily, she watched him come, waiting to hear what he had to say. She owed him an apology, but did not know if she could give it.

He stopped a few feet from her, then wiped a tear from her face she hadn't known had fallen, his action as tender as it had been with Kaci. When he spoke, his voice was soft, and his words completely unexpected. "Can you accept that there's more to our situation than you would have been able to understand that night when we met, even if I tried to tell you? That I was afraid you would run from me if I told you who I was and that's the only reason I didn't?"

She nodded slowly. She could.

"Can you believe that I only want what is best for both you and Kaci, and that I won't turn you in to anyone and that I haven't told anyone where you are and I will do whatever I need to do to help you?"

She nodded again, a mental weight rolling off of her. She could believe that. He'd proved it again and again. He'd probably even saved their lives. Her eyes rolled to the bloody tear in his sleeve. Her fault he was walking around with that hole in his arm.

His face showed stark relief for a second, then he slowly

raised his arm and took her hand. This time, his touch was still intimate, but completely innocent. He was telling her all was forgiven by him, and they were back on the same footing as before, or could be, if she let herself go there.

He gave her that grin, the one that meant he was going to try to talk her into something, and that she would be helpless to do anything but agree, and said, "We have a lot of talking to do tonight. I want to get going so we can get to Grand Junction before I get too tired, but let's have a short driving lesson before we go. Cooter's a stick, so it'll be hard at first, but I firmly believe people who learn on sticks or tractors are better drivers."

Cerise touched his upper arm, stopping his backwards motion. She stepped in close to him and stood on her tiptoes, raising her lips to his. Wanting to tell him thank you and I'm sorry and every single thing rolling inside her without speaking a word. With her own touch that meant more than she could say in words.

He looked down at her, that grin still on his face, impossibly handsome, then slowly lowered his face to her. She savored everything about the moment as long as she could. The chill in the air contrasting with the warmth of his body next to hers. His slow, languorous descent that brought more of the delicious, masculine scent that was so uniquely him, the orange light streaking across the sky, and the whirring of the hover camera as Kaci lost herself in play twenty feet from them. His lips met hers and she let her eyes slide closed to better focus on their first real kiss. *Her* first real kiss.

Her body responded immediately, stronger than it had before, demanding she run her fingers up his back, to his head, knocking his cap to the ground. He cupped the nape of her neck and pulled every inch of her body directly up next to his, then probed the seam of her lips gently with his tongue. She gasped and opened to him, loving the velvet smoothness of his tongue, loving the way every slide of it slipped sensation across all her nerve endings, whimpering as she began to throb for him.

He broke the kiss but did not pull away from her, staring into her eyes, his mouth working like he wanted to say something. He changed his mind and kissed her again, once, then threaded his fingers through hers, bent to pick up his cap, and pulled her across the field under the streaked sky.

CHAPTER 28

*E*lla hurried out of her and Trevor's house, knowing they were all waiting on her at the van for their weekly trip to the police station so Trevor and Crew could catch up on paperwork. They went in the evening, so as not to be a distraction to the rest of the officers. She was surprised Trevor wasn't at the door, waiting to help her over the perfectly flat and dry ground, like he had since the moment she'd become pregnant. Now that her belly was visibly rounded and they'd discovered there were two babies in there, perfectly healthy, anyone watching the two of them would have thought she was made of china, liable to break at the slightest bump or bruise.

The cold air hit her in the face at once, but she noticed it wasn't as cold as it had been. Spring would show its face soon. As if agreeing with her, the clear sky above streaked with pinks and oranges of the setting sun. She turned to watch for a moment, loving a winter sunset, knowing Trevor wouldn't let anyone chew her out for being the late one. Ha! Not that anyone would. So far, their tiny family got along well, no fights, nobody getting on anyone's nerves. It helped that everyone had their own space, now that Crew and Dahlia's cabin was done.

Thoughts pushed into her brain and she looked around, dismissing the sunset. Someone else's thoughts. Her eyes settled on the van, counting the people in it. Three. No, four, Crew and Dahlia were entwined in the very back seat, looking like one person. She spotted Trent, Trevor, and Troy just behind the van, Trevor with his hands on his hips, Trent sitting on his haunches, the bit of white at the tip of his twitching tail catching her eye, and Troy pacing nervously behind Trent, his nose to the ground. She had learned to shield herself from an open *ruhi* conversation, allowing others their privacy if they hadn't shielded it themselves, but her own name caught her attention and she stared, knowing from the tone of Trent's rumbling voice and the cautious way he picked his words, what this was about.

Troy's worried about her, Trent said. *I am, too. She's hiding something and it's eating her up inside.*

Trevor's worry threaded through his words. *What could she be hiding? I'm always with her.*

Troy whimpered and Ella read plenty into the sound. He didn't want to betray her, wanted to let her tell Trevor when she was ready, but he was scared of her secret. So was she. She started down the walk toward them, relieved the secret would be out, but scared of what she knew was coming.

Troy spoke. *I think it's about her sister. Something big. And awful.*

Ella broke in to the conversation. *Get in the van. I'll show you what my secret is.*

Troy dropped to his belly on the ground, then rolled on his back, covering his face with a paw, while Trent swung his head around to meet her gaze, his more dignified apology written all over his face.

Stop, Ella implored. She hated to see the boys sad. *You were right to tell.*

Troy jumped up and ran to her and she dropped to her knees to hug him around the neck. He nuzzled her hair, then wriggled until he got his nose close to her belly. *Anybody in there? It's Uncle Troy and I've got lollipops!*

The babes kicked at once and Ella grinned past her dismay, imagining their little bodies turning and writhing, trying to get to Uncle Troy. They hadn't talked back, but Ella was holding her breath for the first word. No one had ever heard of pups speaking in *ruhi* in utero, but Trevor believed it was possible. Of course he already thought his pups were the strongest and smartest and cutest things that existed in all the universe, and he'd only seen them on ultrasound.

She took Trevor's hand when he offered it, followed him to the van, and laughed at Trent's jab at his brother.

Uncle Trent's here, too, with toothbrushes.

***

Ella held her breath as they walked through the sterile hallway of the nursing home, the faint scent of disinfectant tickling her nose. She hadn't been to see her sister since her own belly had started swelling, knowing Shay's was soon to follow.

She pushed the door open slowly and encouraged her mate to enter before her. Shay lay on her back, fingers curling into the air, eyes closed, mouth partially open, the mound of her belly straining at the sheets.

Trevor stared for a long time, not saying a word. She could *feel* him carefully concealing his reaction, but he needn't have bothered. She knew what it was. That's why she hadn't told him for so long.

Finally, he turned to her. "This is why you asked Wade to come."

She nodded, searching his face. "Everyone needs to know."

"How long have you known?"

"Since the day we were mated."

He threw his head back and stared at the ceiling. "Ella, why didn't you tell me? It would have been simple then, to have the baby—"

Ella cut him off. "Don't finish that sentence. We are not doing that."

Trevor's eyes widened. "You can't possibly…"

Ella paced the room, keeping her emotions under control. "I've had months to think about this, and the only answer is the one I've come up with." She faced him. "That's my niece or nephew in there and we are not killing him or her!"

Trevor grabbed her hand. "Think of who the father is!"

"You don't know that! I think we should talk to her boyfriend. Maybe he already knew she was pregnant."

Trevor shook his head, inadvertently squeezing her fingers. "I'll find him. I'll ask, but if he says no—"

Ella pulled her hand away from him. "If he says no, we still aren't killing defenseless babies."

"Ella, be reasonable, who is going to take care of these babies? Your sister is a vegetable."

Ella pulled herself up to her full height and stared him down. "I am."

Trevor put his hands to his head. "You can't possibly think I'll allow Khain's spawn in my own house! To be raised alongside my pups!"

Ella took a step backwards, fighting to keep her voice level. "I admit, that would complicate things, but we don't even know if that's true, Trevor." She took his hand between both of hers, trying to remind him of their connection. "If it's not true, the baby comes home with us, can you at least consider that?"

Trevor shook his head, his eyes rolling. "How would we possibly determine that?"

"I don't know. Let's talk to Wade." She knew he would agree with her, even if he wasn't on her side. Because she'd secretly asked him if Rhen would agree with aborting babies that Khain fathered. Wade had stared at her for a long time, but never asked why she wanted to know. He'd sat in repose that very night to contact Rhen and come back to her with this message: *Rhen says that to destroy a baby based on an act it may one day commit is to destroy yourself as well.*

She'd known that, but having Rhen's words on her side had given her confidence. Now Trevor needed some time to realize it on his own. She could give it to him.

He grabbed at her like he was drowning. "Ella, I don't think I can do it. I can't bring a baby into my home that could be fathered by him."

She opened her arms, determined not to fight. "I'm not asking you to. If we find out the baby is Khain's, we'll reconsider. I'm just asking you to put killing the baby out of your mind. It's the one thing you cannot do."

His face was stricken, and it hurt her heart to see, but she could not help him. She'd had to find her peace with it, and he would, too. She knew there was a chance she was making a huge mistake, one she might one day have to pay for, but in her mind, there was no other option. Family was family, and babies were precious, no matter what.

Wade's voice cut into their minds. *I'm here, but I'm in the lobby with Crew. There's something I need him to do.*

We'll come to you, Ella sent, seeing the overwhelmed expression on Trevor's face and knowing he was in no position to answer.

When they got to the lobby, Crew was pacing, a wild expression on his face, Wade watching him, arms crossed. Crew stopped and faced them all. "I don't feel good about this. I can probably do it, but it's like spying."

Wade inclined his head, his expression grave. "I need to know he's ok. I'm feeling danger heading toward him at an alarming rate, but I can't tell where he is or what the danger is."

Crew set his lips, then sat on the couch, his elbows on his knees, holding his head in his hands. "Give me a minute."

Wade pulled Trevor and Ella to a back wall of the empty lobby. Visitor's hours had just ended, and the nurse at the desk was gone.

Wade nodded in Crew's direction. "I asked him to check in with Beckett, if he could. It's not something he's attempted before, but I think he can do it. If I'm feeling this low-level unease I've felt about Beckett since he didn't show up for work two days ago, then Crew has to be able to get more. His connection with Beckett is strong, and I know Beckett has looked up to him like the older brother he lost when he was young."

"Where is Beckett?" Ella asked, glancing at Trevor. His face was still white, his eyes distant. He wasn't with them.

"Not sure. Nebraska the last I heard. I'm almost positive he's found his one true mate and she's in trouble. He hasn't told me anything."

"Nebraska!"

Wade cast her a look. "I don't have any idea what he's doing, or why, but there's a lot involved. The woman we think is his mate was in prison, then taken to the hospital for an injury, and he freed her, helped her escape."

Ella's eyes went wide. A criminal? Was their tiny family about to get disrupted if Beckett brought her back to Serenity? So far, she loved both her new sisters, but this one sounded scary.

Crew heaved himself out of the chair, his short dark hair sticking out in crazy tufts, his face twisted. "I got him. He's fine. He's... kissing a female. His one true mate. Don't ask me to look again, because I won't."

Wade stepped closer to him, visibly relieved. "Are you certain she's his mate?"

"I'm certain he believes so."

"Where are they?"

"Colorado, in the middle of a field, about to head west."

Wade nodded thoughtfully, speaking to himself, his eyes on the floor. "I've got some work to do, looking into that incident that landed her in prison, and I want to send a team out that way to be close in case he needs help. I just wish I knew exactly where he was headed." He looked back up at Crew. "Did you see it?"

Crew frowned. "Vegas."

"Good wolf. Would you be able to tell if he were in trouble?"

"Yeah." Crew's voice was sour as if he hated what he had done. "I throttled the connection so hopefully I won't be able to tell what he's thinking unless his emotion is high. I can't stand this, though. It's not right."

Wade clasped his shoulder. "I know. I won't ask you to do it one minute longer than is necessary." He turned to Ella. "Now, about your sister. She's pregnant."

He stated it like a fact, making Trevor jerk.

Ella could only nod, ready to fight them all if she had to. No one was killing that baby.

CHAPTER 29

Cerise blinked and opened her eyes, looking at the clock set in the dashboard of Beckett's truck. Almost one in the morning. She had been able to sleep, gotten just about three hours. She probed her tender temples gingerly, and read the highway signs, trying to figure out where they were. To her right, Kaci watched YouTube endlessly. To her left, Beckett concentrated on the road.

She studied the casual way he held the steering wheel, and the minute adjustments he made to the gas, wondering if she'd ever be that comfortable driving a car. She'd thought their lesson had gone horribly, but Beckett had insisted everyone's first time was like that. She'd only been able to shift into second one time, the rest of the times she'd stalled out immediately. But the thrill had stayed with her a long time and Beckett had promised they would try again soon and she would be better at it by then. Muscle memory, he called it.

He noticed she was awake. "Mornin', darlin'," he drawled, grinning at her. She smiled back and pushed her hair out of her face, anticipation pulling at her. Soon they'd be in a hotel room together. Answering questions. Would he still like her when he heard the answers? The danger they'd gone through twelve hours before now seemed far away, and like an accident or an afterthought, something that would not happen again. But he didn't feel that way. He'd wanted her to sleep during the drive if she could so she could stay awake and on guard while he slept at the hotel, saying he only needed three hours to be at his best the next day.

Beckett took an exit. "You woke up just in time. We're here."

Cerise watched the road slip by as Beckett found the parking lot to the hotel, then drove through it, noting all the exits and entrances, and the first floor rooms with their patios. Finally, he parked the truck near the lobby and facing the street. "You two wait here. I don't want them to see us all together. If you see anyone who looks even a bit suspicious, you lay on this horn, you hear me?"

Cerise nodded, but she could tell he thought it unlikely that she'd need to. She watched him go inside, denying that she was watching his body move in his clothes, then giving up and going with it. He looked good.

Her thoughts turned to the night ahead of them, and she wondered if he were going to try to have sex with her, and if he did, would she let him? If TV were to be believed, men wanted sex constantly, while women were the gatekeepers of sex, handing it out for multiple reasons, like currency. Men used it for pleasure, while women usually used it to get something they wanted. Maybe safety, money, marriage, babies, presents, or promises. She frowned. It was lopsided and didn't make sense to her. Didn't women ever have sex just for pleasure? The movies had made it seem like the women liked it, but then later, a different motive always was revealed. She couldn't think of a single instance where—

The hotel doors slid open and Beckett came out. Cerise took a deep breath and put a hand on Kaci's arm. "Time to go in," she whispered, never taking her eyes from Beckett. The weight of his returning stare settled on her heavily, seeping into her bones. She licked her lips, wondering if she was throbbing again, or if she had never stopped. He looked exhausted, though, his face white, his expression pinched, and she had a moment's worry about the wound on his shoulder.

Beckett helped them out of the truck and grabbed their bags. Within a few moments, they were inside, Kaci heading straight to the bed in the main room with a satisfied squeal, the TV coming on at once. Beckett triple-locked the door, then grabbed a heavy glass table to set in front of it, then cracked the windows in both rooms, moving quickly. Cerise set about finding Kaci something to eat, as they'd skipped dinner.

Beckett interrupted her and pulled her into the other room, sliding open a drawer, showing her what he'd put there. A gun.

He picked it up. "If I sleep three hours tonight, we can drive all day tomorrow and get to Vegas in the early evening." Cerise swallowed hard. She had been the liar after all. "While I'm asleep, you stay alert. Check the windows and the door often. I'm certain I'll wake up if those men show up, but still, if you hear anyone trying to get in, you grab this gun and point it at them." He showed her the safety features. "Will you be able to shoot if you have to?"

She nodded. If Kaci could do it, she could do it. If she had to.

Beckett nodded like he knew she would agree. "Don't let Kaci in here. Don't let her see it."

Cerise bit her lip, a confession leaking from her lips before she could stop it. "I won't. I'm afraid she's scarred from what she already had to do with one."

Beckett grasped her upper arms and stared into her eyes. "Don't you worry about Kaci. She's small, but she's got a warrior's spirit. She'll be fine. We'll be there to help her through anything that comes up, but I know she's going to make it past the hell she's been through with nothing but strength to show for it."

Cerise nodded silently. She could see that. But how could Beckett?

He let go of her and continued on with his room checking and setting everything exactly as he wanted it, then retreated into the bathroom. She gazed at the deadly looking gun one last time before she pushed the drawer closed, then headed into the other room to sit next to Kaci. She heard the bathroom lock engage and her forehead creased.

A sensation rippled through her, dim at first, then growing stronger, and she stretched out her neck, her fingers curling involuntarily into her palms. Something… something good was happening. She stood and drifted toward the bathroom, the sounds from the TV blurring and muting until she could no longer hear them. She reached the bathroom door and pressed against it, almost writhing, unable to stop herself. Something *amazing* was happening in there. Beckett was… doing something. Changing somehow. She could *feel* it behind her breastbone, in her muscles and joints and desires and wants. Animalistic instinct to hunt and run and rut with her mate filled her, making her muscles twitch—

The feeling waned, then stopped like a car hitting a brick wall. She almost collapsed to the floor, but caught herself, then backed away from the door. *What had she been doing? And that word again? Mate.*

She ran to the bed and sat on it, trying to look nonchalant, taking deep breaths, getting herself under control again bit by bit.

The bathroom door opened and Beckett came out in a new shirt. He grinned at her and held out his hand. She reached to take it, but Kaci interrupted her thoughts.

"Cerise, can I talk to you?"

Cerise let her hand fall away from Beckett's. "Of course, Lemon." She moved to sit next to Kaci. Beckett tapped the brim of his cap and moved into the other room. She watched him until she couldn't see him anymore, then turned her attention to Kaci.

She screwed up her tiny face, then muted the TV. "You scared me today, in the field."

Cerise sighed. "I'm sorry, Lemon. I was angry. I let my emotions get the better of me. It won't happen again."

Kaci's eyes brightened. "I saw you kiss him. Are you going to marry him? If you do, can I live with you instead of going to California?"

Cerise smiled and ran her hand down Kaci's cheek. She was so innocent, her only education of the world what she could glean from the TV. "No, I'm not going to marry him." Her heart seized at the statement and her throat thickened, like she'd told a lie. "Your parents miss you, Kaci, they have to be looking for you. It won't be fair for me to try to keep you."

Kaci gave her a skeptical look and Cerise bore it. She

knew Kaci didn't believe her parents would want her. Sandra and Myles had never seemed to. Only Cerise had cleaved to her, been kind to her, encouraged her to grow and be herself.

But Kaci just shrugged. "What was it like to kiss him?"

Cerise licked her lips, not sure what to say. But there was only the truth. "Wonderful."

Kaci watched her for a long moment and Cerise wondered what she was seeing in her face.

Kaci nodded once, sharply, like she'd found what she was looking for, then unmuted the TV and returned her attention to it.

Cerise touched her arm. "You good? I need to go talk to Beckett."

Kaci didn't even look at her. "Kiss him, you mean."

Cerise stood. Maybe. Hopefully. "Just talk, Lemon. We have some stuff to work out.

But when she entered the other room, Beckett was laid flat out on the bed on his belly, face pressed into the pillow, boots still on, cap next to him, snoring softly.

CHAPTER 30

Cerise prowled through the two rooms, past Kaci sleeping in one, the TV still on to provide light but the sound muted, then past Beckett sleeping in the other. Exhaustion pulled at her. She'd let Beckett sleep for five hours, figuring he needed it, but she couldn't give him anymore. She would fall asleep standing up soon.

She crossed next to him on the bed and gazed down at him. He'd barely moved, only turned his head to the side. Her hand reached out to touch him, but she stopped, went to the door between the two rooms and pushed it closed until there was only an inch-wide crack left, then went back to Beckett. She'd been eyeing his big body the entire night, wanting to touch it so badly, but loath to disturb him. Now she had her chance.

She knelt beside the bed, stretching her hand to reach the bare heel of his foot. She had taken his boots and socks off when he'd first fallen asleep. She touched him there, just below the ankle, then grazed her fingers up his skin, to his calf, which was covered by his pants. No matter, she squeezed it lightly, feeling the hard muscle there, then continued up his thigh, hoping he wouldn't take offense at her exploration. She didn't think he would, thought in fact he would savor being woken up to her touches. Her fingers followed the line of his thigh to the curve of his ass and she cupped him there, loving the firmness of his flesh. He was perfect, every inch of him. She wondered what he would look like naked and blushed, dipping her head, her core swelling as she contemplated it. The tanned skin, the muscles, the curls of downy hair she'd seen on his belly, that had dipped below the sheet to his—

Oh, she couldn't think about that. It made her breathe too heavily, her body giving her away. She grazed her fingers up his back, lightly pressing to get a feel of his muscles under his shirt, then reached his neck. His eyes were open and on her, she could feel it, but she didn't look. She ran her fingers up the back of his head, loving the rasp of his short hair, following the curve down to his forehead, then slipping one finger down his cheek before she met his eyes.

"Hi," he said, then moved onto his side and pulled her into the bed before she could respond. He tucked her body alongside his and nuzzled her collarbone. Her breath came in pants, dismaying her, although she'd known this would happen, had wanted it, but what bothered her was how *much* she wanted it. Like she would die without it. Without him.

It wasn't a safe or comfortable way to feel for her and she fought it, but knew she was doomed. If, for some reason, he didn't want her back, or only wanted her to use her body for sex, she would be crushed. Destroyed, under the freight train of her fledgling and inexperienced desire and need to be loved.

***

Beckett captured Cerise's lips with his own, dismayed to scent her arousal disappear. Was she scared? He pulled back and looked into her eyes, trying to understand what had caused the shift. He'd woken up the second she put her fingers on his ankle, wanting to stretch under her touch, to arch into it, but holding himself completely still, willing her to continue in any way she would. His cock had gone arrow-straight and board-stiff, but he was used to that happening when she quirked a brow or cocked a hip or even just sat quietly.

Now she was tense in his arms, and her expression seemed pained, saddened. "What's wrong, darlin'?" he asked, keeping his voice soft, like he was charming a wild animal.

She didn't answer, only looked at him with those big eyes, her strawberry blonde hair falling over her forehead and curling around her shoulders. He ran his fingers through it, smoothing it back from her face.

"I tell you what," he drawled, thickening his accent the same way he'd done for Kaci, but keeping his voice low and soft. "You ask me a question, any question you want, and I swear on my life to answer it honestly." He watched her face, hoping to see the tension there ease a bit, but it didn't.

She didn't even hesitate, almost whispering, "The big picture on your living room wall, where did it go?"

He had to stop and think for a second. That seemed like a lifetime ago. "I gave it to my best friend, Crew, as a house-warming gift. He just moved in with his new wife,

Dahlia. That was always his favorite picture and I wanted him to have it."

Now her tension eased and he was glad to see it go. He traced the worry lines on her face with his finger. "Can I ask you one?"

She nodded, the lines deepening again.

"That man Kaci shot when he was pounding your head against the wall, you lived with him, right? What did he do to you?"

Her voice hitched and caught, but she forced out the words. "Myles. My father. I know you said he isn't, but I always thought he was. He hit me, yelled at me. But mostly ignored me."

"Anything more?" Beckett forced his fingers to stay relaxed and his voice calm.

She shook her head. "Nothing sexual."

His own tension uncoiled somewhat. "And Kaci?"

"He hit her, too, but not often. Mostly we stayed out of his way. He tried to… do more, that morning that she shot him, but I stopped him."

Beckett could see it in his mind, exactly how they'd each protected the other. Exactly how Myles had invited his own death. Begged for it, really. Compassion for these two girls who'd done the best they could with a bad situation flooded him.

He nodded. "Your turn."

Again, she didn't hesitate, didn't have to think. "What were you going to say in the field after you kissed me?"

Beckett watched her face as he spoke, worried she wouldn't like it. "You're mine," he said.

But her expression went hopeful and some tension left her. "Am I?"

"I want you to be." He traced her lips with his fingers. She pursed them and kissed him, her eyes locked on him.

He moved slowly, not wanting to startle her, tucking his hand at the nape of her neck, pulling her in. This time she kissed him back, hard, clutching at him with her hands, exploring his mouth and tongue the way she'd walked her fingers up his body, her breaths coming faster and harder as his cock went ramrod straight again, pushing against her soft middle. She met it, did not seem scared of it.

After what seemed like only a few minutes, but what might have been as long as thirty minutes of the hottest make out session he'd ever been involved in, he pulled back from her. "Cerise, you tempt me so much."

"Tempt you to do what?" her voice soft but curious, her eyes watching him boldly. Something had changed between them during their kiss.

"Tempt me to take you, to make you mine."

"You mean sex."

He groaned and pressed his length against her. "I do mean sex."

"What is it like?"

"You've never?"

She shook her head. "You're the first man I've ever kissed."

He groaned again, having sensed it somewhat, but now the confirmation floored him. He had so much to ask her, but he couldn't sort any of it out in his mind. "Have you orgasmed?"

She bit her lip in that nervous way of hers and shook her head, her eyes wide. He cupped her plump ass and pulled her ever closer. "I have to give you one. Will you let me?"

Nibble on the lip. Eyes half-lidded as her scent flared,

filling the room, making him crazy. So much for their plan to talk.

"Will you—will we have sex?"

He shook his head. "We can't. It's too dangerous. If we do, I'll lose control, we'll be vulnerable." He lifted his head and looked around the room, just realizing where they were and remembering what he needed to guard against. He tried to scent past her sweet smell, then lowered his head, satisfied they were safe, no one was within a mile of the place who meant them harm. "I should check on Kaci," he said.

She shook her head. "I can feel her. She's sleeping in the bed where I left her."

That cryptic statement brought Beckett back to reality, to what he needed to do. Feel her? "Whose turn is it to ask a question?" he asked.

Her eyes flashed. "Mine."

He lifted his chin. Go.

"Why did you take my handcuffs off me, in the hospital?"

He stared at her for a long time, ignoring the pulsing of his cock in his pants. Did she even know what she could do? He spoke carefully. "I wasn't sure at the time, but now I think you compelled me to, somehow."

Her eyes flew wide and she gasped, her expression returning to the one he'd seen in the field when she'd tried to run from him. He spoke in a rush, grasping her arm. "I'm not blaming you. I'm totally ok with it. You were in survival mode. You've been in survival mode your whole life, but that's over now. I know you're special, different, and I know why."

"Why?" Her eyes were wide, her face pinched and scared.

He gave her a teasing grin, trying to lull her back into comfort. He needed her open and communicating with him.

He would try to calm her. "It's my turn. You have to save your question for your turn."

She stared as he waited for her agreement, then she finally nodded.

He let out the breath he'd been holding. "Are you attracted to me?"

She bit her lip, nibbling, then released it. One nod, straight up and down, her mind back on him.

He ran his fingers up her back, into her hair, ever so lightly. "Your turn."

She thought for a moment, her eyes going dark, then light again. She didn't ask her earlier *why* again. "You said I wasn't related to Myles. How could you know such a thing."

How much to tell her? Could she handle it? He didn't know. He'd tiptoe up to it and see how she reacted. "I smelled it in your blood on the wall of your trailer. That morning, when I woke, I followed your scent through my basement and the tunnel, then through the woods, and found Myles's body. I'm special, too, but in a different way."

"You… followed me? You could smell that?"

He nodded, waiting for her to speak again. If she asked another question, he'd answer it. They were so close to the dangerous stuff, that he thought she'd ask when she was ready to hear the answer.

She dropped her eyes and stared at his chest for a long time, running one finger over his shirt. He pulled it over his head and threw it on the floor. Her eyes widened and her finger began to trace his muscles. Her sweet scent flared at once, making him grin.

"Your turn," she said, her eyes trained below his neck.

"Where are we really going?"

"Loma Linda, California. To Kaci's parents' home. Myles

and Sandra stole her out of her bedroom when I was young, eleven, I think."

Beckett needed a moment to recover from that. He put his hand carefully at his side, so he didn't accidentally hurt Cerise with the anger pooling in his muscles. After a few moments, he was able to calm himself. When he was able to focus on her again, he realized she was crying. He touched her chin, brought her gaze up to his. "Hey, look at me, it's not your fault."

Her fingernails scrabbled across his chest as her hands clenched. "It is my fault! I tried to take her and run the next night, but they caught me! I tried again when she was older, and the police found me. I told them the whole story but they didn't believe me. They said I was making it up. This big, awful, mean cop took me back home and told me if I ever made up stories like that again, he'd throw me in jail and make sure they hurt me in there. I did try one more time, years later, but the police caught me again. That same cop was there. He did put me in jail, even though I wasn't old enough. He took Kaci and put her in foster care and she was bitten by the other kids in their care, even on her poor face! They let me out, let me go home, and we got Kaci back, but I was so scared I couldn't try again and then I got sick. I don't know how long I was sick for, but I think it was almost a year. I almost died, and if I would have, Kaci would have, too. They would have killed her, I know it. She's small for her age, and weak, and they were killing her with their threats and their beatings and their negligence!" She buried her face in his chest and sobbed. "I don't even know why they took her in the first place. They didn't want kids. They never wanted either of us."

Beckett pulled her to him and put his chin on the top of

her head, all thoughts of attraction driven from his mind. He couldn't even protect her from what had already happened. All he could do was do his best to comfort her.

CHAPTER 31

Cerise felt it pour out of her, like festering blood from an infected wound, hurting so badly, but cleansing like fire at the same time. The hate, the pain, the horror of their lives. Beckett took every bit of it, letting it flow through him.

Beckett spoke as he smoothed her hair. "You did so much, Cerise. You kept her alive. You kept her sane. You gave her a reason to keep fighting, to keep living."

Cerise didn't think it was enough, but she had done her best. She forced herself to stop crying. "My turn," she said. She'd told him the absolute worst of what she had to tell, and he was still there.

"Go."

"Would you have helped me in the hospital of your own free will if I hadn't made you?"

He didn't even hesitate. "Absolutely. That's why I was there, looking for you."

She bit back the why and waited for his question. When it came, she didn't understand.

"Who fed you the mushrooms?"

"What?"

"Someone was cultivating poisonous mushrooms in the forest behind your trailer. I smelled them in your blood. The scent was old, but you had consumed them for a long time."

Cerise put a hand to her head. "Oh, God."

Beckett held her.

"Why? Why would she try to kill me?"

"Who?"

"Sandra. Myles's wife. I thought she was my mom, but you're saying she wasn't."

"She wasn't. No relation at all. Don't try to figure it out too much. The answer could be as simple as she was crazy or on drugs, or there's something at work here outside Myles and Sandra that we don't understand yet. Someone pushing them to do the things they did to you and Kaci."

Dizziness overtook her. She squeezed her eyes shut and held on to Beckett until it passed.

Beckett spoke. "Did you know she's dead? Buried in the back yard?"

The dizziness hit her again, harder. "No," she choked out. "We thought she hadn't been able to stand Myles anymore and had taken off. We had no idea she was dead. But she disappeared around the same time that I got better, so it all makes perfect sense." She clutched Beckett's arm, trying to concentrate on the feeling of the soft mattress and pillow beneath her, trying to ground herself enough that she could recover from the revelations. She felt no sadness, no pain at this final loss of Sandra.

She took deep breaths, running it all over in her head, until she felt somewhat normal. Now the only thing left was to ask Beckett what *special* meant as it related to her and to him. Her dismay began to leak away and excitement took its place, bit by bit. What he was going to tell her was going to change everything for her, she knew it, making what she had gone through pale in comparison to what was in store for her.

Every dream she'd ever had about what her life could look like opened up before her. Friends, laughter, love, happiness, hobbies, a nice home, pets. Would Beckett be with her? A boyfriend? A husband?

But Kaci. Cerise felt for her, found her still sleeping soundly, the sense of her small body burrowed into the big bed in the next room making her realize that Kaci was not included in whatever the *special* thing was. She and Kaci had been brought together by accident, not fate, as Cerise somehow knew she and Beckett had been. She shook her head against Beckett's chest, not wanting to know what was special about her, what was special about Beckett, just yet. If she could get Kaci home, see for herself that her parents were loving and kind and wanted Kaci back, then maybe she could face the rest of her life without her little sister, the only person she'd had to love for so long. Maybe then she could accept Beckett and whatever he was promising with her soul and heart open.

She bit her lip, then looked Beckett in the eye to ask her next question, not even having to think about it. "Are you attracted to me?"

He groaned, long, low, and sexy, and she almost couldn't handle it.

"So much, darlin'. You're more beautiful than I ever could

have hoped for. So sweet and innocent, and you smell like a candy store."

She picked apart his words. He sounded like he'd been waiting for her for a long time. But it wasn't her turn to ask a question. She held her breath and waited for his.

He nuzzled her, then pressed a kiss to her lips before he asked his question, his voice a low rasp. "What happens in your body, when I do this? What do you feel?"

He kissed her again, leisurely running his tongue over her lips, tasting her, taking her, making her forget everything except his voice, his scent, his body, his attention. He pulled away and waited for her answer. The intimacy of the moment let her speak honestly. She grasped his hand and held it to her throat. "I feel a quickening here, a tightening, which I think is a hope you'll never stop." She moved his hand to her breast. "I feel an aching here, a straight desire for you to touch me." She skimmed his hand lower along her belly as he stared into her eyes, encouraging her. "I feel butterflies here, my skin and muscles jumping, begging for you to touch them." She lowered his hand between her legs and pressed it there, the sensation of his thick fingers almost against her skin flooring her. "And I feel a throb here. A delicious promise of something I don't fully understand."

He beamed at her like she'd answered the hardest question of the spelling bee correctly.

Her turn. "Will you be gentle with me?"

His fingers turned and cupped her sex, creating a delicious friction there. She gasped and arched into it, hoping he would bear down, show her what she'd been missing. He nuzzled her neck. "Yes," he rasped. "So gentle."

His fingers disappeared from her core and she mourned the loss of them until she realized he was stripping her pants and panties off of her. She helped, then stilled, biting her lower lip. He replaced his hand. "Can you be quiet?"

"Quiet?"

"You might feel the urge to cry out."

"It's that… intense?"

He nodded. "It can be."

He pulled the hand that had been cradling her neck out from under her and palmed her right breast with it. His thumb grazed her nipple and she threw her head back at the intense pleasure of both his big hands on her. He moved slowly, expertly, dipping one rough finger against her softest skin, probing there until he found wetness. His next pass was like velvet, creating bliss she couldn't even understand. She whimpered and brought her head down to face him. "You should stop. I don't think I can be quiet."

He didn't stop. Instead, he dipped his finger between her folds again, the drag and push electrifying her, spreading sweet sensations through her entire core as his fingers worked first one nipple through her shirt, then the other.

Her hips thrust at him as her back bowed and more small noises came out of her. "Beckett!" Worried but unable to stop, she implored him. "Will I lose control? I don't want to scare Kaci, or wake her."

"Kiss me," he said. "When it gets so intense you think you can't stand it, bury your face in my shoulder. You can bite me if you want. I won't care at all. I'll love it."

His fingers never stopped their magic while he was speaking, and still she was whimpering. "What will happen?"

"What you're feeling right now? It will build and build until you think you're gonna explode or pass out, but you won't do either. There will be a peak where it will feel like a kind of break or snap inside you, and the pleasure will come in thick waves. That's when you should bite me. Bite as hard as you need to."

Cerise licked her lips. He looked so eager at the thought of all of it, which eased her shyness over the new experience. She did as he had said to do, kissing him. He kissed her back in the same way he was fondling her, lazily, thoroughly, but never slowing, never stopping. Her body took all the sensation and asked for more, rocking against him, encouraging him with her small whimpers, clutching at his tight, muscular shoulders to pull herself closer to him.

As he'd said, the pleasure built, climbing peak after peak, until she *knew* she was going to pass out, knew she would die of it. And still he kissed her, still he dragged his fingers across the naked bud of her hidden flesh that she'd never noticed before.

Her breaths came faster in her throat, little pants with a whimper at the end of each. He spoke into her mouth. "Now, darlin', bite me now, or you're going to make noise."

She could scarcely follow directions, scarcely think well enough to do more than react, but she managed to bury her head into his chest, not able to reach his neck, but finding the curve of his pec muscle with her mouth. She bit, not wanting to hurt him, but unable to care at the same time—

It hit, stunning her with the new sensation, so exceptionally pleasant and all-consuming, a solid push of ecstasy that incapacitated her completely for a few precious moments. She cried out against his chest, biting and moaning at the same time, until finally it eased, tapered off, tiny pulses of pleasure reminding her of what had happened.

She relaxed, dropping to the mattress, as Beckett disentangled himself from her, and began to smooth her hair back.

When she could, she opened her eyes. Beckett had the

biggest grin on his face that she'd seen yet, so pleased with himself she couldn't help but giggle.

He propped himself up on one elbow. "Was it good?"

Her mouth dropped open until she realized he was teasing. "Very good. Can I make you do the same thing?"

His hand dropped to his zipper and he adjusted himself. "I'm embarrassed to say that your pleasure made me come in my pants like a teenager."

"Oh! Is that bad?"

He shook his head. "Not unless you tell someone about it."

Her eyes widened. "Who would I tell?"

He pushed himself out of the bed to clean up. "Don't tell anyone, especially not the guys I work with. I would never hear the end of it."

Real life came crashing down on her. She moved to the center of the bed and buried her face in the pillow, turning her head to talk for only a second. "Your friends? In Serenity? I'm not ever going to meet them, am I?"

He was digging around in his clothes, but turned to her, puzzled. "Of course you are."

"No, I've got to go back to prison. I know I'm in trouble for what I did. If not for shooting Myles, then for escaping."

Beckett crossed to her and took her hands in his. "Don't worry about it for one more second, Cerise. My boss is the Deputy Chief of the Serenity Police Department. He knows about you and I promise you that you won't spend one more second in jail."

She stared at him, wondering if she could possibly believe him, when Kaci's small form stirred in the other room.

They could be in Loma Linda before midnight, if they hurried.

CHAPTER 32

*B*eckett let Kaci and Cerise's laughter wash over him, soaking it up as best he could. It was hard to believe that if everything went well, they could be saying good-bye to Kaci in a few hours. An unfamiliar tightening of his throat made him swallow and look out the side window for a moment.

Ahead of him on the dark but busy freeway, the lighted exit for Loma Linda finally appeared. He made his way to the right lane.

"Ok, I've got a good one," Kaci said. "Would you rather find true love or a million dollars?"

"True love," Beckett said immediately, even though it wasn't his turn.

Cerise's voice mingled with his, almost harmonizing. "True love."

Kaci didn't say anything for a moment, and Beckett

wondered if the game had stirred the sadness that had been growing in her over the last two hundred miles. Cerise had been trying to keep the atmosphere light, but they all felt it.

Kaci spoke. "Yeah, me too. But it's harder when you didn't grow right."

Cerise put a hand on her arm. "Kaci…"

Beckett snorted. "Are you kidding me, Kaci? Guys love short girls."

Kaci leaned forward to look at him like she didn't believe him. "You think boys will be interested in me?"

"Of course. You'll grow, darlin', and if you don't, it won't matter, because petite is hot. So's tall. So's thin and thick. Believe me, boys love girls in all shapes and sizes."

Kaci's face pinched and she ran her hand over her face. "Do you… do you think I'm pretty?"

Beckett grinned at her, giving her his very best one, the one that had never failed to get him female attention. "I think you're gorgeous." He leaned over Cerise and pinched Kaci's chin. "I especially love your freckles, and your red hair, and your smile. If I were 19 years younger, I'd snap you up."

Kaci gave him an appraising look. "You're 30?"

"Yup."

Kaci pressed her lips together, her demeanor changing slightly. "Man, that's old."

Cerise barked out a laugh, then clapped her hand over her mouth, looking at Beckett, her eyes twinkling merrily.

Beckett sat back in his seat, swinging the truck to the right to catch their exit. "I guess it is. I'll have to find me a lady my own age." He winked at Cerise and her cheeks colored prettily, making him remember what she'd looked like when she'd orgasmed around his fingers. Shit, that had been a sight.

If they could catch some alone time that night, he planned on doing it again and again.

"So what's the address?" he asked.

Cerise's forehead creased with worry and she recited an address. Beckett handed his phone to Kaci. "Punch it in the GPS for me." Kaci had discovered she had an uncanny ability with anything technology related, even teaching Beckett a few things about his phone.

Kaci did, then looked at Cerise. "Wait, is this the address that was written on Zeus's tag?" Cerise nodded, nibbling on her lower lip.

Beckett didn't like the look of that. "Who is Zeus?"

Cerise waved a hand distractedly. "When Myles and Sandra stole Kaci out of her crib and put her in the back seat with me, she was asleep, but she had ahold of a small horse stuffed animal. It had writing on the tag. The name Zeus, and that address."

Beckett looked at the phone screen. They were close to the address. "That's what we're basing this on? What if they've moved, or what if that wasn't the address to their home?"

Cerise nibbled harder. "I think that is their address."

Beckett nodded. He wasn't going to argue. They would know soon enough. "It's almost midnight, are we just going to knock on the door?"

Cerise stuck her thumbnail in her mouth and began to chew on it, staring out the front window. "Yeah."

Beckett shrugged. Ok. This was her show. He was just there to keep them safe.

"I gotta pee," Kaci said, also sounding nervous.

Beckett swung into a gas station. Kaci had the bladder of a gnat, but he thought this time might be more of a delaying tactic. He could tell she didn't want to leave Cerise, and was more scared of meeting her parents than excited. He stopped and the girls jumped out, heading to the outside door marked *Women.*

Beckett waited, then got out also, leaned against his truck, and took a deep breath, sorting through the scents as best he could. Busy city streets always masked scents to some degree, but he did not smell *foxen* or *bearen* in the vicinity. Good.

Cerise and Kaci barreled out of the bathroom, Kaci holding her nose. "Smells like dead flowers covered in shit in there," she said, her voice nasally. "Newsflash. Spraying perfume without cleaning the bathroom doesn't mask scents near as well as this place thinks it does."

A flash of understanding speared through Beckett's brain. One he'd almost woken up with that morning, but hadn't been able to put together until just now. The dead/flat *foxen* smell had been a masking scent, like a hunter who sprays deer urine on his clothes. A masking scent he'd smelled before.

The night his father and brother had been killed. Those fuckers from the rest stop…

Cerise came straight up to him. "Are you ok?"

His eyes rolled as he tried to figure out if he was or not. They *had* been after him! So why had they tried to get Cerise and Kaci? Just because they were with him? He gave his phone to Kaci and waited till she climbed in the cab, then clamped down on Cerise's wrist and pulled her to the back of the truck. Why hadn't he called Wade? Told him exactly what he was up to? Wade would have sent a team out to help him.

He stiffened. That was exactly why he hadn't called him. Because a team, even of his friends, being near Cerise would have triggered him in ways he didn't want Cerise to see. Or Kaci. They didn't need any new violence from males in their lives. If they saw him acting like Trevor had with Mac, or like Graeme had with him, just because a male got too close to Cerise? He never would have been able to gain that trust back.

Shit. Now he had no choice.

He pulled Cerise face to face. "Listen. I want you to carry a gun. I'm going to give you one when we get back in the truck. I think I've met up with those males from the rest stop before, a long time ago, and they might come after me again." Although he couldn't see how they would find him. Not until he got back to Serenity.

He lifted his head to scent the air, then looked her in the eye again. She was shaking her head. "I don't think I should. I've never fired one. I might be better off using…" she held up her hands.

"They got you the last time."

"I wasn't ready. Didn't think he'd hit me." Her face and voice said she didn't know why she'd thought that. Her past experience had taught her the opposite.

Beckett took her wrist and pulled her hand to his mouth, kissing the fingers gently. "Don't hold back, you hear me? Don't hesitate to kill if you can. These men are murderers."

Cerise nodded, her eyes far away, as if she were remembering something she'd rather forget.

"Can you kill, do you think?"

Cerise stared at him, worrying her lower lip with her adorable white teeth. "Maybe. I could tell someone to jump off a roof and they would do it, I think. Or tell their heart to stop beating? I could try it." It was obvious she didn't want to. But he thought she would if she were faced with the worst.

He nodded. "Wait here." He ran to the open door of the truck and wrote something down on a scrap of paper, then ran back to her. "If something happens to me, you call this number and talk to Crew. He'll take care of you."

Cerise took the paper and put it in her pocket without looking at it, her expression dubious. He caught her face in his hands and kissed her, hard, then spoke again. "I mean it, Cerise. Promise me you will. He won't just give you some money or put you up in a hotel room for a night. He'll take care of you for life. Kaci, too. Get you a house, give you money, everything."

Her eyes were wide and scared. "How do you know he would do that?"

Beckett shook his head. She still didn't know what she was. The simplest answer was probably the best. "Because I would do the same for him and anyone he cared about."

She nodded once. "I promise."

CHAPTER 33

Beckett stared out the side window as they cruised past the house once, slowly, his window down, cold air hitting him in the face with a story. Nothing to be worried about. Three newspapers lying at the end of the driveway. One dim light visible glowing past the shades, but the rest of the house dark. Someone had left in a hurry? Or someone was holed up inside? He parked Cooter in front.

Cerise and Kaci stared at the house for a long time, until Cerise said, "Here we go!" in a falsely-cheery voice, and motioned for Kaci to get out.

Beckett hopped to the ground, eyes, ears, nose open. Head on a swivel. But he scented nothing but humans, their emotions dulled by dreams.

Cerise and Kaci walked to the front door, hand in hand, then stood there. Beckett joined them. "You going to knock?"

Cerise shook her head. "No one is inside."

"How can you—?" Beckett broke off, mid-question. Oh.

Cerise let go of Kaci's hand and stepped off the porch. "I'll be right back."

Beckett grabbed her. "Wait, you're not leaving my side."

Cerise twisted her hand in his grip and grabbed him back, looking sweetly into his face. "I just want to see if it's the right house or not. I promise I'll be right back. And I'll be ok."

Beckett let her go, his heart following her down the steps and around the corner of the house. He'd never quite understood, before, what it was like to be in love with someone. He'd always enjoyed women, but could take them or leave them, not caring if he hung out with the same woman twice. But this. This was like being stabbed in the chest every time she left his sight. How did people live like this?

Small fingers curled around his and he glanced down to see Kaci's pixie face looking up at him, her eyes dark and bottomless with nerves. In that moment, he could see in her face the woman she would become, and he hoped he could be around to help guide her there. A rush of affection filled him and he squeezed her hand, as fresh understanding filled him. The opportunity to feel love for even a moment was worth a lifetime of potential pain.

His brother's face filled his vision. The memory of his brother shoving him out the back door. *Run, Beckett. Me'n Pa'll hold them off.*

Cole had wanted him to have a chance to grow up. To experience life. Even though he'd only been a few years older than Beckett, he'd understood more about love than Beckett had. "Thanks, bro," he whispered, his eyes on the twinkling stars above them.

Kaci squeezed his hand and he smiled at her.

The door behind them opened and they both whirled around. Cerise was standing there, her expression horrified. "It's the right house," she said, holding up a pamphlet.

Beckett ushered Kaci inside, then closed the door behind them. What were they doing? But the pamphlet took his mind off the breaking and entering for a moment. He read it over Kaci's shoulder.

MISSING
Lillian Roth: Aged 11
Taken from her home in Loma Linda at 14 months old. Age now: 12

Two pictures sat side by side below the words on the paper, and both hurt Beckett's heart equally. One showed a chubby toddler in white pajamas with feet, taking an unsteady but adorable step, a horse toy clasped in one fat, raised hand.

The one next to it was labeled, age progression photo. What Lillian may look like now.

It showed an obviously computer-enhanced, but totally human picture of a pretty girl with long, flowing red hair and a shy smile. Beckett frowned at the freckles on her cheeks, wondering how they had known she would develop freckles.

The picture was eerily accurate, except Kaci's actual eyes looked larger and her cheekbones much more pronounced. Beckett looked from the picture to her, then realized what it was. Kaci looked slightly malnourished, while the girl in the picture did not.

Cerise knelt and gathered Kaci into her arms. "We found them, Lemon. You're home." Kaci balled the piece of paper up in her fist and buried her face into Cerise's shoulder, the smell of her indecision so strong Beckett could identify it. Beckett stepped deeper into the house, seeing and dismissing the stack of more signs on the table, then frowning. He scented *wolven*.

He moved into the kitchen, then down a hallway to a bedroom. He bent over the bed, smelling both sides. A human male lived here, along with a half-breed *wolven* female. Non-shifting.

He couldn't scent that, but if she were shifting, he would know that she existed. All living female *shiften* who could shift around the world had notoriety, half-breed or not. But the concoction Khain had spilled into the drinking water, tainting it, had seemed to treat non-shifting half-breed-or-less females the same as it did the males. It had made some of them sick, but most had noticed no ill effects.

Beckett grinned and headed back out to the girls. If this was her parents' bedroom, Kaci was one quarter *wolven*. He knew he liked her for a reason. One-quarter was normally not enough to pick it up by scent, the *wolven* nature so very buried under the human.

Beckett stopped mid-stride, the coincidence bearing down on him. A certainty gripped him, running cold fear through his veins. He had to get to his phone.

He burst into the living room, finding Cerise holding up a DVD case. 'Lillian' was written across the top in block letters. She opened it, but it was empty. She went to check the DVD player below the TV.

"Kaci, I need my phone." Kaci pulled it out of her pocket and handed it to him silently, her eyes on Cerise.

Beckett pulled up Wade's number and began to text him, his thumbs flying over the tiny keyboard. He didn't want to call, his conversation would scare the girls.

Wade. In Loma Linda. The guys who killed my father and brother tried to attack us in Colorado. They tried to take Kaci and Cerise from me.

He paused, wondering if Wade even knew who Kaci and Cerise were, then shook his head and finished his message. He would have put it together by now.

There is some sort of a connection between the three of us. Kaci was kidnapped as a baby, probably by these guys. Maybe Cerise too. Deatherage? I will be here for a few days. Send me help. And contact local PD so they know who I am if I call. Tell them to stay away from Cerise if they come to us! You know why.

He typed in the address they were at, then turned around as the laughter and coos of a baby filled the room. Cerise had pressed play on the DVD player, and Kaci-Lillian was racing across the screen, as fast as her roly-poly legs could take her.

"Lemon do it! Lemon do it!" she cried, her toy horse in her hand. The camera panned to a woman who was trying to sweep the kitchen floor. She laughed and smiled at the little girl and handed her the broom as the camera panned in on her face. Her red hair, generous smile, and freckles covering her cheeks, chin, and forehead were so reminiscent of Kaci that Beckett knew immediately who she was. Kaci's mother.

She helped Kaci sweep the floor, holding her horse so Kaci could grab the broom with both hands, then she put the broom aside and picked Kaci up, kissing her under her chin and making her laugh. She spoke to her obviously-revered child. "Lemon did so good! Such a helpful baby!" The unseen man spoke, and his voice was playful. "Put her down, Sharon, I want to see her sweep some more."

Kaci sank to her knees on the floor in front of the TV, her

mouth open in an O, her eyes liquid pools of what could have been. What should have been.

Cerise drifted to him, and took his hand. "That's why I call her Lemon. She said that from the very first day. It was the only word she would say for a while, and then she stopped talking completely. When she was four or five she started talking to me again, but only when we were alone. She never spoke to Sandra or Myles." She bit her lip. "I never knew it really was her name."

She looked at him, tears in her eyes. "Thank you for getting us here. We never would have made it without you."

Beckett was about to reply, when a strange scent reached him. Humans. Lots of them. All men. Strange because it was the middle of the night and he was inside a house with the windows closed. He crossed to the window and peeked outside, but saw nothing.

He pulled out his gun anyway, his phone in his other hand, his thumb poised. But who to call? Wade? Or 911? Wade hadn't returned his text yet.

He decided. 911. But first, "Cerise. Turn off the TV and take Kaci somewhere to hide. Don't argue with me, just do it. And don't come out until I tell you it's all clear. No matter what you hear."

Cerise moved toward Kaci, her face full of fear, but she didn't move nearly fast enough.

"Hurry!" he hissed at her, instinct telling him it was already too late. She moved then, snapping the TV off and grabbing Kaci under the armpits, heading for the hallway at the same time as the front door and the back door burst open.

Beckett leveled his gun, but a stinging pain caught him in the ribcage, then another in the thigh. His vision blurred and his muscles relaxed. He fought to stay upright. He looked down at his leg. A dart stuck out of it, with a red feathery tuft at the end of it. Tranq… and he couldn't shift because of the humans…

He fell to the ground, his brain refusing to work, watching Kaci and Cerise's feet as they disappeared up the stairs at the end of the hallway.

CHAPTER 34

*C*erise covered Kaci in blankets in the very back of the closet. "Shhh, don't say a word," she breathed. She would peek out. See what was happening. She'd heard the doors fly open, but no gunshots. Beckett might need her help.

Before she could move, heavy footsteps strode into the room. A male's voice. "Mudge. Mudged. Pudge. Nudge. Mudgett!"

She shrank back into the closet, knowing she'd heard that voice before. The cop who had shown up both times she had run away with Kaci. The one who had put her in jail. Put Kaci in foster care. He was behind it all. No wonder their luck had always seemed so poor. He had rigged the system.

"Come out, come out, wherever you are," he sang and she could tell he was right outside the door. He ripped it open, and smiled down at her, making her guts twist. He'd grown his hair long, pulled it back in a ponytail, and he had a dark goatee now, but she would recognize him anywhere. Same conniving look. Same big-framed body. Same flat, dangerous stare. His lips were split, bloody, and his skin seemed to be bruised.

In his right hand he held a chain, like a thick necklace chain, and at the end of it was a kind of jewelry, a piece of gold or metal that was just over an inch high, a snarling wolf on one side, an angel in flowing robes on the other. It was glowing.

"That's mine," she cried, even though she'd never seen it before.

"Indeed it is!" the man said. "Let me introduce myself. I know we've meet before, but your manners were ghastly back then. Hopefully they've improved. I'm Grey Deatherage, and I've been keeping this safe for you until you were old enough to use it."

He bowed at the waist like he was meeting royalty, and not bat-shit crazy. Cerise stayed still, praying Kaci would not move or sneeze or give herself away, but the blankets behind her moved. No!

Kaci pushed her way out, her small face twisted in anger. "Hey dickhead, fuck you!" she cried.

"Oh, Kaci," Cerise breathed. She'd just seen the man behind Grey Deatherage. A short man, but with a mean face and a gun in his hand, pointed at her.

Grey backed up and the pendant swung below his fist. "Both of you, out here," he said, his voice a pained snarl.

Cerise saw no point in resisting. She crawled out.

"Sit on the bed."

They did, holding hands tightly, Cerise awash with fear, Kaci seeming only angry. Dimly, Cerise took in the surroundings. It was a large, long room, the only room at the top of the stairs. The walls were sloped, like the roof was directly outside. An attic bedroom.

The crazy cop only stared at her. So she spoke. That's what they always did in the movies. Keep 'em talking. Till someone came to the rescue. Beckett? Please let him not be dead. Her heart twisted at the thought of it. She put it aside. "You're the reason Myles and Sandra stole Kaci, aren't you? You made them to do it. Why?"

Deatherage smiled, the pendant he was holding still glowing, but the light pulsing on and off now. As she watched, she realized it was in time with her heartbeat.

He turned dramatically and locked eyes with her. "And you, sweetheart. Don't forget yourself in this crazy play."

Cerise's eyes narrowed. Did he mean he'd had them steal her, too? When was that? How old was she? Where did she come from and who were her parents? She couldn't think about that right now. Couldn't be distracted by it. She had to figure out a way to use her power, like Beckett had said. Get them both to jump right out the damn window.

Grey pressed his hands together, letting the pendant swing. "So, Cerise, is it?" he said, like he'd never met her before. "We have business, you and I. It's simple, won't take more than a minute or two of your time. If you do as I ask, I'll leave the girl here. Let her reunite with her family, who will be back soon. They regret having to leave, but they are following a *very* credible sighting of her a state away. If you don't…" He turned and nodded at the other man in the room, who swung the cannon-sized muzzle of the gun till it pointed at Kaci's knee.

Cerise held up her hands, stark terror pulsing through her chest, her face going almost numb with it. "Ok! Don't point it at her, please!" The gun moved slightly to the left. "I just—" More talking. Keep him talking. "What happens to me if I do what you want?"

Grey's eyes settled on her. "Nothing, m'dear. We'll take a little trip. You may even enjoy it."

She couldn't think of anything else to say. What would he want of her? "And Beckett? What happens to him?"

Grey and the other man exchanged a smirking look. "Unfortunately, he's going to have to go meet an old friend. That old friend will probably have some harsh words for him. You may not see him again. But no worries, there are hundreds of strapping young *wolven* just as eager as he was to make your acquaintance."

Cerise frowned. What in the hell was he talking about?

Grey laughed, a surprisingly sane sound, but he didn't look at his buddy this time. "Ah. You don't even know what he is. What a surprise it will be for you when you see. If you see. Whatever did you two talk about on that long drive across the country?" His eyes narrowed, his voice growing mean. "Or were you too busy rutting? Got any pups in there yet?"

Cerise flushed as things began to fall into place for her. She didn't know how any of this could be true, but somehow, it was the only thing that made sense. Beckett wasn't human.

She bared her teeth at Grey, thinking how much she would like to see him jump off the roof. But she liked him better this way, seeing the real him, not as some fake, pretending he was not completely evil.

The pendant flashed, catching her attention. She locked eyes with the wolf, then the angel, then the wolf, as it turned, emitting a rainbow of light. She could feel its power, almost hear it speaking to her in a glut of feelings and images.

Grey snatched it behind his back, breaking the spell.

"Listen to me, little girl. You're going to do exactly as I tell you to, or you know what will happen. Are we clear?"

Cerise nodded.

"Good. I'm going to hold the pendant up. You are going to stay where you are and look at it only, not touch it. You're going to repeat the words that I say and nothing else. Do you agree?"

Cerise nodded again, an eagerness stealing through her. She would get to look at it again? Talk to it? Suddenly, it was all she could think about.

"Perfect." He brought it out slowly, and all of Cerise's thoughts fell away. On some level, she heard Grey's words move through her consciousness.

"Say exactly what I say: Oh great Matchitehew, I summon you to this time and space and implore to your calmest nature. I have a *sacrifice* for you, the booted wolf who is said to be the one to save the savior in the future. If you will come to me, and leave all else unharmed, I will give him to you, in good will."

The pendant spoke to her, soothed her, opened her mouth and encouraged her to speak the words. She did, haltingly, tripping over the words sacrifice and *booted wolf*, but the pendant assured her all would be fine and well and she could continue.

As soon as the last word left her mouth, the air around them began to ripple as if it were water.

A wind picked up in the enclosed space.

Something was coming.

CHAPTER 35

*C*rew leaned back in his chair, frowning. He hadn't been able to sleep, and he wasn't sure why, but now he knew. Something was wrong with Beckett. He bore down on the feeling, sending his consciousness out, searching for exactly what was wrong, when Dahlia came down the stairs, wrapping a robe around her. She saw his face and stopped, then sank down on the stairs. He returned his concentration to Beckett.

What he saw made him shoot to his feet and run for the radio. It crackled in his hand, Trevor's voice. "Everyone to the main house. Wade's on his way, says Beckett could be in trouble and we need to brainstorm how to get to him quickly."

Crew pressed the button on the side, already heading for the door and motioning for Dahlia to follow him. "Beckett *is* in trouble. Wade has to get someone to him *now!*"

Without waiting for an answer, he pulled Dahlia outside

in her slippers and they ran for Trevor's. Behind them, he could hear Graeme and Heather coming fast. He pushed open the back door, leaving it ajar, counting heads. Trevor, Ella, Trent, Troy, Mac, Bruin, and Harlan were standing there, Trevor and Ella in sleep clothes, Trevor with his phone to his ear. Mac held a finger to his lips and Crew could hear Wade talking through the phone.

Trevor lifted his chin at Crew. "Wade says he got a text from Beckett but can't reach him now. He wants to know what you know."

Crew spoke up so Wade could hear him through the phone. "Beckett's been shot four times, and drugged somehow. He's in a basement, there are humans all around him. He's digging bullets out of his legs and they're just laughing at him, like they are saving him for something, but even if he gets the bullets out, he can't shift. He's losing blood fast. They're saving him for something, not killing him outright, but he doesn't expect to live through whatever they're saving him for."

Trevor listened to the phone as Wade spoke urgently. "Wade's got Loma Linda PD on the way to an address Beckett gave him, but they are ten or more minutes out. They had an armed robbery on the other side of town an hour ago, officers and civilians shot."

Mac snorted. "Nice coincidence."

Crew leaned against a barstool. It didn't look good for Beckett. His best friend…

Graeme grabbed his shoulder. "Crew, if you were there, in California, could you find him? Locate him like a beacon?"

Crew nodded. Graeme squeezed his arm. "Give it to me. The location. The essence of it."

Crew had never tried such a thing, but if Graeme thought

it would work... He grabbed Graeme's other arm and stared into his eyes, letting everything he'd seen in Beckett's mind flow through him, out of him... into Graeme?

Graeme nodded sharply. "Got it. I can take two with me."

Troy barked sharply and stepped forward, as did Trent. Mac held up his hand, his voice tight. "You know I'm going, sparky."

Graeme only hesitated for a second, his eyes playing over everyone, then landing on Bruin, but he spoke to Mac. "Mac, you're gonna get burnt. Maybe bad."

Mac winced but didn't back down. Graeme nodded. "I gotta take the bear, too. He's got the least chance of being burnt."

Bruin shot next to Mac, a look of disbelief on his face. "Fuck yeah, I'm *in*."

"Shift, both of you." Graeme turned to Crew, his face twisted. "Protect Heather and the bairn."

Crew nodded tightly, knowing exactly what Graeme hadn't said. *If I don't return.* "With my life."

Graeme pressed a kiss to Heather's lips, then turned to Mac and Bruin. Everyone had scattered away from them. Heather uttered a little cry and openly gaped at Bruin, then backed away, out the door behind her.

Mac didn't look any different than Trent and Troy, just white to their black, but Bruin, he was monstrous. His shoulders stood five feet high and his head was as big as a man's entire chest. Bigger. He sat back on his haunches rather like a dog and lifted his paw, his curved claws jutting out like thick knives. He turned his head to the side and waved his massive paw back and forth, as if to say, *are we going yet?* The effect was almost comical, but still no less terrifying. He could tear Mac's head from his shoulders if he wanted, without even exerting himself.

Graeme spoke to them. "I'm going to transform and wrap you in my wings. Bruin, I'm not sure how well you will fit, and both of you will still be burnt. It won't last long. Don't squirm, because if I lose you in-between, you'll incinerate instantly."

Troy retreated to the couch, looking almost glad not to be going, although he'd been outraged a moment before.

Graeme spoke to Trevor. "Warn local PD we will be there, human or beast, we won't know till we get there."

Bruin's voice floated in Crew's mind. *Tell them to bring clothes.*

Graeme gathered their clothes up from the floor. "No need." He looked around. "Stand back."

He waited till everyone was clear of him, then transformed. One minute a man, the next a dragon the size of a pony, the clothes he had been holding no longer visible.

Neat trick, Bruin said.

The dragon unfurled his wings, knocking two chairs across the room, and sliding the dining room table three feet to the left into the wall.

Come to me.

Bruin started forward first, then Mac. Graeme wrapped them in his wings, curling the leathery skin around Mac two or three times, but only once around Bruin.

And they were gone. Winked out of existence like a light turning off.

CHAPTER 36

*H*eat. Pressure. Nothingness. Searing pain.

Then Graeme was running, running fast on powerful dragon legs. A voice to his left screamed, then another called out, "It's the dragon, he's returned! Tell the King!"

Graeme sped up. Mac tried to yell at him, to tell him to let him out, that those god-damned wings were strangling him. He couldn't breathe! Graeme stopped. Side-stepped. Then the darkness overtook them again.

Heat. Pressure. Void. Burning.

Mac gritted his teeth, his own fangs punching through his lips, the burning too much—

Until it was gone and he knew they were back home. He tumbled as the wing he'd been wrapped in unfurled to spill him into the snow. He rolled, putting his burning skin and fur out, the pain gone, numbness covering him. He'd been burnt so badly over his entire body he couldn't even feel the burnt spots anymore. He relaxed, letting go, letting the snow soothe him, the darkness of the night take him—

"Mac!" Graeme whisper-shouted at him urgently and shook him. "Shift, you have to shift now to heal yourself."

Mac looked down at his body. His legs were twisted and too short, all his hair gone. He didn't want to see anymore. He clamped down on the animal in his mind, who for once went willingly. The shift hurt, took so much longer than normal, but when he pushed to his hands and knees, his skin was whole, his hands and feet back.

"What the fuck, sparky," he gasped, almost retching in the snow. "Remind me not to sign up for your frequent flyer program."

He looked up. Graeme and Bruin were already crouching next to a house as humans, Bruin showing more skin than Mac wanted to see, Graeme dressed in what he had been wearing at the house. Fucker. Mac envied him that ability, to keep his clothes somehow. They were peering in a basement window. Mac crawled over to them, ignoring the cold of the snow against his naked skin. It was better than burning, any day.

Inside, on the floor, he saw Beckett in a pool of his own blood, holes in each of his arms and legs, surrounded by six human males, all carrying assault rifles, most with another gun on their belt. Beckett's fingers were in a messy red hole on his leg, his face screwed up in pain that had to be almost as bad as what Mac had just gone through. While Mac watched, he pulled a twisted piece of metal out of the hamburger that used to be his leg as the humans laughed, and one pointed his gun at him again.

"Fuck that noise," Mac growled. "We're going in, now."

Graeme nodded. "Me and you in the window. Bruin, you'll have to go around to the door, your bear won't fit."

Bruin nodded and changed, loping away mid-shift. Mac shifted, too, but his transformation took time, while Graeme's was instant. The tinkling of glass breaking was the first thing Mac heard as a wolf, the yells, shouts, and screams of the men in the basement the second, as Graeme separated their heads from their necks with bites and swipes of his powerful wings. By the time Mac was in the room, all the men were twitching on the floor, dying or dead.

Mac shifted and crouched by Beckett, who looked right through him, no sign of recognition on his face. "Come on, tough guy, you got all your bullets out of you yet?"

Beckett rolled his eyes, looking half-crazed. Mac took his hand, tried to catch his eye. "Stay with me, wolf, all you gotta do is shift and it will be all better."

Beckett nodded, his body shaking for a moment. He stared at Mac, his mouth drawn, cords standing out on his neck. "Grey's here. Upstairs. He killed my father. He's got Cerise and Kaci."

Mac nodded, not knowing who Cerise and Kaci were. One of them had to be Beckett's mate. "I don't need the news, tough guy. Let's meet your wolf and then we can go tear Deatherage's fucking head off just on general principles."

Beckett shook again, like he couldn't quite manage the shift. Mac got down on his hands and knees and grabbed Beckett by the back of the head, putting their foreheads together, talking directly to Beckett's animal. "Come out, fucker, you got your mate to save. If you don't come out, right now, you're going to die, and so will she!"

Beckett threw back his head and roared to the ceiling, as his animal took over, muzzle lengthening, hips twisting, holes mending, wiry white fur appearing, except for his feet and half-way up his legs, where the fur was black.

"Yeah, right on" Mac encouraged, stepping back, about to shift himself, when he caught a noseful of an acrid, fiery smell he knew all too well.

Graeme's scaly head swung around from where he stood at the bottom of the steps, his eyes meeting Mac's with surprisingly readable emotion.

Khain was in the house.

CHAPTER 37

Cerise clutched Kaci's hand, knowing the girl would be terrified. She tried to pull Kaci to her, but she resisted with surprising strength. Cerise frowned and checked her expression. Her head was up, her nostrils flaring, a look of realization on her face, almost like something was happening that she'd expected for a long time.

Grey had hidden the pendant from her view again, breaking its hold on her, and now that Kaci didn't seem to need her, her thoughts doubled over on themselves in fear. She had just doomed Beckett somehow, she knew it. He was the booted wolf, and she'd offered him as a sacrifice.

Her gaze travelled over everything in the room, the two men who stood in front of her, the human now looking terrified, his gun hand shaking, his eyes wide and rolling to the ceiling as he crouched and scanned the rippling air. She dismissed him. He was going to pee his pants or run any second.

And when he did… Her gaze fell on Grey. His eyes were narrowed in excitement, no fear there. He had his head up like Kaci, his nostrils flaring also. She frowned. Were they smelling something she wasn't? She thought maybe she smelled a bit of smoke from somewhere.

Behind them, there was one window. If she could touch Grey, she could *push* him to run at it, crash straight through it to the ground below. She tensed her muscles, ready to run, but before she could, whatever had been coming, came.

A set of nasty, onyx-black claws ripped through the air like a wall of fabric at the end of the long room, creating a sort of hole in reality that allowed… something to push its wrinkled snout through. Cerise's senses went dim, as terror pushed to the forefront of her consciousness, making her shake. She'd seen a movie about Wendigos a year ago, an evil, cannibalistic monster that looked almost like a giant deer that stood on its hind legs with long fangs and arms, something Kaci had found in Sandra's stash of DVDs. They'd only watched it once, and only for the first hour, when Cerise had finally snatched it out of the DVD player and cracked it in half, but the image had stayed with her, giving her nightmares for weeks.

This… *thing* looked a bit like that. Its beady animal eyes rolled over everyone in the room, then settled on her. Its oversized nostrils pulsed and she knew it was smelling her, appraising her. She pulled herself into a ball, and whimpered. This was bad.

The man with the gun ran past the monster, just as she'd known he would. The monster let him go, then pushed its entire body through the rip and stepped onto the floor, bowing its head so the protuberances there (horns?) didn't scrape the ceiling. Blood and tissue showed at its ribs, where the skin didn't quite meet.

In a blink, the monster was gone, and a man stood where it had been. A large man, bigger than Beckett or Grey, but not as big as the monster had been. Dark hair, manic eyebrows, unnaturally muscular body, his intense eyes still locked on her, like no one else in the room existed. Her muscles turned to water and she wondered if she and Kaci could survive a jump out the window themselves. Better than staying here.

Grey spoke up, like he was greeting a treasured guest. "We meet at last, Khain the Destroyer."

Khain the Destroyer ignored him completely and took a thundering step toward Cerise.

Grey got in front of her. "I've been doing much work for you. Perhaps you've noticed?"

Khain stopped at that and swung his gaze to Grey, but he didn't speak. Only took him in, assessed him.

Grey lifted his chin, preened. "That's right. We have similar aims, me and you. It is time we knew each other. Maybe formed a gentlemen's agreement."

"Work for me?" Khain's voice was awful, and Cerise resisted the urge to clap her hands over her ears.

Khain and Grey were between them and the only door out of this room. She turned and looked at the window behind them again, thinking it was their only choice. But when would be the right time? She inched toward it. She would slide it open and look out. Maybe there would be something to climb down.

Grey nodded eagerly. "You know the angel fathered the one true mates to help the *shiften* in their mission to thwart you, but I've spent years locating them. I've had them stolen from their mothers and swiped their objects of power." He held up his hand, but Cerise could not see the wolf/angel pendant because his body was in the way. Anger burned in her at his words. He'd done that to her?

Instead of heading out the window, she was going to *push* him. Make him fight Khain, and then she and Kaci would run out, find Beckett. She edged toward him, trying not to catch anyone's eye.

"Kaci," she whispered, touching her on the arm. "We're going to run for it. Get ready." Kaci didn't even seem to hear her. She was snarling, her eyes locked on Khain, her lips pulled back from teeth that looked longer than she remembered. Cerise pulled back, scared for a moment, Kaci looked so fierce.

The man/monster spoke to Grey. "You called me here."

"Yes, I offer a member of the KSRT. He's alive and you may do with him as you wish. We just have to go to retrieve him."

Khain looked over Grey's head, his terrible eyes finding Cerise. "I will take the Promised instead."

Grey faltered for a second, whipping his head around, then back to Khain. "No, I need her for a short while longer, then you may have her."

Khain batted him aside like he weighed nothing and took another step towards Cerise. She put her hands up, her pulse racing, the sound of her heartbeat like a bass drum in her ears.

Kaci leapt to her feet and stood in front of Cerise. "Don't touch her, you pusbag!" she screamed, her spittle landing on Khain's face. Cerise saw it burn there, like acid.

"Kaci, no!" Cerise stood and tried to pull Kaci behind her, but Kaci was falling to the floor, her body twisting. Cerise shrieked and tried to grab her as the monster/man reached out a hand…

Before Cerise's eyes, Kaci transformed into something else, her face and body growing hair, her clothes ripping off her as her body changed shape, arms becoming forelegs, ears moving to the top of her head, strong white teeth growing, fangs lengthening, until she crouched as an animal. Dog or fox or wolf, Cerise couldn't tell, she looked like a mixture of all three. She was medium-sized, but did not look awkward or pinched as an animal, like she had as a human. Her fur was red and threaded through with black down her back. Her eyes were a gorgeous honey-color, her nose black, her muzzle white. Cerise's limp hands slipped off of the Kaci-wolf. She couldn't get them to work right. Her legs gave out on her and she tumbled backward to the bed, just as Khain grabbed for her, missing her by inches.

The Kaci-wolf thing snarled and leapt into the air, clamping on Khain's forearm with its teeth, a terrifying growl coming from its—her throat. Khain's lips twisted and he tried to shake her off, but she held on tight. He lunged for the wall and slammed her body into it. Still she held on. Cerise regained her footing and launched herself at Grey, who was pushing himself up from the floor. She grabbed his shoulders and shouted into his face, *pushing* at about 75% strength. He had to be a wolf, too, and instinctively she knew she wouldn't be able to *push* the man/monster, so she went for Grey instead. "Save Kaci! Kill that thing!"

Grey lurched forward, pulling a gun from a holster on his side, his face resistant like he knew he had no chance, but he couldn't resist. He socked the gun against Khain's chest, but Khain stopped pounding Kaci into the wall long enough to backhand him across the room. Cerise ducked, in case the gun went off, then tried to think of what to do next. Guaranteed he was one of those wolf things, maybe she should make him shift and fight that way. Kaci still hadn't let go, in fact seemed to be hurting the monster.

A pounding up the wooden stairs caught her attention and she stopped mid-stride, her gaze shooting to the door. In streamed another wolf, white with black on its legs, then another, this one all white, then a—oh god, a *bear* who had to squeeze and shimmy to get through the doorway, and… Cerise felt her knees weaken again. A dragon. That's what it looked like, red and scaly with wings and a hooked snout. Whose side were they on? Had to be hers.

They all ran for the man-monster, and his face twisted in something like rage with fear mixed in when he saw them. He bellowed and whipped his body around in one final heave, as Kaci's jaws met, cracking his bone. She flew across the room and hit the wall near the door, crumpling to the floor, the monster's hand and wrist still in her mouth.

The first wolf leapt and hit the man-monster in the chest, while the second went straight for his gut. The bear snarled and launched itself at Khain's legs, while the dragon grew to twice the size it had been, filling the room, hooking a clawed wing around Khain's neck and slashing.

Again that bellow, and the man changed, grew, and twisted, now he was only monster, black blood leaking from exposed ribs and new holes. He grew three times his size, bigger than the dragon, punching through the roof of the house, his body rippling to try to shake off the wolves, the bear, and the dragon, who were rending his flesh till oily blood flew. Cold air enveloped them all.

Cerise covered her arms with her hands, shielding herself from the blood, and ran for Kaci, dropping onto her knees next to her, shielding Kaci's limp body with her own.

The monster bellowed again, kicking and lashing out,

ripping through more of the roof. Car alarms from what sounded like every car on the street, maybe the block, went off, horns and whoops rising into the sky. Police sirens swelled and neared.

The monster, bent over as its back arched out the roof like a dolphin showing only a curve above the water, plucked the two wolves off of him with one hand, throwing them. Cerise heard a voice in her head shout, *Bruin, get back, he's going to run.* The dragon let go and parried back on strong legs, its wings stretching side to side.

The monster reached out the one hand he had left, grabbed a dazed Grey with it, and disappeared with a pop of air slamming into the space he'd just occupied, leaving only the gaping hole in the roof and spots of rancid black blood on the floor to prove he'd been there at all.

CHAPTER 38

*B*eckett was the last to shift to human form, as if he was the most shaken, possibly the only one to realize just how close it had really been. Mac and Bruin were already dressed by the time he shifted, his eyes on Cerise the whole time. Cerise was trembling, her arms wrapped around a compact red female *wolfen*. *Kaci.*

Beckett grinned, grabbing a sheet from the bed and heading toward his girls. Kaci had taken Khain's hand right the fuck off. Good deal. Warrior. He'd known it from jump.

Beckett knelt next to Cerise, pulling her up. Her eyes met his, and they were stricken. "I think she's hurt. She won't wake up."

Beckett shook his head. "She'll be fine, Cerise, I promise you that." He looked around at Graeme. "Graeme, we need you."

Graeme came to them, transformed at once, into a

dragon smaller than a Labrador Retriever, then bit open his foreleg and dripped blood into Kaci's mouth.

Cerise watched, her eyes wide, but soothed. She clutched at Beckett. "You didn't tell me you were a wolf, and that your friends were wolves and bears and…" Her voice dropped to a whisper. *"A dragon."*

Beckett laughed. "They ain't got nothin' on you, darlin'. You're half angel." Cerise's eyes rolled toward him and her fingernails dug into his shoulders. He grinned and nodded. "I ain't funnin' ya. You'll see."

Outside, cars screeched to a stop, many of them, the sounds loud in the room courtesy of the new sunroof Khain had installed. Car doors opened and shut and they could hear the low grumble of men talking urgently.

Graeme stepped back and transformed. "That should do it." He looked over his shoulder at Mac and Bruin. "Come on, you two. We've got some explaining to do."

Bruin snorted. "So that was Khain, huh? He didn't seem so tough. Did you see me bite through his kneecap?"

Mac raised a hand in the air and the two high-fived. "Yeah you did, bear, you fucked him up."

Bruin snorted again, this time it sounded more like a growl. Beckett leaned against the wall and watched them file toward the door, as his muscles shook out their tension. He had no idea how they'd found him so quickly, but he would be forever grateful to them. Even Mac.

As they got close, Bruin looked like he was going to stop and speak to Cerise. Beckett stiffened involuntarily. Mac grabbed his friend around the shoulders, then addressed Beckett, nodding at Cerise. "You claimed her yet?"

Beckett snarled by way of answer and Mac nodded. "Right-o, tough guy. Get on that shit. We're out." He pushed

Bruin out the door and the sound of their oversized boots clomping down the stairs reached Beckett.

Cerise flashed him a look. "They're leaving?"

"They won't go far."

The Kaci-wolf opened her eyes and lifted her head, her black nostrils flaring in spurts.

"Kaci!" Cerise cried, pulling her into a hug. Kaci let herself be hugged for a moment before she tried to pull away. Beckett snatched up Khain's withering hand from the floor next to her and flung it across the room. They would deal with it later.

Kaci stepped over both of them, then ran to the hand, sniffing it, growling low in the back of her wolf-throat, then stared at the hole in the ceiling.

"He's gone, Kaci, you all chased him off," Cerise said.

Kaci cocked her head and looked at Cerise strangely.

Cerise spoke to Beckett. "Can she understand me?"

Beckett nodded. "Yeah, but it might take her a while to realize she can, if it's her first shift, which I'm assuming it is. Twelve is awfully old to shift for the first time. I've only heard of it happening in legends, never seen it. She can't be more than a quarter *wolfen*, so I'm surprised she shifted at all, but seeing Khain has been rumored to do that to half-breeds before. Quarter-breeds, too, apparently."

"When will she shift back?"

Beckett shook his head. "I don't know. I shifted within a few hours of being born. I don't remember what it was like the first time."

Cerise touched him on the chest, her gaze astonished, as she looked at him in a new light. She swallowed a few times, before she could speak again. "And what is Khain? He, ah, he wanted to take me with him."

Beckett bared his teeth and growled, he couldn't help it. At the noise, Kaci turned in a tight, frantic circle, snapping at the air, her amber eyes searching every corner of the room.

"Ah, shit." Beckett crawled to her on his hands and knees, the white sheet draped around his middle, puddling under him and impeding him.

He was going to have to help her.

***

Cerise clutched herself in a hug, worry for Kaci rippling through her. There was no human intelligence in her face, like she'd seen in the other beasts. Kaci was all animal, her lips pulled back from her fangs, pacing back and forth.

Beckett reached her and spoke in a low voice, swaying his head with her movements, trying to catch her gaze. "Listen Kaci, your animal wants to run, and it deserves a run, but not yet. It's time for you to come back to us. After you've shifted a few times, we'll take you to the woods, I'll run with you myself. But now, it's time to cage it, get control of it. You are only as strong as your willpower, and you have to be the one in charge. Or you will lose yourself."

As he spoke, Kaci slowed, then stopped, standing in front of him, panting, her pink tongue rolled out. Beckett moved in close until his forehead touched hers. He rubbed his face on her cheeks. "I'm going to shift, and then we are going to come back together, you hear me?"

Kaci didn't move, only stared at Beckett, their foreheads seemingly fused together. Her left ear twitched, then fell still.

Cerise heard shouts from the living room, then a woman's shrill cry. *Hurry, Beckett*, she thought, not knowing why.

Beckett's skin rippled, and as she watched, he changed,

turned into that gorgeous, huge wolf she'd seen before, the one with the boots. *The booted wolf.*

He crouched, his belly almost touching the floor, his back end in the air, his wolf-forehead still pressed against Kaci's. He made a noise, that sounded almost like a bark but was deeper, and growlier, scary and beautiful at the same time. Kaci whimpered, then made a similar noise back.

Footsteps pounded up the stairs. Cerise looked up to see one of the men from earlier, the lighter-haired one, holding his hand up, slowing the ascent of two people. The man's face was set, the woman's a mess of hope and contradiction.

The guy stopped them, but the woman peeked over his shoulder, seeing Beckett and Kaci in the middle of the room. She didn't even care about the hole in her roof, she had eyes only for Kaci. Cerise watched her for a moment, then tore her gaze back to Beckett and Kaci as energy shifted and power flowed.

Beckett began to transform, and Cerise thought it was slower than she'd seen it before, beautiful, a thing of wonder and beauty. Then Kaci's fur rippled along her back, and her own transformation began, fur disappearing into skin, hair growing, hips and hands and feet changing shape, until Kaci collapsed on the ground in a heap.

"Lillian!" the woman cried, and even Beckett's big friend couldn't hold her back. She ducked under his arm and swept into the room, sobbing, grabbing up Kaci and hugging her like a baby.

"Bob, go get her some clothes," the woman forced out over her sobs. Bob swiped his eyes and ran from the room. Beckett wrapped his sheet around him and backed up to sit next to Cerise.

Cerise's heart overflowed with so many emotions as she

watched Kaci being hugged by her mother that she couldn't even place them all. She raised a trembling hand to her face and wiped her own tears away. Beckett hugged her with one arm, and they both watched as Kaci put her head down on her mother's shoulder and curled her arms around her back.

Kaci met Cerise's eyes, and Cerise saw a whirlwind of emotion in her face, too. Was the strongest one contentment? A realization of something she'd been waiting for, for a long time?

Yes, Cerise realized. Kaci looked more than content. She looked at home.

CHAPTER 39

Cerise lazed on Kaci's parents' couch, seriously close to falling asleep, her body limp and exhausted. It was almost nine in the morning, she hadn't slept yet, and there'd been an army of cops tromping in and out of the house, occasionally asking her questions through Beckett, who wouldn't let any of them get near her. They'd talked for hours, though, and she loved everything she'd discovered about him.

His friend with the accent, the dragon, had disappeared, but his other two friends walked through occasionally, the bear grinning like a loon any time anyone mentioned Khain, and the other one giving Beckett noogies and calling him tough guy every time he went past. Beckett had shrugged at her once. "It's better than hardhead, I guess, or redneck."

"Make a hole!" a male voice called from outside, loud enough for her to hear it inside, and the front door opened.

A silver-haired man stood there, his shrewd eyes taking in everyone.

Beckett raised his hand and tapped the brim of his cap with two fingers, then sketched the new guy a salute. "You took long enough, Chief, we're exhausted."

The chief ignored Beckett, his eyes falling on her. He raised his chin and even gave her a small smile, then entered the kitchen, headed straight for Sharon and Bob, Kaci's parents, who were huddled together, Bob holding Kaci now. They were talking to a cop in uniform, and Kaci's eyes were closed, her breathing even, like she was asleep, but Cerise saw her steal glances at her mother occasionally.

Cerise smiled. Kaci'd taken to her parents so easily, all her trepidation fallen away as soon as she met them. They were good people, and their love for her was obvious in the way they looked at her, touched her, and couldn't let go of her long enough to put her down for some shut-eye. They weren't going to miss another second of her life.

Beckett sat down next to her. "That's Wade. He's my boss. He's the one who already got your name cleared from killing Myles and escaping prison." He spoke softly. "Does Kaci look different to you?"

Cerise pulled herself into a seated position and scanned Kaci's body and face. She did. Fuller, somehow, and taller? "She grew?"

"I'd have to see her standing to be sure, but she looks like it, doesn't she? Gotta be at least five or six inches."

Excitement hit Cerise. "She does! Look at her cheeks! Her face has filled out, and her knees! They look normal, not too big for her legs anymore." And her hair had grown! It curled down her back, as thick and long as her mother's.

Beckett smiled at her. "Could have been the shift, or the

dragon blood. But I don't think she's going to be worried about her height anymore."

Cerise grabbed his arm and hugged him in delight. This was what Kaci should have looked like all along. Strong, healthy.

Kaci's eyes blinked and she lifted her head, staring intently at Wade, who was now talking directly to Bob and Sharon. They had revealed earlier that morning that Bob was a language and computer expert, and he'd been hired by Grey over a decade before to work on his codes. Sharon had gotten suspicious about the content of them based on a few off-hand things Bob had said to her, and stole into his office one night to read everything, even though Bob had only half the story, what looked like every other page of the memoirs.

As a half-breed, Sharon had never been deeply involved in the world of *shiften*, not knowing really who was in charge of what. She hadn't told her husband what she was before that night, not thinking it important since she could not shift and her children would not be able to shift. But when she'd been trying to decide who to take their suspicions to about Grey's real motivations, she'd told him everything. Kaci had been stolen that night. They'd never connected the two events, and with their furor to get their daughter back, their decision to tell someone something had gotten lost in the years of pain and searching.

Wade was speaking intently to them and Cerise stilled, trying to hear his words.

"We'd like you to come to Serenity. We'll put you up in a house, provide you full time security in case Grey ever reappears, or Khain decides to retaliate against you in some way. Lillian is important, and we want to keep her safe."

Bob held up a hand. "Wait a minute. I know your story.

You wolves have no females, and that's why Kaci is valuable to you, isn't it? Well, you can forget it. I know you don't have any males under thirty years old, and none of them are going to be sniffing around my daughter."

Wade shook his head. "It's not like that. When Lillian is old enough to mate, she gets to choose who she wants to be with. If she's interested in a full-blooded *wolfen*, that's up to her, but that's not why we are inviting you to Serenity. We want to train her, we want her to work with us."

Sharon went white. "You aren't talking about the war camps."

Wade shook his head. "No. No war camps. She would work with instructors one on one, experts in their field. We need females in the department. She's only one, but there will be more eventually, as the one true mates are being found, and two of them are pregnant already. We have the future of the police department, the *shiften*, and the entire world at the forefront of our minds." Kaci's eyes flickered with something like excitement. Cerise held her breath.

Wade looked around to see who was listening, then stepped closer and lowered his voice. Cerise had to strain to hear him. "I also would like to ask her if she would be willing to speak to the police departments in the area, maybe consider a teaching circuit around the country."

Bob shook his head, confused. "Teaching what? She's just a little girl."

Wade nodded. "I know she is, and she should have time to play, and run, and grow, but there's something you may not understand. She's one of only five *wolven* in the entire world who have faced Khain and lived to tell about it. Two of those *wolven* are non-shifting wolves, not able to speak. One of them is Beckett, and he's got a busy job with the KSRT," he said, waving his hand at Beckett. "The other is," he looked around, spotted Mac down the hallway, making a rude hand gesture at Bruin and laughing.

Wade frowned. "The other isn't that great of a teacher." He looked back at Bob and Sharon. "We would like her to, very occasionally, share her experience with other *wolven*. What it was like. What Khain is like. She is the only *wolfen* alive who has ever severed one of his appendages. It'll grow back, I'm sure, but you have to understand how valuable that is. She's a fierce little girl whose going to grow into a tough police officer, and others will benefit from her knowledge."

Kaci picked her head up off of Bob's shoulder. "I want to do it…" her voice trailed off . She injected strength into it as all eyes swung to her. "I want to do it, Momma. Daddy."

Sharon took her hand. "If Lillian wants to, we are on board, right, Bob?" Bob nodded vehemently, hugging his daughter closer.

Cerise couldn't help herself. She burst into tears and buried her head in Beckett's chest.

She wouldn't be losing Kaci after all.

She was going to get her freedom, her sister, and her… wolf. It couldn't be better than that.

CHAPTER 40

erise half-slept through their trip to the hotel, Kaci's last words ringing through her mind. "I love you, Cerise, you were right about my parents, but call me Lillian, ok?"

Cerise had gathered her into a hug. "Can I still call you Lemon?"

Kaci-Lillian had nodded, her face serious, then Kaci had kissed her on the cheek and run back to her parents, her knees straight, her gait fluid. Sharon had smiled at Cerise and mouthed, "Thank you for everything, talk soon."

Cerise had almost floated out of there, holding Beckett's hand as he led her to his truck. It was all thanks to him.

He pulled up in front of the hotel where they were going to sleep. After that, she didn't know what would happen. He sat in the parking stall for a moment, then ran a hand over the back of her head. "You wanna come in with me, or stay here?"

"Am I safe here?" she mumbled, her head against her window, floating in that state between asleep and awake.

"Yeah, my friends are parked behind us. They won't let anyone near you."

"The wolf and the bear and the dragon?"

"Just the wolf and the bear. The dragon is home already with his mate. Your sister."

That woke her up. A little. She lifted her head. "My what?"

He grinned and she felt her body respond to him even in her exhaustion. "I told you that, didn't I? You ain't the only one, darlin'. You got three sisters at home just dyin' to meet you. And more coming soon, I'm sure."

She laid her head back against the window again for just a moment. He had mentioned there were others like her, but she hadn't quite made the connection they were her sisters. Her eyes slid shut…

"Stay here, I'll be back in two shakes."

And before she knew it, he was, knocking on the window so she would move away from it and not fall out when he pulled the door open. She was about to get out when he gathered her into his arms and carried her. She lay her head on his chest, remembering exactly how safe he'd made her feel before, and how much more safe he made her feel now. He'd never let anyone hurt her again.

Inside, he laid her down on the bed and stripped her shoes and pants from her, then covered her with a blanket.

"You coming?"

"Be right there. You sleep."

She did. The faint light from the covered window shifted every time she woke for just a moment, from morning light to afternoon light, to evening orange, until one time it was completely dark. She lifted her head and blinked at the darkness, but she could feel Beckett was behind her, and something hard was against her ass. She put her hand back there. He was naked, and oh lord, that was his cock, fully at attention. She curled her fingers around it and fell back asleep.

When she woke again, light shone around the drapes. Beckett was hovering near the door, talking quietly into his phone. "I want to drive. Take our time. Cerise deserves some downtime after what happened. And we need a couple of days in Chicago." He stopped and listened to whoever was talking, then spoke again. "You can't spare them for a few days? Come on, Wade, be reasonable." Another pause. "No, seriously, I don't even want to leave this room until at least tomorrow."

When he spoke again she could hear the grin in his voice. "Alright, got it. Whatever you say. Ok, for sure. See you then."

He hung up and came to her, still naked, head bare for once, cock soft. It was the first time she'd actually seen it, and as she eyed it, it grew exponentially. "Oh my," she said, licking her lips. It jutted straight out from his body, just that fast, and she could almost hear it call to her, she was that curious about it.

He slipped into the bed facing her, pulling her close to him, drawing lazy circles on her hip with his finger-tips. She put one finger to his lips. "Hold that thought," she said, and jumped up to do her thing in the bathroom, getting back into bed with him as quickly as she could.

She lay down and looked at him shyly. He pulled her close.

"Can we do that thing where we ask each other questions again?"

He nodded.

"You go first," she said, feeling shy, not knowing how to start, now that they were actually alone together.

He didn't hesitate. "Do you know how much I want you?"

She shook her head.

He took her hand and put it on his cock. She ran her fingers over the velvety skin, exploring fully. He arched into her touch, his eyes never leaving her face. "I want you so much I've barely slept. I've just been lying next to you, listening to the sound of your breathing, imagining how it would be when we were finally together."

She licked her lips, nibbling on her lower lip for just a second. "Can you be gentle with me?"

He nodded. "I can be gentle. As long as I can have you." He brushed her hair away from her face. "Can I make love to you?"

She nodded and he smiled, leaning close. "You're mine, Cerise."

She sighed as his lips caught hers. She wanted to be his. Wanted to never leave the protective circle of his arms. Wanted to learn more about the pleasures he'd given her the last time they'd been in a hotel bed together.

His tongue dipped into her mouth, swirling, exploring, sliding over teeth and tongue and lips, the sensations rocking straight through her body. She mimicked the movements of his tongue with her hand, pulling and caressing his cock. He groaned into her mouth with every tug.

His big hands dropped past her collarbone, down her chest, finding one of her breasts, and he tugged on the nipple, making her gasp, then he pulled away, to hook his fingers under the hem of her shirt. She put her arms up, and off it came, her bra following. He gazed down at her breasts and a grin spread across his face. Her favorite grin. "You're beautiful, darlin'. Perfection from head to toe and everything in between."

She let her eyes drift closed as his words washed over her. Perfection. She could get used to hearing that.

His mouth went to her breasts instead of her lips and she arched her back, rolling on the bed. "Oh, Beckett," she breathed, as he expertly plied her nipples, swirling his tongue around each tight bud, making her body tingle in response.

"Yeah, darlin'?" he asked, a grin in his voice, raising his head. She looked at him in shock, then shoved his head back down. He chuckled and spoke against her nipple. "Don't stop, got it. Sorry." He didn't sound sorry.

He lavished attention on both breasts, his fingers drawing delicate circles around her belly now, grazing her hips occasionally, never dipping lower, as much as she wanted him to. "Beckett, please," she finally groaned.

"Please what?" he said, the tease still in his voice.

She growled at him and he laughed again, his hand going exactly where she wanted it. He ground his palm against her for a moment, making her gasp, and then he pulled away from her breasts, shooting her a look that made her shudder, all serious now. He moved on hands and knees like some big jungle cat, or maybe a dangerous wolf, to kneel between her legs. She watched his muscles flex, not knowing what he was doing.

But when he dropped his head to her clitoris and kissed her there, she couldn't help but cry out. Nothing to bite on this time. She didn't care. Her pleasure came so much quicker, taking her by surprise, the pleasure building and taking over, until she was weak with it, toes curled into the mattress, back bowed, fingers tearing at the sheets…

The orgasm rocked her, making her lose all sense of who and where she was as she cried out, giving herself over to it.

It ebbed enough that she could come back to reality, and when she did, Beckett was pushing her legs farther apart with his knees, his thick length in his hand, his breath coming hard and fast. The sight of him grasping his cock was erotic as hell and she couldn't stop staring. He ran the head of his cock along her sensitive folds and she gasped. "Beckett…"

"Gentle, Cerise. I'll be gentle. But I can't wait for this. Don't make me wait."

"No, I want it." She urged him forward, arching into him, encouraging him. She did want it. She wanted to know this final act intimately, to leave who she was behind, and to fully realize who she would be. Beckett's lover. His… mate.

He bent over her, still holding himself with his right hand, pressing against her again and again, his eyes glued to the spot where their bodies were meeting. She'd rarely seen him serious, and she took the time to study him, really study his strong jaw, his molded lips, the expression in his eyes. He looked like a starving man staring at the most delectable dinner imaginable. Her.

"It might hurt," he said. "I know it's your first time. But it shouldn't last too long."

"I'm ready," she said, knowing he would do whatever he could to minimize the pain for her.

He pressed inside, just a little bit, and it felt good, so good, until he moved inside her more. Then it pinched her, and she felt something give way inside her. She bit her lip. He saw immediately and stilled, staring into her eyes. "I love you," he said, then looked surprised, like he hadn't meant to say it. She bit her lip. She hadn't expected to hear it. But it felt so good. And right. Did she love him back?

Before she decided, he was moving again, the ache fading, the pinch receding. It didn't quite feel good, but it didn't feel bad, either. He pressed farther inside her and she sucked in a breath. She was so full. So stretched. She had never imagined anything like this. This complete and utter joining with another person.

He lowered his body to hers and kissed her lips, until she was lost in the sensation, meeting his tongue, enjoying his taste, loving his body, and when she came up for air, she realized he was moving inside her, slowly, gently, but definitely moving. The slip-sliding of skin against skin made her smile, as a wave of pleasure began to build in her again.

She held onto his shoulders, pushing and pulling at him, lifting her hips to meet his. He kept his pace gentle, light, thorough, letting her make it more. She gasped as a wave of pleasure pulsed in her. "Can I…?"

"Come again? Yes." His face tightened as if he was determined to make her and he stirred himself inside her, making her cry out. He didn't tease her though, his expression saying he was beyond teasing, and completely lost to her. As much hers as she was his. That was a good way to be.

She met him, thrust for thrust, not hard, never hard, but insistent, until she began to pant again and he noticed. "Come for me, darlin', I want to feel you come all over me."

She nodded, digging in to his shoulders, letting him take her… and in a moment she was there. She threw back her head, keened out a lusty cry at the intensity of it all, dimly aware that Beckett had let go also. His breath caught in his throat and he groaned in time with her. Inside her, hot seed spurted against her inner core, and it felt right, like she was finally doing exactly what she'd been meant to do in her life.

CHAPTER 41

erise sat in the passenger seat of the truck, watching as Beckett packed their last bag in the back. She'd wanted to help but he'd said no way, she was only allowed to relax. They'd made love four more times the day before, then once more last night when she'd woken and turned over just to touch him. She was sore, but content, and now they were headed home, the long way, as Beckett put it.

He climbed into the truck, grinned at her, then said, "You ready?"

She nodded eagerly. She *was*. Ready to meet his friends, to see her sisters, to become a part of his life, fully and completely.

They drove for hours, her occasionally checking behind them to be sure the tiny white sedan was still shadowing them, him just trusting it was. He'd told her the white wolf's name was Mac, and the bear's name was Bruin, and they were having some sort of a bromance while they waited for their one true mates to show up.

He told her all about Rhen and Khain and the creation story, and the *wolven*, *felen*, *foxen*, and *bearen*, and the one true mates. She shivered every time she thought about it, about who she was and how she fit into this larger picture.

After they'd skirted around Las Vegas, she'd fallen silent at the sight of the big city, staring out the window. But a thought niggled at her and she had to ask it.

"Beckett?"

"Hmmm?"

"You've been gentle with me because I've asked you to be, right?"

He grinned at her. "Yup."

She looked away, musing, then spoke. "I can't help but wonder if it's fun if you're rough, too."

Instead of answering, Beckett swung the truck into the right lane, then took the next exit, speeding up instead of slowing down.

"What?" she asked, scared for a moment.

He grabbed her hand and placed it on what had grown behind his zipper.

"Ohh," she said, then giggled. "Am I about to find out?"

"I can't leave you wonderin', darlin', it goes against my nature."

He found a motel in record time, and she went in with him to get their room, sneaking glances at his pants, excitement blooming in her at the way his hardness never faltered.

Once outside, he didn't even stop at the truck, he bent at the waist, threw her over his shoulder, and took off at a run to their room. She could see the two males sitting in the white car, watching them. She blushed, but before she knew it she was inside a small, dark room.

Beckett put her down and began to strip off his clothes, kissing her while he did so, then pushing her against the wall and pinning her hands over her head. She gasped, liking rough already. He stripped off her shirt, then her bra, and she stepped out of her pants, then bam, back against the wall she went, arms above her head, as Beckett nudged his hard cock against her belly.

"You want it rough, Cerise?" he asked, his voice a low, raspy whisper.

She swallowed hard. "Not too rough."

His heavy eyes assessed her. "You sure? You sure you don't want to be fucked hard?"

Wetness bloomed between her legs and she whimpered. Apparently she did want that. "M-maybe," she said.

"I won't hurt you, darlin', but I'm ready to switch it up a bit if you are."

She nodded but he was already kissing her again, pinning her to the wall with his big body. He picked her up again, then flung her on the bed. She laughed as she bounced, then flipped over to her hands and knees. As long as they were trying new things…

A thick growling filled the air and she flattened herself reflexively, looking over her shoulder. Beckett's lips were lifted and his canines showed, looking like fangs, his eyes locked on her backside. She flipped over to face him. He shook himself and seemed to come to his senses.

He flung his cap onto the floor behind him and rubbed a hand over his short-cropped hair. "Shit, I gotta tell you something. I-ah-there's a thing we *wolven* do, and when you are on your hands and knees like that I can't help but want to do it."

Cerise nibbled her lip, waiting to hear what it was.

He rubbed his head again. "It's called claiming, and it's where I bite you." He touched the back of her shoulder, where it met her neck. "Right here."

He dropped to his knees, placing his hands on her legs and staring up at her, his face completely open and vulnerable.

"What does it mean?" she asked.

"Everything," he said. "Once I do that, we won't ever separate. It's like marriage, but there is no divorce."

She nibbled her lip. "Do you want to?"

He breathed out, hard. "So much. I ache to, Cerise, but I don't want to push you if you aren't ready. You're new at this, it's a bit vio—"

She held a finger to his lips, shushing him. She trusted him implicitly. Slowly, she pushed herself back up onto the bed, then turned over, practically wiggling her ass at him. His growling started at once and she bloomed for him, surprised at how swollen her sex got, and how fast.

He grasped her hips, pulling her toward him, his fingers digging into her skin. He didn't say a word, seemed unable to speak, but then he thrust violently and she cried out at the pleasure/pain of it. She'd wanted rough, and oh, she did like it. He thrust wildly, and she almost forgot about the bite, until he fell upon her, so close she could smell him.

His teeth found her shoulder and pain erupted there, but then pleasure did, too, filling her body, consuming her from her core outward. She threw back her head and screamed with it as all pain was driven from her. All the pain from her entire sad life. Gone.

***

Beckett claimed his mate, finally, his past falling away, every mistake he'd made in his life, every time he'd second-guessed himself or those around him. Now was his time, and he was doing everything right. His teeth violated her skin and his cock violated her body, but exactly how it was supposed to be. From her back, gossamer wings of brilliant purple light and feathers erupted, wrapping them completely, lifting them from the bed, as she called out his name and screamed out her pleasure.

Beckett thrust one last time, hard, hard enough to please her, and his own orgasm rocketed out of him, filling his mate, claiming her thoroughly. He gently pulled his teeth out of her flesh, as her wings rocked them one last time, then set them down as lightly as a whisper floating on the breeze. His bite mark began to heal over at once, leaving a staggered scar behind.

She dropped to the bed, and he went with her, disentangling himself from her, but pulling her close to him.

She snuggled into his arms. "I love you," she said.

He grinned.

He knew she did. He was a loveable male.

Her male.

CHAPTER 42

*M*ac stared at the door Beckett and his mate had disappeared into, his mind sour. Why the fuck did he have to be on babysitting duty? Just because he hadn't wanted to take the express ticket back through fucked-up firetown with Graeme, didn't mean he should be the one watching Beckett hotel-hop.

"What do you think they're doing in there?" Bruin asked.

Mac laughed. Bruin had to be joking. Mac never could tell for sure, but most everything Bruin said was good for a laugh, joking or not.

Light erupted from the top of the motel directly above Beckett's room, shooting into the sky, so bright they both had to shield their eyes. "Fuck," Mac swore. "Took him long enough. All these fuckers are slow as shit. When I meet my one true mate, I'ma hit that the first night."

Bruin bobbed his head. "Hit her with what, your Vienna sausage dick?"

Mac shook his head. "Yeah dude, just cuz I ain't a bear don't mean I got a small dick."

Bruin snorted his bear snort, then opened his door and unfolded his body from the little car. "We're gonna be here for a while. I'm getting a room." He flipped Mac the bird, then took off at a run, calling over his shoulder, "Last one in the pool is a brokeback bee."

Mac flung open his door and yelled after him. "What the fuck is a brokeback bee?"

Bruin slowed to a walk and turned to face him, his face deadly serious. "A bee with excellent taste in independent films." He flipped around to face front and loped inside.

Mac shook his head slowly. "Bears are weird as shit," he said, not without affection, then hauled himself out of the rental car.

He could use a few days off, he guessed. Maybe meet some chicks.

The thought of his own one true mate slid through his mind but he let it go.

The wait was too painful to dwell on, so he would do what he always did. Crack jokes, crack heads, and hope she was around the next corner.

EPILOGUE

Cerise's guts rolled with a feeling she hadn't had in weeks. Dread. They were in Cooter, driving the back roads outside of Serenity. Beckett had said he had something he wanted to show her, and she'd been in a pensive mood, so she hadn't asked what.

On her left, coming up, was the gate where she and Kaci (*Lillian!* she reminded herself for the hundredth time) had tried to rehome Zeus. She twisted in her seat and craned her neck to see all of the grassy field, but no horses were visible.

Her heart jumped in her chest as something like surreal appreciation flooded her. She never imagined she would see these fields again like this. Free. Happy. Fulfilled. With a purpose. And a man.

She peeked at Beckett, then smiled and put her hand on his, which was resting on the stick between them. He grinned back at her, his manner easy. No, not a man, a wolf, which was infinitely better. She loved his hidden nature as much as she loved him, and couldn't wait until they had their own little home on Trevor and Ella's land with privacy to explore their new relationship. It was being built, would be done in a few weeks. The best part was, Kaci (Lillian!) and her parents would move into a cabin on the same property.

She opened her mouth to tell Beckett about Zeus, when he slowed, then turned right on the old county road that led to the driveway of the trailer she and Lemon used to live in.

She knew immediately where he was taking her and she pulled her hand back to herself, curling it into a fist and covering it with her other hand. How did she feel about this? *Ok.* Not scared. Not angry. Not happy. But ok. Beckett was with her and that meant she could handle anything.

In a moment, the mostly-hidden driveway swung into view. She could feel Beckett's eyes on her as he turned the big truck into the wooded plot of land, which would soon open up into the clearing where the trailer sat. She looked around with her new perspective. She was no longer victim, or captive, or oppressed and poisoned girl, desperate to save another girl. Now she was someone's mate. Someone's sister. Her own person with voice and power. As that person, this drive wasn't scary. It was just… sad.

The trailer appeared, the saggy roof, the tarps in the windows, even the electrical cords that ran from the street were still there.

Ghosts were too.

She opened her truck door and slid out onto the ground, wrapping her light jacket tighter around her. Spring was coming, but it wasn't quite there yet. Feeling Beckett watching her, she took one step, another, and another, and then she was standing directly in front of *it*. Her home for so many years.

A place of incredible pain… and a resilient, sisterly love she would always cherish.

Beckett came up next to her and took her hand, and they stood in silence for several moments, each with their own thoughts.

She stared at the trailer and let her mind wander, go where it wanted. She expected it to crawl through the worst of her memories in that metal tube, but instead, it brought up images of her vacation in Chicago with Beckett. They'd taken their time crossing the country on their way back to Illinois, stopping at whatever silly tourist attraction caught her eye. Then he'd bypassed Serenity altogether and taken her straight to Chicago, where they'd stayed at the Langham hotel, a far cry from the motels they'd been hitting on the way back from California. She'd never been so spoiled in her life, sight-seeing during the day and making love at night. They'd only been able to stay for three days, but they'd packed as much good fun as possible into each day, even taking several new pictures with his drone to replace the one he'd given to his friend.

"Want to go in?" Beckett asked, pulling her back to reality.

Cerise shook her head. "I'm done here. This life is over."

Beckett's tone hardened. "I brought gasoline."

Cerise turned to him, her mouth agape. "You what? Why?"

"In case you wanted to burn it down. I brought baseball bats, too. We could smash all the windows that are left, if you want."

"You'll lose your job!"

He grinned his cockiest grin. "The booted wolf? No way. I've got prophecy on my side, baby."

Cerise did her best to ignore the pull that grin had over

her body and gave him the sweet smile she reserved just for him, then shook her head. "I really feel ok about it. Like, it was a horrible thing to go through, but if not going through it meant I wouldn't know Kaci, I mean Lillian, then I would choose to do it all again. Or if it meant she would have had to have gone through it on her own? I would choose it again a hundred times to have been there with her."

Beckett stared down at her, his face uncharacteristically grim. "If we're dreaming, why don't we dream that neither of you had to go through this?"

Cerise nodded slowly, then turned to face the trailer one more time. "We could. But is that really how life is supposed to be? Are we supposed to live pampered lives where everything is perfect for us all the time? Or could the only reason life exists at all be to challenge us? To show us what we are capable of? Imagine if Lillian had never lived through any of this? Would she have the strength and courage that she showed two weeks ago? Would she have this awesome new career before she even turned thirteen years old, these full-grown police officers looking up to her, being in awe of her?"

Cerise faced Beckett and squeezed his hand. "She wouldn't. She'd be talking about boys and maybe getting into dangerous stuff, defying her parents, because she never had those defining moments that showed her what's really important. I'm not excusing what Myles and Sandra did, I'm just saying I've decided to only look at the benefits of what we endured here. Not the bad stuff."

Beckett shook his head, then inclined his head and captured her lips for just a moment. A sweet, sweet kiss she would never tire of.

He pulled back and looked into her eyes. "You are amazing, you know that?"

She shook her head. "Not me—" Her thoughts broke off as he raised his head and frowned, his nostrils flaring. "What?" she asked.

"Horse," he said, then turned toward the trailer.

"No way," she breathed, then pulled away from Beckett and took off at a run, ducking around the right side of the trailer, hurdling weeds and piles of melting snow.

When she reached the back of the house, the tiny yard was empty, but she could feel... something. "Zeus?" she called. The sound of heavy feet thudding over the forest floor reached her and then he broke from the cover of the trees, his big tan head stretching her way as he trotted to her.

Beckett skidded to a stop behind her and grabbed her by the shoulders, startling Zeus, who turned quickly, his agitation obvious in his twisting ears and tossing head.

"It's ok, Beckett," she said, peeling his fingers off of her. "You stay here. He's shy."

Beckett snorted, but stayed put. Cerise stepped forward, slowly. "Zeus, he's ok, really. What are you doing here? You were supposed to stay with those other horses."

Zeus quieted and stood his ground, letting Cerise get close. She put a hand on his once-again too-thin side, then made her way to his head and pressed her forehead against his cheek. She'd missed him more than she'd realized.

"Whose is he?" Beckett called from his spot near the trailer.

"No ones, I guess. Me and Ka-Lillian fed him for a long time. He just showed up one day and never left. We tried to rehome him but I guess it didn't take."

"Sounds like he's yours."

Cerise ran her hand over his strong chest. Hers? No. She

was nobody. Just a poor—. She cut the thought off mercilessly. Had she not been listening to herself?

"I've got a friend with a horse trailer," Beckett said. "Just sayin'. Trevor's land isn't fully fenced, but I bet we could convince him to do it. Or if Zeus likes the forest, he could hang out in there. We'll just have to make sure he's out of it when the wolves run."

Cerise's fingers tightened against Zeus's chest. Did Beckett really mean it?

***

"Thanks Blake, you really made my female happy," Beckett said, eyeing Cerise at the side of the trailer, speaking softly to Zeus, her eyes light, a constant smile on her face.

"No problem, Beck. I'll have him checked out by my equine veterinarian and then get him over to Burbank's place by dark."

Beckett went to Cerise and nodded at Blake, who was getting in the truck. Cerise whispered one more thing to Zeus, then backed up. The truck pulled out and they both watched it go.

Cerise's hand snuck into his. "He must have been in a trailer before. He doesn't seem nervous."

"He doesn't," Beckett agreed. He took one last look at the trailer, then faced his woman. "You ready?"

She leaned into him and he thought he was getting a kiss, but, too late, he realized she was digging his keys out of his pocket. "I'm driving!" she shouted, and ran to Cooter.

He climbed into the passenger seat, a stupid smile pasted on his face. "I'm never gonna get to drive my truck again, am I?"

She flashed him a look of pure joy and his stomach twisted with love for her. She was gorgeous, sweet, strong, and all his.

"Eh, I might let you drive on Sundays," she said, depressing the clutch and the brake pedal, then twisting the keys. She yanked the stick into reverse and backed perfectly down the driveway. A natural.

Once out on the main road, she turned on the radio and bounced in her seat as she drove, singing along to Starboy by The Weeknd. He'd learned she favored pop and hip-hop just a bit more than country music but he didn't hold that against her.

She stopped at a stop sign, judiciously looking each way before continuing, even though the only other vehicle in sight was behind them. Instead of stopping there, it pulled up alongside them in the wrong lane of traffic, stopped, and revved the engine.

Cerise frowned and looked out her window, then looked back at Beckett. "That truck's just like yours!"

Beckett was already eyeing it. A year older. Painted a stupid orange color, with tires two inches bigger. Amateur. He checked out the driver. Hillbilly, with a big grin who had pulled up for a drag race and now was checking out Cerise. Beckett's upper lip pulled back from his teeth and he growled involuntarily. Did somebody need to die?

Cerise shushed him. "Why is he revving his engine?"

"He wants to race you."

"Oh!" Cerise threw Cooter into neutral and revved her own engine, grinning crazily. "Come on, then!" she shouted, and shoved it into first, tires squealing as she took off.

Beckett grabbed the door handle, holding on tight, as Cooter fishtailed through the intersection and the other truck left the line. "You're gonna get me fired!" he shouted, laughing anyway.

She flashed him the quickest of grins, shifting into second, barely letting off the gas to do so. "The booted wolf? The tempest in the storm? No way, baby!"

"Shift, shift!" he shouted as the engine screamed and she shot down the road.

But the other truck had already given up. She whipped her head to look over her shoulder and slowed. "Ooh, should I let him catch up? That was fun."

Beckett relaxed, then looked at the truck, which had stopped and was reversing to change its direction. "He's outta here. You won't ever see him again, darlin', not if he sees you first. You spanked him good." *Rank* amateur.

Her new phone he had bought for her chimed. She handed it to him. "See if it's Lillian."

Beckett pulled up the message, unable to help the smile that spread across his face. Lillian's parents had decided while their cabin was being built, the three of them would travel, taking Lillian on her first vacation. The picture she had texted Cerise showed her in front of a roller coaster, her parents flanking her with their arms around her shoulders and wide smiles on their faces. Trent and Troy were on both sides of the family, looking impressive as shit even in their orange service dog vests, and Harlan was standing off in the background, his eyes sad but watchful. Beckett held the phone up so Cerise could see it.

"Oh! Cool. Do you think they let Trent and Troy ride the roller coaster?"

Beckett snorted. "Ha, if they do, I hope they send us pictures."

"Tell her about Zeus!" Beckett sent a quick text.

Lillian texted back. *Holy fucking shit!! I want to come home right now!* Beckett grinned. Lillian's mom hated the swearing, but hadn't been able to break her of it yet.

Within twenty minutes, they were home. Or where Beckett was starting to consider home. Yeah, he'd agreed to move into the freak commune. How could he refuse it when he had this precious female to consider, to protect? Their cabin would be within an easy walk of both Crew's new place and Lillian's new place.

And it had two extra bedrooms. Just in case, you know, he and Cerise needed the extra rooms for anything. Not anytime soon, but yeah, he could see it happening. Maybe he had even dreamed about it once or twice. A sweet and sassy little girl with an innocent face and strawberry-blonde hair? Or a hard-charging little boy with a cocky grin? Beckett knew exactly what he wanted to name a boy. Cole. After his big brother. But first he still had to introduce Cerise to many things. They had time.

Cerise pulled up the driveway and parked Cooter next to Mac's pimp-mobile. These days, more of their work was done in Trevor's dining room than at the police station. They made their way inside the house, where Ella met them at the door. She hugged Cerise and Cerise kissed her growing belly. Beckett watched them, surprised again by the dynamic between them. With Heather and Dahlia, Cerise seemed to have fallen into an easy friend-sister role, but with Ella? She had turned into the mom of the group, taking care of everyone, and Cerise seemed to cherish it in a way that the other two women did not.

"Guess what," Ella said, crossing her arms over her belly.

"What?"

"We finally heard from the prison. Cici has recovered

well. They say her personality is a bit different, but she doesn't have any neurological deficits from her strokes."

The women moved to the couch and Cerise flopped down on it, her eyes rapt. "Strokes?"

"Yeah, she had a few, but they didn't harm her long term. The guards say she's quiet now. Different than how she used to be. Not so reactive and liable to fly off the handle."

"Interesting," Cerise breathed.

Beckett sat down next to her and took her hand. "That reminds me. We should do a test. See if you can still *push* me or not. We haven't tried since Chicago." She'd been able to, but only for a second before he'd thrown it off. They hadn't tried anyone else yet. Ella and Heather were out, since they were pregnant, and all the males had been busy.

Cerise turned to him. "Ok, smart guy, you ready?"

He nodded.

Cerise's face tensed and he could feel the power emanate from her, like a magnetic field. "Quack like a duck," she said.

He grinned and stuck his hands in his armpits, flapping his elbows. "Quack, quack."

Her face fell immediately.

"Nah, darlin', don't fret, that was just funny. Give me another one."

She touched him again. So much power. She was getting better at it, stronger. "Run through the house naked."

Beckett stood and stripped as Ella fell over on the couch laughing and hid her eyes. Cerise looked like she was going to cry.

Beckett made a loop around the kitchen, then out the front door, running through the melting snow in bare feet, then in the back door, ignoring Graeme's roar from somewhere behind the house. "Get yer bloody clothes on! There's lasses about!"

Beckett skidded to a stop in front of the couch and pulled his clothes back on as quickly as he could. He didn't need Graeme trying to kick his ass… He'd go toe to toe with anyone else, but Graeme? Who wanted to be flash-fried? He dropped onto the couch and grabbed his boots, already pulling one on.

Cerise grabbed him by the hand, her face stricken. "Did you even try to resist?"

Beckett stuck his foot in his second boot, flashed a look at the door, then leaned back and spread his arms like he'd been on the couch the whole time. "Shh," he whispered to Cerise. "That one was funny, too. Had to do it."

Graeme came in the back door, fuming, followed by Mac and Bruin. Beckett avoided their eyes and turned to Cerise intently. "Give me a good one. Something deep."

Cerise pursed her lips and thought for a moment, curling her fingers in his. "Love me forever, protect me always, and buy me pretty things."

Beckett rolled his eyes. "Now *you're* not even trying. It's got to be something I'm not going to do anyway."

Mac dropped onto the end of the couch and Bruin leaned against the wall. Graeme had disappeared into the kitchen. "What're we talking about?" Mac asked.

Ella stifled her giggles. "Cerise is using her power on Beckett to see if she can make him do stuff."

Mac shot to his feet and he and Bruin crowded close to Cerise, making Beckett growl and show his teeth. They both took a step back but held out their hands.

"Oooh, do me!" Mac crowed.

"Me too! Me too!" Bruin was shifting from side to side

like a little boy who had to pee. Beckett expected him to clap his hands together and jump up and down any second.

Cerise looked at Beckett with one eyebrow raised and he considered. He thought he could stand to see her touch them, but did he want to? Then he had a brilliant idea…

He whispered something in her ear and a slow smile spread over her face, then a blush. She shook her head. He nodded his. "Just do it. It'll be awesome."

She stood and grasped each of their hands lightly, with as little contact as possible. *Good girl.* "You two, kiss," she told them.

Beckett grinned and nodded his head as Ella giggled again, but didn't look away this time. Graeme appeared from the kitchen, his eyes on Mac and Bruin, his face unreadable.

Cerise let go of them both and took a step back, her expression a strange mixture of awe and terror.

Mac turned to Bruin as Bruin turned to Mac and they entwined arms, stepping closer, their eyelids going heavy. Beckett burst out laughing. If they actually did it… he needed his camera!

But Cerise couldn't go through with it. She touched them again, quickly. "No, don't!"

Beckett fell onto the couch, holding his stomach, barely able to breathe, about to cry he was laughing so hard.

When he recovered enough to look around, Mac had retreated to the bottom of the stairs and was leaning against the banister, dry-heaving.

Bruin was right where he'd been before, leaning against the wall, his expression unbothered. He shook his head at Mac. "I don't know why you're freaking out. I totally brushed my teeth today."

Beckett stood up. "My fault, my fault. Sorry. Won't happen again. So I'm guessing you couldn't resist?"

Mac bent over one more time, pressing his hand to his stomach. "Did I look like I could resist?"

Bruin shrugged. "Eh. I think I could have. Let's go again."

Trevor tromped down the stairs, frowning at Mac. "Puke on my floor and I'll kill you." He held up his phone, pointing the screen at Beckett. "What's this about a horse?"

Beckett sat down next to Cerise and pulled her into his arms. "His name is Zeus, and he's big. But he's part of the family."

His family. He grinned and buried his face in Cerise's hair, savoring her sweet licorice scent. He could get used to being a part of the family.

Notes from Lisa xoxoxo

I enjoyed the way this book came together a lot. My defining scene for it was the one where Beckett and Cerise first meet and she inadvertently wakes him and he asks her if she's going to kill him. Everything else came from that one image in my mind. I love the story that grew around it, and am just thrilled for Kaci and Cerise. Beckett was gonna be ok, as long as he found his otm, but I was worried about the girls for a while.

Thank you so much for reading, and I really hope you enjoyed Beckett and Cerise's story. <3 <3 <3 <3

Made in the USA
Lexington, KY
22 May 2017